Blue DAWN

Praise for
Blue Dawn

Sinmisola Ogúnyinka is an accomplished author of inspiring and intriguing fiction.

–Joanne Troppello
Publisher of *Pandora's Box Gazette*

A thoroughly compelling and gripping read, *Blue Dawn* is a poignant tale of sacrifice, love, a mother's grief, and her battle for justice. It is an amazing reminder that even in tragedy, God has a wonderful way of turning things around. Highly recommended!

–Abi Dare
Bath Novel Award 2018 Winner

Blue DAWN
A Novel

Sinmisola Ogunyinka

NEW YORK

LONDON • NASHVILLE • MELBOURNE • VANCOUVER

Blue DAWN
A Novel

Published in New York, New York, by Morgan James Publishing. Morgan James is a trademark of Morgan James, LLC. www.MorganJamesPublishing.com

ISBN 978-1-64279-497-7 paperback
ISBN 978-1-64279-498-4 eBook
Library of Congress Control Number: 2019901677

Cover Design by:
Rachel Lopez
www.r2cdesign.com

Interior Design by:
Bonnie Bushman
The Whole Caboodle Graphic Design

In an effort to support local communities, raise awareness and funds, Morgan James Publishing donates a percentage of all book sales for the life of each book to Habitat for Humanity Peninsula and Greater Williamsburg.

Get involved today! Visit
www.MorganJamesBuilds.com

Dedication

For Mom, the best one ever

Chapter One

A homicide officer draped Shakira with a dark blanket to keep away the cold. She'd never understood why they did so till now. Despite the blanket, she froze inside out.

Men and women who worked the crime scene walked in and out of her beautiful Katy, Texas, suburban residence. A place she and Deon and their two beautiful daughters had built with love and warmth—and once called home.

The strangers did their work with stiff detachment. If she hadn't opted to teach special-needs kids, could she have done this? Never.

"Ma'am? Would you like a cup of coffee?"

Shakira stared at the face of the cop. He couldn't be more than twenty. She turned away, assuming he'd understand. Why didn't they leave? Where was Deon?

The questions had hardly left her thoughts when the front door burst open and Deon ran in. Another cop grabbed him at the waist.

Shakira rushed to him and hugged his neck. The dam of her tears broke. Her daughters couldn't be dead. Someone had to wake her from this dream.

"I don't know what they're saying, baby! They said the neighbor called. I don't know where Florence is. I wasn't at work. I had to—"

Deon made a deep, guttural, wounded sound, and this brought a new dawn of realization to Shakira. Her head felt light and she fainted in his arms.

When she came to, she lay on her couch and a paramedic attended to her. What was she doing here? She viewed her surroundings and tried to sit up. She blinked rapidly to get her orientation.

Two policemen strode in.

"You'll have just five minutes to speak with her," the paramedic said in hushed tones.

"Thank you," one of the officers said. The two men flashed their badges and mumbled names. "Ma'am, we need to ask you some questions."

Shakira sat up, disoriented. "Could I have some water, please?"

The first officer who had spoken, a man in his middle age with a spread to go with it, and a near-feminine face, poured some water into a glass placed on a side stool and gave it to her.

Shakira drank it all. The cool liquid soothed her parched throat. Had she cried so much? She had never wept like this in her life. "What's going on?"

The second officer stepped forward, seeming to be in charge. He had the face and build of a veteran. She could well imagine him in a naval suit. His age was hard to tell.

"Where's my husband?" She couldn't help it. All she needed right now were answers more than they did.

"Ma'am, a neighbor called to report your babysitter left the house and hadn't been back for some time. When was the last time you spoke with her?" The veteran-looking officer sat, and his partner followed suit poised with a pen.

How many tears did a person have? She sniffed. This couldn't be happening. Things like this didn't happen to good folks who paid their taxes and did community service every month.

"Are they really—gone?"

The two men exchanged glances, and the soft-spoken officer nodded. "You need to give us information on your babysitter. She may have the answers we need."

"Six hours ago, I left home. Kissed them both goodbye." Shakira swallowed. "Florence stood by, as she usually did. Complacent."

"Did she say anything to you? Her plans?"

Shakira shook her head. "No, she works four hours till my sister comes by. Until I get off." She closed her eyes, willing her mind to coordinate. "What did she do to them?"

The veteran-looking officer spoke. "The coroner is working on the facts. I believe we should have the report in seventy-two hours."

"Was there anything unusual about your babysitter, Florence Odu, when you left her with the girls?"

"Nothing."

"When did she start to work for you, ma'am?"

Shakira drew in her breath. She needed air. "Less than a month."

"How did you find her?"

"Referral. A lady at the—" She blinked huge tears away, yet they fell all the same. "I want to see them."

No one spoke a moment. The veteran cleared his throat. "A lady at the—?"

"I want to see my husband, please."

The officers exchanged glances again. The kind-looking one closed his notepad, but it was the veteran who spoke.

"We are so sorry for your loss; we'll do our best to solve this riddle." He bowed his head slightly. "Thank you for your time."

They left and she closed her eyes. She wanted to scream.

"I want to see my husband."

Chapter Two

Deon walked into the living room moments later, and Shakira rushed into his arms. His eyes were sunken, and he seemed to have aged ten years.

She couldn't recognize his thin, raspy voice. "What day is it?" When she didn't respond, he closed his eyes, and his lips trembled in suppressed emotion. "Has anyone spoken to you?"

Shakira nodded. "Policemen."

She stared long at him. This couldn't be happening. What would they do? As though he read her mind, he opened his eyes and stared back.

"We just have to wait?"

"I guess," she whispered. "*Oh* dear."

Both sat with tears in their eyes till two men walked in.

"Good evening, Mr. Smith. I'm Detective Chris Gray. My partner is Lieutenant Bruce Will."

Deon took the hand the detective extended. "Hey."

Gray had kind eyes. "We spoke with the cops who first arrived at the scene. And we hope to speak to you both." The detective glanced between the couple.

Deon swallowed. "We are ready. How can we help you?"

It would get ugly, she knew, and she hoped she could get through all of this, but who knew what to do? She had never fainted, never believed she could, yet there was no way to control her body or what she felt.

"We want you to know. The Sheriff's Office is committed to solving this crime." Gray nodded as though to affirm to himself. "Now, we'd like to hear a little about the relationship your babysitter had with the girls. Anything unusual?"

Shakira cleared her throat. "In what way?"

"How did they behave around her?"

Deon gave Shakira a questioning look. "We, *um*—"

She stared at her fingers. "We leave the house as soon as she comes."

"She worked five days a week?"

Deon nodded. "Five days, yes."

Gray directed his attention to her. "What about the hours she worked?"

"Four hours a day. My sister stays with them the rest of the time. Before I return."

"What is your sister's name?"

"Kenya Brawn. She helps out with the girls."

Deon cleared his throat. "She's a great help."

"Do the girls talk about their time with Florence?"

Shakira drew in her breath. The name gave her nightmares. "No. You need to find her."

Will took the focus away from his jotting. "We will."

Gray paused for a second. "You said Florence was referred."

"I'm sorry, I can't remember the name of—"

Deon sat forward. "The agency may not be registered but I think the name is Home Helps."

"We found them in a classified ad and wrote to them." Shakira noticed Will stared hard at them. "I needed to work—"

Deon cleared his throat. "Wanted to work."

She shrugged. Deon didn't agree with her getting a job. But his real estate business had suffered a hit from the economic meltdown. Her income helped more than he cared to admit.

She closed her eyes briefly to let the anger wave pass. This was not the time to argue. "I needed to work, and so we needed childcare." The tears threatened. "Maybe I shouldn't have taken up the job. If I hadn't, maybe those babies would still be—alive." She sobbed.

The remains found by the police in the bathtub couldn't be her gorgeous daughters. Surely they had to belong to someone else.

No one spoke for a time. Deon sat beside her, so rigid her skin tingled. His silence expressed all the months they argued about her getting a job, and fighting over money, and eventually leaving the girls to a stranger. Deon would now blame her—

"We couldn't afford a proper agency or the popular ones. Babysitters cost so much. These home helpers weren't quite legalized, but they promised to get someone for us."

Deon clamped his hands over his head. "And they did."

The two officers exchanged a brief glance. Lt. Will closed his notepad with a snap. "The police department has made arrangements for you to stay in a motel till you can come back home."

Shakira sobbed. "Where's my mother?"

"I'm sure you will see her at the motel."

"Has she been told? Latoya was named after her."

Gray cleared his throat. "We believe the family should know by now. The news media are all over the place."

"The news?" She wailed. "Does all of Katy know now?"

"We're using the media to alert the public that Florence Odu is wanted for questioning."

Deon's head jerked up. "You mean she hasn't been brought in?"

Detective Gray pinched his nostrils. "We've issued a BOLO, but she's eluded us."

Shakira said, "What's a BOLO?"

Deon growled. "Eluded? What do you mean eluded?"

The detective frowned. "Huh? BOLO is, er, be on the lookout."

Chapter Three

The following days came and went in a haze. How did people live through these times? After staying at the motel for three days, they could go back home. But the moment Shakira stepped into the living room, pain and anger overwhelmed her. She saw Leila run to her screaming, "Mommy!" Couldn't take it and decided to go and stay with her mother.

The coroner's report was released to the press, and Shakira learned the circumstances surrounding the death of her two daughters. Evidently, Leila, the three-year-old, must have taken Latoya, her eighteen-month-old sister, into a filled bathtub and then got in after her. Both drowned within minutes. Time of death was estimated at 9:48 a.m., barely two hours after she and Deon left home. Her lips trembled and she couldn't control the shaking of her hands as a representative of the police department made a statement.

Florence Odu, legal permanent resident of Nigerian descent, instantly made it to the list of Texas's most wanted. Regional and local news channels broadcast the story for a few days. The two Smith girls were buried in an emotional interment five days later. The mayor attended and the governor sent a moving message. Shakira wafted through those days and details like a ghost, refusing to see it as her story, or taking part. She removed herself from the scenes and conversations, hidden in a place of no emotion or feeling. Somewhere she wouldn't feel pain.

Deon refused to stay with her mother and moved back home after the funeral. Shakira could not bear to be in the same house where there had been so much joy in her life at first, but after two weeks she returned home.

Every night was difficult as she tried to cope with the loss of her beautiful daughters. In her mind, she kept hearing water fill the tub where their lives had been cut short. Shakira wanted to have the tub removed, but a trauma specialist advised they keep it to help bring closure.

Day after day, the police tried their best to find the woman believed to have last seen the Smith girls alive, but she had not been sighted since the day of the tragedy by either the neighbors or the agency she worked for.

Shakira was given leave from her job at the school. She thought she'd manage to work after a week but couldn't bring herself to face the children she taught. Her therapist, Dr. Brickam, advised her and Deon to join a victims' group, which they did, and to return to work. He did, she couldn't.

Instead she sat in front of the TV all day, every day, seeking news about the case. But after less than a month, the tragedy became just a scroll on the screen and eventually disappeared as a whole. Other crimes made news.

Frustrated, she sought out the two officers assigned to the case.

Detective Gray attended to her in his cubicle. "We are doing everything we can to find her. Did you notice a ransom has been placed on her?"

Fifty thousand was a lot of cash. Shakira had been elated when the ransom was announced. No one would have information and not give it for such an amount of money.

"So has anyone come forward with information?"

"Unfortunately, no. There has been a torrent of leads though."

"But she can't just disappear?"

"Everyone is searching for Florence Odu. She can't hide for much longer. It may please you to know the Interpol is involved after the—"

Shakira blinked. "Interpol? What has Interpol—she left the country?" Her heart skipped several beats. "She left?" *Oh no.* Florence couldn't leave. How could she leave?

She stared at Gray. The officer nodded, and Shakira bit her lower lip hard. Florence was gone and they couldn't find her. She was free. They would never find her. Interpol never found anyone. She had escaped.

"When?" Shakira said in a whisper, barely able to discern her own voice.

"November the eighth. She traveled with her Nigerian passport."

Shakira shut her eyes tight, and this time a screech escaped from her soul. Florence Odu had left the country the same day she killed those babies.

Chapter Four

Shakira was in Leila's room, rearranging her wardrobe, when Deon returned home from his real estate job. At some point, they had locked the girls' rooms but reopened them at her insistence.

"Hi." Deon stared at her. "You're here?"

She spared him a glance. "Hi." His curly hair was matted around his temples with sweat, and he seemed work-weary.

"How was your day?"

Shakira finished folding the last dress and moved to the bed. Several of Leila's favorite toys were strewn all over the floor. She picked them up one by one and arranged them on the bed.

Deon sniffed. "Why are you here?"

"Why?" She smirked. "Why not? The room has been like this for ages." Her eyes shone. "You should see Latoya's room now. Beautiful. Exotic."

Deon sighed. "How much longer?"

"Just five more minutes—you go ahead and warm dinner."

He trudged out, and she stared after him. What did he mean by his question? Dr. Brickam recommended she drop the habits of bathing the girls' dolls, singing the dolls to sleep at night, doing laundry, rearranging the rooms. She couldn't. Those chores kept her busy.

Deon dished out leftover barbecued chicken and steamed vegetables onto his plate. She hated to see the pathetic meal available to him, but she hadn't cooked anything since. Hardly ate anything too. For a moment, her heart thumped with guilt, but she pushed the feeling aside.

He glanced at her. "Care for some?"

She shrugged. "A little will do."

He brought out a plate. "The offices in downtown Houston got bidders today. Great offer too," he said.

"Wow."

"I think we should go to one of these tropical islands once I get a check. Just for a week or two. Just soak in the sun at the beach." He put the plate of food before her. "What do you think?"

"Not with those girls still roaming around." She took a bite of the chicken and dropped the fork on her plate. "Tasteless."

He frowned. "Roaming?"

"I read in ancient mythology that the spirits of the dead never rest until they find justice."

He put down his fork too. His pale skin became red. "I don't think you should read such things. They mess with your mind."

"I think you should. You've forgotten so soon."

His dark-green eyes flared. "How can you say that?"

It always amazed her that he took the most remarkable features from his Austrian mother, beautiful green eyes and near-white skin. But his dark curly hair was entirely from his African-American father.

Leila and Latoya had those eyes too, but their skin had been much darker than Deon's. Ironically, the girls also had their grandmother's long silky hair. Seeing him reminded her of them so much.

"Soaking in the sun doesn't sound to me like someone who remembers anything."

"Don't you think we need to get away? Be together. We still have each other."

Shakira shook her head. "We have nothing." She pushed the plate away from her. "All we had is gone. Nothing."

He closed his eyes and bit down on his lower lip; his jaws twitched. "We have each other. I still have you, and I love you, Shakira."

"I was at the police headquarters today." She cleared the plates and emptied their unfinished food in the trash.

Deon opened his eyes. "Why did you go there?"

"You ask why all the time. You know why."

"Sarcasm is not helping this conversation." Deon took an empty glass and pushed it under the tap. Cold water gushed in.

"Well, don't ask."

He sighed and drank all the water. "So, any news?"

"Florence left the country." She stood at the sink and took in some gulps of air to calm her nerves.

Deon went still. "She'll never be found," he whispered.

"That's what I told Detective Gray, but he says Interpol is on it."

Deon staggered to the kitchen table and found a seat. "No wonder everything has been quiet."

Shakira focused on him. "The reward means nothing to Stone-Agers living in some jungle. They probably don't even see the news." Sweat broke out from her forehead. "She left the same day. She killed those babies and ran."

Deon swallowed. "Our babies, darling. Not those babies."

Shakira burst into tears. "Why? What had those little girls ever done to harm anybody? They were the sweetest things in the world. Why?"

Deon pulled her close and hugged her to him. The rhythm of their cries blended till it became one sad music.

The following morning, Shakira insisted they visit the officers again to get more facts about the home country of the woman they now hated.

Lt. Will gave them the low-down on Nigeria without mincing words.

"On the west coast of Africa. It's believed to be the most populated country in the continent with about 170 million people. Figures vary. They have some educated leaders. A Nobel laureate comes from there—"

Shakira gaped. "They speak English?"

"They speak English," Deon said.

She flared, her emotions raging. "How do you know?"

Deon sighed. "I spent the night reading about the country."

She swallowed. "Oh."

She'd cried half the night like she did most nights. He didn't come into the room till the early hours of the morning, and she had assumed he'd gone to sleep elsewhere. It hadn't mattered. Dr. Brickam encouraged them to grieve together, but she couldn't share her grief with anyone. Not even Deon. He couldn't understand what had been taken away from her.

Deon addressed Lt. Will. "What we need to know is how much progress is being made looking for this woman."

Lt. Will frowned. "To be honest, this case is no longer in our jurisdiction." The couple stood, but he waved them to their seats. "Please. I didn't say we are not getting updates, but the best person to speak to is this guy." He scribbled a name and number on a piece of paper and gave it to Deon.

Deon stared at the paper for a moment. *Inspector Fraser.* He took Shakira's hand in his and gave a curt nod at Lt. Will. "Thanks for your help."

Chapter Five

Inspector Jorgeian Fraser of Interpol spoke confidently about the case, and this seemed to please Deon. He clapped and laughed for the first time in the house, and even carried Shakira into their bedroom and planted a kiss on her lips. But she wondered why. Fraser was only a voice on the line. He could be sipping coffee and browsing through *Men's Health* as he spoke. They were concerned parents. A phone call couldn't be enough.

Shakira squeezed out of his embrace. "I think we should call back to set an appointment."

Deon's eyes widened. "With who?"

She rolled her eyes. "Jorgeian Fraser."

He shrugged. "We just spoke with him, and he's on top of the case."

Shakira paced the space between the king-size bed and her closet. "So? We didn't know the case had left the jurisdiction of the KPD until we went to sit across from the officers."

"Jorgeian Fraser is in Washington DC. You want to fly across the country to sit in front of someone who knows his job? What will this do to the case?"

She held her head. Couldn't he understand? "It would give us a face and an identity and not just a case number," she cried.

Deon told her he needed to seal the deal for the glam offices in downtown Houston. His deal meant everything for their finances. Shakira couldn't wait an extra day to see Fraser, who agreed to meet the following day. The trip meant everything to her peaceful existence.

She traveled alone to Washington DC.

Being a home-girl, born and raised in Texas, Shakira found DC a bit overwhelming. Fraser worked in one of the stately buildings housing Interpol. He was the epitome of a triple-A geek. His age was hard to determine, but he could be fresh from some academy and sounded just as eager and confident about his assignment. Perhaps this was his first case? Was this good or bad?

Fraser wore professor glasses, which he tilted to rest on his nose. His straight dark hair hung in heavy bangs across his forehead but interestingly did not interfere with his deep blue eyes. A committed agent of international law enforcement, Shakira thought with some false humor.

"I'm so pleased we could meet at such short notice," she said as she took the seat opposite him in the Starbucks across from his office. He had chosen to meet her in a neutral place for reasons best known to him.

"Sorry for your loss, Mrs. Smith," Fraser drawled. A true Southerner? His accent hadn't seemed so thick when they spoke on the phone. "You flew in all the way from Houston?"

"Yes. Those babies were all we had—have, our only children."

Fraser pushed the glasses onto the bridge of his nose. "I understand such a great tragedy. My family was killed in an accident caused by a careless driver."

"Did you get closure?"

Once upon a time, this tragedy would have moved Shakira to tears and physical pain for Fraser, but after her experience, she felt nothing. No grief compared with losing one child. And two? How did she still manage to talk normally?

"Closure is a big word, Mrs. Smith. When you watch two people you love die, nothing gives closure."

She could identify. Nothing gave closure. "Was he apprehended? The driver?"

"She." He inhaled. "My twelve-year-old daughter. Ran the car over my mom and her mom. She's in a mental hospital today."

"Must be—hard," Shakira said, genuinely mortified. How horrible.

"Yes. Hard is a good word." He cleared his throat. "So what do you want to know about the case of the Nigerian woman?"

How could he sound so casual? If he had a twelve-year-old daughter and came across like this, then he couldn't be too old. Maybe in his forties? He appeared much younger. How could he look so much younger with such a tragedy in his life?

"What can Interpol do?"

He nodded as though to convince himself first. "Find the fugitive and extradite her. Bring her to the United States to face justice."

"Is it so simple, Inspector Fraser?"

"It's what we do every day. In the last forty years, the Interpol USNCB, uh, United States National Central Bureau, has recorded immeasurable success. We dig till we find."

Shakira sighed. Perhaps Deon was right. But she'd needed to see this man for herself. "I took time to read about Nigeria. It is a large country. It has over two hundred languages. They have a corrupt government and security is lapse."

"And we have agencies we work with in Nigeria. The police work well with us."

"The police in the country are corrupt."

"But we get our job done."

She sighed. "Has Interpol—your office—ever caught any Nigerian like in this case?"

"Mrs. Smith, I have worked for Interpol in three countries including Nigeria over the last ten years. If you've lost a needle in Nigeria, I'll find it for you."

Shakira tightened her lips. "So why is it taking so long? It's been over a month now. Almost Christmas. She could leave Nigeria and go to another country."

"We will find her. I assure you. And she will face justice."

"How do you do it? How do you face these evil people when you find them?"

Fraser sighed. "It's part of the closure I get every day. The freedom to bring justice to the earth is my peace."

"There is no peace anywhere."

"Except in the one who made you?"

"You're religious?"

"I got peace, Mrs. Smith. Peace that passes human understanding." He nodded. "This peace is what we truly all need."

Shakira closed her eyes. "The woman took everything from me. The most precious people to me. They were innocent children who never hurt anyone."

She talked about Leila. How caring and protective she was of her sister and her parents. Leila was the child who thought she could mother anyone. And Latoya was just so adorable, a calm baby who never fussed.

Inspector Fraser let her talk till her voice shook. Then he placed his hand on hers and squeezed gently.

"Mrs. Smith."

She dabbed at her eyes. "Yes?"

"Move on."

Chapter Six

hakira returned home ill. She couldn't hold anything down and had a splitting headache. When she couldn't sleep at night, Deon rushed her to the emergency room.

Reports from tests conducted in the night showed she was pregnant and needed to be on bed rest. She couldn't understand how the baby could have survived through the rough times of her life, days and nights of endless grieving. The result showed she was almost two months along.

She didn't want a baby. The doctor recommended she stay on, get admitted to the hospital, for a couple of days, but Shakira refused and signed herself out.

While Deon was at work, she drove 168 miles out to a thrill park and got on the most dangerous of the rides. She hoped to bleed her baby out, but this didn't happen. When she got back home, she mixed and drank stuff she found online and ended up in the emergency room again. She lost the baby.

Deon was beside himself with anger and disgust when all she needed was his comfort. But he had none to give. His hopes had lifted when the result of the tests showed she was pregnant. At least they could have something new to look forward to, and he told her as much. His gentle words resonated as he tried to convince her it was good news. With the deal sealed on his property, and the confidence from Fraser, and news of the baby coming, things indeed seemed to look up so soon after the tragedy.

But he only had vain hopes. Shakira saw nothing bright or hopeful. Those babies were not coming back, which meant everything. Though Fraser had promised to give her regular updates weekly, it meant nothing either. She had no plan to move on to anything. The eighth of November was frozen in time. Nothing could move the date.

Kenya came over to stay with her. In the weeks following the tragedy, her sister had been drilled like a suspect. Kenya wasn't the one who found the bodies, but that didn't matter because she was meant to be in the house after the babysitter left. A neighbor called after she saw Florence Odu hurriedly leave the house and the police came over to check out the house. They found the babies in the bath. Like everyone else, Kenya felt the story was clear enough, expressing her frustrations and grief. After the police cleared her, she stayed away, nursing her ego and mourning the girls she loved as her own. But after Shakira's miscarriage, Dr. Brickam put her on suicide watch, and Kenya volunteered to stay with her kid sister.

Shakira nursed a cup of coffee early one morning while Kenya made breakfast. "You've been through pain, Kenya. You know what loss is."

Kenya sighed. "It is indescribable."

"No one wants to understand. The worst is my husband. The father of those babies." Shakira shrugged. "He hasn't spoken to me since I came back from the hospital. What would we do with another child? Another potential victim? He refuses to see reason."

It had been a few days since the incident at the park, and Shakira had refused to talk about it. Deon took time off work, hoping she would respond to treatment, face the reality, and agree to go to the tropical island he suggested. Dr. Brickam had commented that if Shakira continued to see Leila and Latoya as "those babies," distancing herself from the crime, healing would take longer.

Kenya flipped eggs in the pan.

"What are you doing in my house, Kenya? You don't sleep at night. I see you watching me."

Kenya shifted slightly then put two slices of bread in the toaster. She poured some milk in a mug and put it in the microwave.

Shakira patted her arm. "Dr. Brickam sent you?"

"To look after you, yes."

"Seriously? I'll be fine, Kenya." She poured another cup. Kenya made to stop her but changed her mind. It was her fourth cup. The only thing willing to stay in her stomach was thick black coffee.

"Everyone is worried."

"The other day, Deon said I just committed murder. Can you believe he compared what happened to those babies with what happened to a piece of tissue?"

Kenya flinched. She made to remove the milk, but Shakira saw it.

"I can't understand it. When someone says *move on* when the bodies of those dear babies are still warm. Move on to what?"

Kenya opened the refrigerator and poured freshly squeezed orange juice into a glass. "Who said move on?"

Shakira told her about Fraser.

Kenya gasped. "I wonder what he first thought."

"What he first thought when? There are no first thoughts." She watched Kenya arrange a tray with the milk, juice, toast, and eggs. "The first thought is, what's going on, where am I?" Kenya placed the tray before her. She pushed it away.

"You've not eaten anything in almost a week, Shakira."

She laughed. "*Ya been heee tha long?*" she slurred with her dry humor.

Kenya kept a straight face. "You'll be sick."

"No. I won't. My body wants to live. My soul wants to live. My spirit wants to live. I want to see the woman who killed those babies come to justice. I want to see her roast on Texas death row."

"Shakira!" Kenya exclaimed. "You will seek the death penalty?"

"Yes."

Her parents had fought alongside Amnesty International on the death penalty. Before his death, her father had taught them to fight capital punishment. She expressed strong opinions for the cause of life without parole instead of death. But all ended on November the eighth, a day frozen in time.

Kenya poured a cup of juice for herself and drank it slowly.

"If you don't agree with me, then you don't understand it yet. I do. Now I sanction it. A person who would take the life of another is not fit to continue to live." She took a deep breath. "I don't know why I never saw it this way." She glared at her sister. "We were so blinded by our sheltered lives. We couldn't see the pain of others."

"So you ought to understand both sides now," Kenya said. "And this woman ran away, but I've wondered if this could have been an accident and she panicked?"

"There are no two sides, Kenya! Only one. The side of pain. The side of justice." She closed her eyes. "Fraser talked of peace, but there is no peace."

Deon walked in. "Good morning, Kenya."

"Morning, Deon. Hope you had a good night?"

Shakira opened her eyes. "He always has a good night."

Deon walked to the table and picked the glass of orange juice from the tray. "I am not your enemy, baby. Don't fight me." He drank the juice and took a piece of toast. "Thanks for breakfast, Kenya."

"It's my breakfast," Shakira said.

Deon gawked at her. "Then why aren't you eating it? Trying to kill the last member of my family?"

Kenya's hand flew to her chest. "Deon, please."

"You don't have family you don't want. It don't mean nothing to you who dies and who lives!"

"Shakira!"

"Let her talk, Kenya. Maybe then she can let off steam." Deon squeezed the toast into his mouth and chewed awkwardly.

Shakira shrugged. "I have nothing to say."

Deon drank milk. "No new exploits?"

Kenya walked over to stand between them. "Enough, Deon. Shakira, eat something, and you have medication to take."

"Yes, big sis." Shakira took the fork on the plate and pushed the eggs around, then stood up and walked out of the room.

Kenya followed her.

Chapter Seven

Fraser kept to his word and gave updates every week. He sounded positive, they'd made progress. Florence had been found in Nigeria but was not yet apprehended because, in truth, she eluded them and seemed to be one step ahead. Deon took a keen interest in the reports and made an effort to help his wife. He even got her to go back to work.

But after six months, Florence had still not been brought in.

"What's the problem, Fraser? Why can't she be arrested? She's been found, right?"

Fraser continued to assure her he was working toward getting Florence Odu, but she found it hard to believe. A man who told her to *move on* definitely would take her as just another case. Who would see her as an individual? A person with pain and needs.

On the one-year anniversary of the babies' deaths, Deon and Shakira and their families visited the graveside. The local news channels did a recap of the story and informed the public that Florence had still not been arrested.

"A news report on Channel 5 said there are predictions Nigeria will soon split," Deon said.

The family gathered in their home for light refreshments. His father, Braylon Smith, well-respected in Katy, patted Deon's shoulder. "I believe in our system, son. Even if the country tears to pieces, they'll still find her."

"Except it's been a year." Shakira closed her eyes. "I live for the day when she will be brought in handcuffed."

Nancy Graham, Shakira's mother, squeezed her hand. "There will be brighter days ahead."

Kenya walked in with the phone. "Channel 5 reporter."

Deon took the phone and spoke with the caller. She asked a few questions and spoke with Shakira, but it ended up being traumatic for her. She had thought she could talk about the girls after one year, but several times she broke down, and the reporter hung up after a couple of minutes.

Later, in the comfort of their room, Deon pulled his wife into his arms.

"This will end," he whispered softly. He nibbled her ear and traced kisses down her throat. Shakira shifted away. "Baby—"

"I can't." She wrapped the cover around her. "I'm sorry."

"It's been a year."

"I'm sorry."

"You can't or you won't?" Deon pushed the cover away and got up from the bed. "You're not sorry. Just selfish. And uncaring about anyone but yourself." He ran his hand through his curly hair.

"I can't. Don't you understand what this whole thing means to me?"

He flipped on the switch. "Help me understand why a woman will deny her husband affection for one full year." He paced. "Normal people are drawn together when they mourn. You. You push everyone away."

She sobbed at his harsh words. She thought he understood her now. He'd been so kind, helpful. She had gradually gained her momentum, started eating a little more, registered in her gym again, and resumed work.

"I'm not just a woman!" Her voice cracked. "I lost—everything."

"You have me. Don't I mean something to you?"

"I lost everything."

Deon stared her down and then stomped out. She covered her face and wept. If only he could understand. Nothing gave her pleasure anymore. Once Florence Odu was found, and condemned to death, then she could begin to live again. Until then there was nothing for her to do but wait.

The following morning, Deon left the house without saying goodbye. To absolve her conscience, she called in sick, deciding to visit the office of Home Helps, the agency which assigned Florence to their home. She regretted her decision not to do this earlier. Trusting in the system had cost her time, but she wasn't going to waste any more.

She had never met the manager, Theresa Wilcox, and when she introduced herself, the woman stiffened. Theresa was a thin, dark-skinned African woman. She spoke, as most of them did, trying to hide their African accent and copy an American one. Shakira detested her at once.

Her office was small and accommodated only her desk, a cabinet, and two visitor chairs. If anyone else worked with her, they weren't in today. She pointed Shakira to a seat across from her messy desk.

"Sorry about your loss, Mrs. Smith."

Shakira leaned forward. "Please, can you tell me where Florence is?"

Ms. Wilcox smirked. "If I knew, I'd be the first to tell. You cannot imagine the ugly publicity we've gotten since last year. For you to find me here is a miracle." She shook her head. "The FBI, Immigration, Border Agency, IRS, Interpol—everyone has been here. Even the Nigerian Embassy and Immigration Commission visited last week. Two of my best staff have been deported already."

"I wish I could feel sorry for you." Shakira swallowed. "Whatever loss you experienced can be replaced."

"I understand, and I feel so sorry for you. But I cannot help you."

"I know she left an address when she resumed work, but the police found nothing when they searched it. Do you have any address for any of her relatives?"

"I have the same address the police got."

Was Ms. Wilcox lying? "Do you know any of her friends, anyone she associated with? Her address in Nigeria?"

"No."

"Ms. Wilcox, why don't you want to help?"

Ms. Wilcox folded her arms across her chest. "I have given all the help I can—to the police, to Interpol, and to the FBI. I have nothing further to say."

Obviously, the woman was lying. Shakira stood. "Thank you for your time." She walked to the door and would have opened it.

"Mrs. Smith?" Ms. Wilcox called.

Shakira turned to face the other woman. "Yes?"

"Don't come back here."

Shakira opened the door and walked out. She drove to the next block and parked by the road and walked back to a café around the corner from the Home Help office, where she had a good view of the entrance to the office she just came from. She ordered cappuccino and waited.

On her third mug, Theresa Wilcox left her office, got into a car, and drove off.

Shakira waited three minutes then walked back to the Home Help office. She picked the lock, a skill she went out of her way to learn secretly in the last few weeks, and gained access to the office. The Wilcox woman had her files arranged in stacks in the cabinet.

She didn't search for anything in particular but would know what was important if she saw it. As expected, Florence Odu's file was missing. As fast as she could, she skipped through other personnel profiles.

When she walked out of Wilcox's office ten minutes later, soaked in sweat from her hurried and nervous search, Shakira had profile pages of three Nigerian women with her.

Chapter Eight

Nike Abu no longer worked at the daycare address in her file. A phone call later, she met with Shakira at the Katy Mills Mall parking lot.

She was a short, chubby woman with tribal marks on her face. Shakira thought the marks made her look vicious.

"Thanks for meeting me."

"Yes, Mrs. Smith. What business did you say you were doing?" Ms. Abu had a thick African accent, one she probably never could disguise like Theresa Wilcox's.

"I told you I had business for you. I'm after some information."

Ms. Abu scanned the surroundings like she was afraid of being seen in public. "Information? About what? How did you get my number?"

"A friend of mine, Theresa Wilcox, gave me your number. She seemed to believe in you," Shakira said.

The woman smiled, showing off uneven, stained teeth. "*Na wa o*," she mumbled. "So, what do you want to know?"

"Last year, a Nigerian woman named Florence Odu met me for business." Shakira hadn't thought this out properly. "I think she wanted to do gold business."

"Gold business? To buy gold from here or how?"

"Yes, I think—"

"Wait, wait. See, I just came into this country. I don't know what you're talking about." She stiffened. "I'm sorry, I can't help you." She quickly walked away.

"Wait a minute—"

Nike Abu broke into a run. Shakira startled. Nothing seemed unusual. What had triggered her?

Her phone rang.

Deon still had a sulky tone. "Where are you? I'm home."

"I went to the mall." She checked her time. *Wow.* It was almost six. Where had the time gone? She should have been home two hours ago.

She got into her car and decided to pursue the other two leads the following day. Seemed she would not go to work for a second day in a row.

Deon stood on the front porch, arms akimbo. She parked the car just outside of the garage and got out.

"Where did you go?"

"I told you I was at the mall."

She brushed past him and went into the house. She needed water. He followed her. He came up so close behind her his breath tinged her neck. She opened the refrigerator, decided on something other than water, and poured some orange juice.

"What did you get at the mall?"

"Nothing," she said calmly. "Leila loved to go to the mall."

"I called your office. They told me you called in sick. Why would you call in sick and then go to the mall?"

Shakira took the OJ and headed for her bedroom. What could she say? Now the school knew she lied. Well, she *was* sick. Tired of living like a ghost. Hated not sleeping at night. Missed those babies the woman murdered.

Deon followed her. "Shakira, answer me!"

"What? I *am* sick," she cried.

"That's it. I'm calling Dr. Brickam. She's gonna put you back on medication." Deon stomped out of the bedroom. She followed him.

"I just needed to get away from everything." She pulled at him. "After last night, I wanted to rethink—"

"You need to. Since last year, we have celebrated nothing except the birthday of the girls. You threw a party for—" He choked on his words. "Anyway, I hope you've had time to realize we have a life and a future."

Shakira swallowed. The home phone rang, and she heaved a sigh. Deon answered it. She walked back to the bedroom and drank her juice. A headache throbbed at her temples. Her stomach growled because she hadn't eaten anything since morning.

Deon walked in, his face drained of color. She studied him and feared the worst. Had someone died? She couldn't handle any bad news this time.

"Who is Theresa Wilcox?"

Shakira's heart dropped into her stomach. "Who?"

"Where did you go, Shakira? The woman said you broke into her office. Said you stole some files and threatened her staff."

"She's lying." She rubbed her temples. The headache hit harder. "What staff?"

"She called the cops."

"How would she even know I was there? Why do you believe her? You haven't even heard my side!" She unbuttoned her blouse and rolled down her skirt. A hot shower beckoned.

"So, tell me, Shakira. Who is she and what does she want with you?"

"You believe her already. I don't have to waste my breath." She walked toward the bathroom.

Deon caught her arm and swung her around. "She threatened to sue you. You tore off profile pages of three Nigerian women in her employ and met one of them. The woman recognized who you were and ran for her safety. And called Theresa. What did you want with the Nigerian women? Why those three?"

Shakira closed her eyes and allowed his words to swirl around her. Smart woman, yet how could the clumpy thing know who she was? No wonder she ran off. She must be illegal too. But Florence wasn't illegal. She had her green card.

"Shakira? Talk to me." Deon moved closer, and his breath fanned her face.

She opened her eyes and stared into the eyes of the man she loved more than anything. Though she wasn't sure she had capacity to love him anymore.

"She's right." She sighed. He released her and stepped away as though she carried a plague.

"They all know you, Shakira. Why would you think they wouldn't? Every Nigerian woman in the United States now knows you."

"I just wanted to find out where Florence is."

"I hear Nigerians are loyal." He dragged his hand over his face. "Even if they know where she is, they won't tell."

"But why? As mothers, don't they see? As women?"

"Why those three?"

"They were the only Nigerians in the files. Others were from some other countries in Africa."

Deon sighed. "Let it go, Shakira. I pleaded with the Wilcox woman to drop any charges, but you have to release it."

Shakira closed her eyes. She couldn't. "I will."

Deon drew her into his arms and hugged her neck. "They'll find her. I believe they will. Let the authorities do their job and find her, sweetheart."

She wasn't sure even Deon believed his own words.

Chapter Nine

The second woman had left the country a month earlier. It left Shakira with one last name. Eugenia Afokang. Eugenia worked in a playgroup by day and a restaurant in downtown Houston at night. To get off Deon's radar, Shakira called him. "I'm visiting Kenya."

He paused a beat. "When will you be home?"

In her mind's eye, she could see him calculating. "Eight?"

"Too late, Shakira. Wait till I get home and we could—"

"No, Deon. Please give me some space. See you later."

"Shakira—"

She hung up and squeezed her eyes shut. She tried watching Eugenia at the playgroup she worked for but couldn't approach due to her thudding heart. The restaurant then.

There was no harm in going after this case in her own little way. What law enforcement agents couldn't see, she might.

It was close to five. She drove to the Galleria where Eugenia worked. With traffic on I-90 she arrived after six and found a space in the parking lot.

The luxury restaurant was almost full, but a nice waiter found her a table. She placed an order for soda and cobb salad.

When her drink was served, she asked for Eugenia.

"I'll get her for you, ma'am."

Eugenia walked over to her almost half an hour later, a frown on her face. She was dark-skinned and obese but carried herself well, and the white and black uniform all the waiters wore fitted.

"Eugenia—"

One look at Shakira and her jaw dropped. "What do you want?" she whispered.

"I just need to talk with you about Florence," Shakira said, lowering her voice too.

Eugenia's bloated face seemed to explode. She took a step away from the table. "Get away from me."

Shakira stood. "Please. Do you know her? Her family?"

A man in a black dinner suit walked up to the table. His name tag read *Ryan Green*. "Any problem, ma'am?"

Shakira did something she hadn't imagined she was capable of. She demanded that Eugenia be the waitress to serve her table.

Ryan Green obliged. Eugenia's expression changed, like she could burst at any moment. Shakira resumed her seat and squinted at the other woman.

"I will get your order," Eugenia said.

"Before you do, what can you tell me about the Nigerian woman, Florence?"

Eugenia let out a deep breath. "Nothing. I don't know her. I never met her."

"But you must have talked about her, and me. You know she killed two babies." Shakira moistened her lips. "She must have family somewhere."

"I will get your order."

Eugenia left the room. Shakira followed her and caught her midway between the kitchen and the hall on a busy corridor.

"Eugenia!"

"What do you want with me? I cannot help you. Do you want me to lose *ma* job? Leave me alone. I don't know *tha* woman you talk about."

Other servers hurried along. None stopped in their tracks to speak. Another suited supervisor came along.

"Eugenia, please report to the back office. Ma'am?"

"You see *wor* you done. You *gor* me fire. You *gor* me fire."

Eugenia walked away using the dirtiest words imaginable mixed with a language Shakira suspected to be her African dialect. The supervisor ushered Shakira out of the building and politely asked her to go home.

She walked to the parking lot feeling stupid and hoped Eugenia didn't get fired. More importantly, she hoped the woman would not go after her and press any charges. She pushed her key into the lock and jumped when a shadow dashed behind her. Scared to death, she whirled and came face to face with an Asian-American man.

He spoke clean American English. "What do you want with Eugenia?"

Shakira clutched her chest. "Who are you?"

"Call me Sean. I know a lot of people." He smirked. "You're the mother of those little ones, aren't you?"

Shakira swallowed. Her voice sounded thin when she spoke. "Yes."

Sean pushed his hands in his pockets. "Eugenia is a rallying point for those Nigerian—" He used a bad word, and she flinched. He laughed. "Don't feel bad. If she gets fired tonight, it's because she's got too much on her plate." He paced in front of her.

"Who are you?"

"Huh? A helper?" He shrugged. He brought out his hand from his pocket and a piece of paper with it. "Here's someone who can help you. She used to be one of those—women. She will be able to answer your questions." He pushed the paper into her hand and walked away.

Shakira got into her car and drove off. Through the forty-five-minute drive back, she pondered on her luck. She'd stolen a glance at the name on the paper. She couldn't quite pronounce it. The address was in the ghetto. Deon would never let her go to the rough area. She called Kenya.

"Shakira! Where have you been? Gosh! I've been calling you all evening. Deon called. Asked if you were with me, and to talk to you. What's going on, girl?"

"It's a long story but I'm coming to you right now."

"Come fast, girl. Deon said he was coming over. I told him we were over at a restaurant downtown. Whew!"

Shakira giggled. "Oh, thank you for covering up. You are such a darling."

"I hope I won't regret it."

"No. No, you won't."

Kenya was dressed as though to go out when Shakira arrived.

"I had to change in case Deon showed up." She stared at her only little sister. "Where did you go?"

She filled Kenya in. "Look at the name." She showed her the piece of paper.

"*Mow-show-ree-re Oh-gun-yeah-mai*," Kenya read out. "She lives in a bad part of town. I don't think you should go there, pumpkin."

"What do I do then? The case is going cold."

"Can't you call her?" Kenya read through what was written on the piece of paper again. It had no phone number. "Why don't you ask Inspector Fraser?"

"He calls every week, religiously. But I could almost say his exact words in my sleep."

"Going after these people isn't safe or wise. And to what end?"

"I could help law enforcement. I might be able to find something they are missing."

Chapter Ten

*B*ad part of town didn't begin to describe the slum the Nigerian woman lived in. To distract Deon, Shakira made an appointment with Dr. Brickam but left work an hour before the time.

The dirty, angry, stoned faces she passed reminded her of characters in movies set in the Bronx. Maybe a little worse. Part of the numbering of the apartments was worn off, but she finally found the block with Moshorire's address.

She wound her way through a rickety stairway, a stinking corridor, and knocked on the correct apartment door.

The door opened only enough for an eye and a lip to show. "Who?"

"Mow-show—"

"It's Mo. What?"

"I'm from—Sean."

"Who Sean want. I pay his money. Go tell him. I pay his money to the capital." The door would have closed but Shakira put her hand to stop it.

"Not about money. About Florence." To her amazement, the door opened fully.

"Come in. Fast."

Shakira squeezed in and faced a thin woman about her same five-six height, with an old graying wig and bedroom slippers. She wore a skimpy top and shorts. Her face, well, Shakira had learned not to call anyone ugly.

"Sit down. Coffee?"

Her heart warmed at the woman's hospitality, but she couldn't bring herself to taste anything in this dingy, sparsely furnished room. The cover on the settee was torn and dirty. There was no bed or closet, and a few clothes were strewn across a closed suitcase.

"Thank you, no."

"Florence kill your baby and run."

There were two babies. Shakira swallowed, and nodded. "I just need her to answer my questions."

"Nigeria far *oh*. And nobody, not even America, go find her there. I know *wohram* saying. If she enter her village."

"Could you give me the name of the village? Where you think she went?"

"You want follow her? Ah." She made a thin laughing sound. "You can't."

Shakira decided to get whatever information she could. "Did you know her—well?"

"My mother and her mother come from same place. But look me here. Florence no help me anyway. She see *wohrai* do here. She tell my mother." Her voice cracked.

Ah, a grouch. Would this person be truthful? "What do you do?"

Mo eyed her withering body, and Shakira blanched. What man would come near such a woman in such stench? Plates with grime were piled in one corner, and the odor made her turn away.

"It pay my bill. And I will come out when I pay Sean. I will have my freedom, do *wohrai* like."

"How long have you been in the States?"

The question seemed to puncture the other woman's confidence. Tears sprang where they were least expected. Mo sniffed. "A long time. *Buhrai* was here when Florence enter this country. I know *wohrai* do to help her."

Shakira listened hard and tried to figure out her skewed accent and run-over words. She needed all the information she could get about Florence and where she came from.

"Then Flo meet my husband and snatch him. Take *evertin* from me. Throw me out in winter." She bit down on her teeth. "*Buhrai* survive."

Shakira had no pity for her. "How long ago?"

Mo shrugged. "Seven year. Sean see me and give me this place. I pay rent. After living on the road for a year plus. Sean find me. I do *wohrai* like and pay him his capital end of month." She sighed. "It second week now. I have not pay last *mont.*"

With Deon breathing down her neck, she knew she had to leave. "Please tell me where Florence is."

"Efayaw, where her mother from."

"Efayaw?"

"In Cross River close to Bakassi side. Cross River state in Nigeria. If she hide there, no man on earth can find her."

Chapter Eleven

hakira knew what she had to do. She just didn't imagine getting the Nigerian visa would be so expensive or so tough. With her determination though, nothing could stop her now. Her days in Katy were over till she found Florence Odu. It didn't matter what options she had. There were none. She had been on this path of destruction since Florence killed her daughters. She may seem like she had a death wish, but it was the opposite of a desire to live.

Her new allies, Mo and Sean, got her the necessary documentation she needed, and she didn't care if it was forged as long as it got her where she was headed. Mo even provided a name and contacts of someone she could see in Lagos, Nigeria. Shakira was excited for the first time since the murders.

She rushed home with her new documents and pulled out her suitcase. She was half done packing when Deon burst into the room, his green eyes flames of wild fire.

"What's going on, Shakira? You cleaned out the savings account."

She only had her underwear left to pack. "Who told you?"

"I got a call from the bank, standard procedure—where are you going?"

"Nigeria."

She avoided his gaze, but for a full minute she felt the air move in the room.

Deon's voice seemed to come from far away. "Nigeria?"

"It's why I took the money."

She finished up. Her flight was at ten in the night. She'd had no plans to tell him. He would have come home to find a note.

"Shakira."

The brokenness in his voice did nothing to her emotions. She was beyond anything he or anyone else could do and needed to concentrate now and make sure she had everything for the trip. Mo had advised her on traveling light. She may need to shop for local clothes to help her blend in better.

It was a long flight ahead, and she would need her wits about her. She walked to the kitchen and got a glass of milk from the refrigerator.

Deon stood at the doorway. "Does your mom know about this? Kenya?"

"Those who care know." With arms akimbo, she faced him. "I'm doing this for those babies. Heaven will judge me, if I don't."

"What about me? What about us?"

She folded her arms across her chest. "What about us?"

Deon swallowed. "We have a marriage. We had an existence before we had kids."

She shrugged. "So?"

Tears gathered in his eyes. "Don't you care for what we had?"

She sucked in her breath. "What we had was blessed. Till roughly a year ago."

If he refused to understand, there was nothing she could do to help him.

"I release you from your vows to me, Deon. It's the best I can give you now." She brushed past him.

She still had a couple of hours, but it was no use staying. He could try and stop her, but he didn't. She picked up her suitcase and handbag. Leila's favorite teddy, Shrek, was going on this trip for luck. For a moment, her emotions threatened to overwhelm her. She had to be strong for those babies. Now was not the time to concede defeat. The battle ahead was huge, and she was ready to face it or die trying.

She shut the door after her, sure Deon stared at her. She'd never seen him so speechless. For a moment, she thought she might have taken this too far. Deon always handled their challenges with maturity and wisdom, and in fairness to him, she'd not been much of a wife since the tragedy. But she couldn't help this situation. This was thrown at her. How was she expected to cope? Handle such a tragedy—no one had the how-to for this one.

Whoever planned for such a horrible occurrence? Life throws you for a loop and you have to take it. She was taking what life gave her the best way she could.

———

The flight to Lagos was uneventful. Almost twelve hours as she had been told.

A hot, gusty stench accosted her when she stepped off the plane. She wondered if there was a maintenance crew employed. Border control didn't look like any she'd seen in a movie before. This appeared worse than she'd envisaged.

Two hours later, and dripping with sweat from the heat, she finally got her suitcase, thankfully in one piece at the baggage claim. Next, she stepped through customs check to the arrivals lounge.

Mo had given her a number to call. She fumbled in her bag and found the piece of paper with the name and number.

"Taxi, madam!"

She glanced at the middle-aged man who'd spoken. "Yes, please. And I need to make a call."

"Come with me," the man said.

He reached for her suitcase.

Shakira shook her head. "No, thanks."

"Fine. This way."

The taxi driver led her to a row of kiosks and stopped in front of one. "You can buy an MTN line here. And a new phone too."

The kiosk, all branded yellow and labeled with MTN, seemed busy with two salespeople who attended to travelers.

A lady spoke to her. "Yes, madam?"

"I need to make a call." Shakira showed her the number.

"Are you new in Nigeria?"

"Yes."

"It's better you buy a line. I can get you a good bargain with data so you can check your emails and use chats and all."

Shakira beamed. "Really? Great."

The eager sales representative brought out a package with a phone and a sim card. "With 2015 MB data, 3000 call credits and SMS, and a branded smartphone. It's twenty thousand naira."

"Twenty thousand! How much is it in dollars, please?" Twenty thousand! She'd been warned of fraud.

"A hundred twenty-five dollars. We take dollars too." The lady held a phone box. "3000 to make calls and send texts. Plus data. 2015 MB. Like two *gig*."

Shakira thought the eager sales lady spoke too fast. "Oh, okay." With a phone, quite cheap, she thought. She pulled the money from her purse and paid.

The lady put her package in a bag and handed her the phone. "You can dial the number you have now and send messages to any network in Nigeria. And if you need *airtime*, just look for this branded kiosk around town and you'll be helped." She simpered. "MTN is the best network."

"What's *airtime*?"

The lady didn't seem to understand her question. "What? Airtime?"

"Yes. Is it an app?"

She laughed. "No, not an app. A recharge, or refill, of the credit on your phone. For data too. If you run out of data."

"Oh." Shakira sighed. "Thanks a lot." She kept the new phone in her bag, confused already at all the strange information about making calls.

The lady leaned closer. "Would you like to change some US dollars to local currency? I can help. There are many con-men around."

Shakira struggled with a decision to take the offer or not. She'd planned to use Mo's contact for everything she'd need, but what harm could there be, and she'd feel better paying the scruffy-looking taxi driver in the local naira.

"What's the exchange rate?" She hoped it would be as she'd found it online.

"I can give you 155 naira. You can't get it as good in the bureau-de-change."

Her search engine told her 150.

She considered a moment. "I'll change a thousand, if you please."

The lady's eyes widened. "Give me a minute."

She spoke to her colleague and stepped out of the kiosk. With the taxi driver still in tow, the MTN woman led her through a maze to a corner. She waited a bit and then a man came to meet her. The transaction was swift, and Shakira soon had 155,000 naira in her bag.

"The girl cheat you. Is 160 if you go black market. Or 162 *sef*," the driver said and led her out of the building.

She shrugged inwardly. At least she had some cash to spend in the meantime.

The air outside hit her face like a furnace. She'd come from a sixty-five-degree air-conditioned terminal. Not bad regardless, she thought.

"I still need to change more money. Later."

"I can take you to where they will change for you," he said.

It was dusk by her watch. She didn't want to wander around at night, especially because she didn't know where to go.

"No, thank you."

They left the pavement where a few security personnel stood guard and joined a throng of people pressing on every side. Where did they all come from?

"No problem."

She raised her voice. "Where are we going?"

"Car park. Taxi no *dey* wait here." The man walked fast. "Hold your bag *oh*."

He'd hardly finished saying this when her suitcase was yanked from her. She swung around just in time to grab her handbag. Shrek fell. One strap of her bag had been cut. She hugged what remained, bent quickly, and picked up Shrek.

"Wait! Help! My luggage." The driver moved ahead. "*Hey*! Stop!" He didn't. Shakira bit her lip. "Excuse me! *Hey*!"

Chapter Twelve

First, she retraced her steps back to the arrivals area. She had to report that her suitcase had been snatched. Hot tears ran down her cheeks. She pushed against the crowd, her handbag clutched to her chest. All she had now was the money she'd just changed. Everything else was gone with her luggage.

A uniformed man stood at the entrance to the airport.

"Excuse me, sir," she said.

He paid attention to her. His polite manner reassured her. "How may I help you, madam?"

"My suitcase was snatched. Please. Just outside. Over there." She swallowed the lump in her throat. "By the curb."

"So sorry about the theft. I'll lead you to our airport police station so you can make a proper report."

She nodded. "Thank you, sir."

The officer took her two floors up and then three down, and back outside to another section of the airport. The elevators were old. Several times she thought they'd stop midway. Shakira followed the man inside what was much like a cargo container used to transport cars. Two uniformed men stood chatting behind a counter.

"Sergeant, theft." The officer with her saluted, and the others murmured responses. He addressed her. "They will handle your case."

"Madam, what happened?"

Both men looked the same to her, skinny, dark, and with the same shaped eyes as several other men she'd observed.

"My suitcase was snatched from me." Each time she said the words, hot tears clogged her throat and her voice came out muffled. This was not the welcome she had expected of Nigeria.

The second officer arched an eyebrow. "Don't cry, madam. We will find it."

"Here." The first pushed a piece of paper and pen toward her. "Write down what happened."

Shakira wrote with shaky fingers.

"Describe the bag. And put your name, passport number, the flight you came in with, and the location you're going to. How long you will stay, and where you will stay while in Nigeria."

She took out the piece of paper with Mo's contact. While she wrote, a third officer came into the space. The other two saluted.

The new man directed a scrutinizing gaze at her. "Good evening, madam."

She mumbled, "Good evening."

"What is the problem? I am Police Detective Dauda, Airport Area Command."

Shakira thought he sounded important. "I am Shakira Smith. My luggage was snatched."

He asked his colleagues, "Have you taken her statement?"

The first officer responded, "She was just writing it, sir."

"Okay, madam," Detective Dauda said. "Finish up, and I will look at it."

He stood beside her as she finished her statement. He took the sheet of paper and read it. "Hmm, we'll find it." He gave her the paper. "Please write a list of the items in your suitcase. When we find it you can confirm."

His confident tone calmed her raging emotions. She listed her few clothes, nine thousand US dollars and some change, photographs of her daughters and Florence Odu, and a set of simple gold jewelry.

He studied the list. "We will find the bag. Just wait here." He sighed. "Maybe none of the money and jewelry though." He frowned at the other policemen. "If we can act fast enough. Call the chairman of the *area-boys*. I need the bag intact, immediately."

"Yes sir."

The space was narrow and could accommodate no more than two visitor chairs behind the counter. Detective Dauda pointed her to one and asked her to sit down while the officers did his bidding.

Shakira checked her watch. A few minutes to five. It was so dark outside now. She worried about Mo's contact. She needed to get to the place or call the number at least. Maybe the person could pick her up at the airport.

She dialed the number on the paper, and after several rings a female answered the call.

"Hello? Yes?"

The person must be in a crowded place because the noise in the background nearly drowned out her voice.

"Hello. Is this Glory? I'm Shakira. Mo gave me your number. Hello?"

"Yes, this is Glory. Who are you?"

"Mo, from Houston, Texas? She said I should call you when I arrive."

"Oh oh oh. Yes, Mo. Mo," the lady shouted. "Where are you? Where are you?"

"I'm still at the airport. My luggage was stolen." Shakira sighed. "I'm waiting at the police station for it to be found."

"Ah. Ah. No, don't wait. Don't wait. The police will just collect your money. Start coming. Start coming."

Shakira panicked. "I can't leave without my suitcase."

"They can't find it. Start coming. Start coming."

The lady hung up. Shakira stared at her phone. Why did she repeat her words? What would she do now? Maybe she could return to the airport the following day. What a distraction. She wanted to set out on her journey to Florence's tomorrow. It had to wait now. Unless this police issue wrapped up.

She walked over to the detective who stood at one side and fiddled with his phone.

"Excuse me. I need to go to the place where I'm staying. I called just now, and she's asked me to come."

The detective didn't pause what he was doing, which Shakira thought was quite rude. "Where is the place?"

She fumbled in her bag and brought out the piece of paper. He stared at it for a split second and scoffed. "You can't go there tonight. Mile 2? It's too late, the traffic is awful, and this particular area in Mile 2 is not safe, especially for strangers."

She swallowed. "Maybe I could ask to be picked up."

He shrugged. "My advice is you wait till we find your bag tonight, spend the night at the airport hotel, and in broad daylight find your friend."

He made sense. She nodded. "I agree. I'll call her back and let her know."

Glory's number didn't go through, so she sent a message. With this, she returned to her seat and prayed her bag would be found and, by some miracle, still be intact.

Two hours later, Detective Dauda had news for her. She'd dozed on and off several times. She was exhausted, and her body protested.

"We found your suitcase, Ms. Smith. Unfortunately, it was empty."

Her throat went dry. "Empty!"

"Totally." Detective Dauda had the thickest eyebrows she'd ever seen, and he arched them again. She gauged his age at mid-thirties. "I will continue the investigation on this, but at least you can go and rest at the hotel now and go to your friend in the morning."

She sniffed. "I don't know what to do, detective. How can it be empty?" She shuddered. "I'm so confused."

He took her elbow. "What I can do is see you to the airport hotel. You've traveled a long way. You're tired. You need to rest. And dawn breaks soon."

She checked her watch. "It's only about eight. I can try and—"

"Sorry, madam. Nigeria is six hours ahead. You're still on American time."

Shakira wanted to disappear. "Oh yeah." She glared at her watch, willing herself to hold back tears.

"Let me take you to the hotel." Detective Dauda told his colleagues of his plan. Without seeking her permission, he grabbed her left elbow with his right hand and ushered her out.

She needed the support. Needed someone to take charge because she couldn't believe this was happening to her. She missed Deon, wished she'd waited a little longer to get his consent, and probably have him come along. *No*, a voice in her head screamed. She did this for those babies. She couldn't regret it now. Deon would never have agreed to come with her. He wouldn't even fly to DC with her.

Detective Dauda drove her in an old police-branded van to a hotel a few blocks away from the airport and advised her to change her time to Nigerian time.

"This is my card. Call me if you have any problem." He handed her the empty suitcase. "I copied the number on your sheet of paper. I'd like to know you're safe."

When he was gone, Shakira stood in the middle of a clean but small, modestly furnished hotel room. Did the police officer pay for the room? They'd just collected a key at the reception and walked to the room. How generous. She had to thank him.

But now the walls closed in on her. What was she doing here?

She dropped on the double bed made with fresh white linens and hugged a cool pillow. She missed home, and those babies, Kenya, her life. Deon, her only love.

She sobbed. "What am I doing here?"

Chapter Thirteen

A strange noise woke her, and Shakira rubbed her eyes. For a moment, she lost awareness of her surroundings. She checked her watch and gasped. It was 10 a.m. Was this American time or Nigerian time? She couldn't remember if she reset her watch as the police detective advised or not. Her heart thudding, she dragged herself off the bed and walked to the bathroom. Thankfully, hot water ran in the tub. She chose to have a quick shower instead, though she had to wear her dirty clothes again. The warm water soothed her a bit.

Her stomach grumbled with hunger, and she found her way to the reception area where she was told her bill was twelve thousand.

Her heart skipped. She didn't have such a huge amount. Then she remembered it was not US dollars. "Oh, yes." She brought out the money. Mentally, she converted it to the currency she knew. "Please, is there a place where I can get a cup of coffee anywhere around?"

"We have a nice restaurant here in the hotel. And breakfast is still being served," the enthusiastic receptionist said with twinkling eyes. "The door across the hallway." She pointed it out to Shakira.

"Thank you."

After a heavy breakfast of bacon, sausages, omelets, and toast, and several cups of instant coffee, which she hated but had to do with because there was no brewed coffee, Shakira breathed in, satisfied. The buffet meal cost her about thirty dollars with tip, which wasn't bad considering how hungry she was. And though the coffee was decaffeinated, she preferred it to tea.

The receptionist got her one of the hotel-registered taxis, and she headed for Glory's place.

The ride was long and plagued with endless delays caused by traffic jams and bad roads.

Four hours later, terrified she may have been abducted, she breathed out in relief when the taxi driver said to her, "We are in the area."

Shakira absorbed the environment, her lips pressed together so hard she might never get them to separate again. She'd never seen a road so narrow with potholes. Rundown houses merged from line to line, some with their roofs falling apart. The drainages were large and full of dirt and water all running across the road.

Air wafted in from the street laden with a stench so concentrated she held her breath.

"Are you sure this is where you're supposed to go?" the driver asked.

Shakira blinked. "The address on the paper—I guess so."

"This is a rough area." The driver parked the car close to a ditch. "I think you should let them meet you."

"Okay."

"You can call from inside the car, here. I'll wait."

Glory had not picked up her calls in the morning, and Shakira had taken the risk to come without being sure. But she couldn't have stayed in the hotel either.

After three tries, Glory answered. "*Aha*, where were you? I waited for you yesterday."

"I'm sorry. I—I told you my suitcase was stolen. I had to—"

"What about the money? The money you were to change?"

Shakira sucked in her breath. "Gone. All gone."

"*Ah!* What kind of bad luck is this?"

"But I'm here now. On your street."

"On my street? Where?"

She tapped the driver. "Where are we?"

"Tell her in front of the famous brothel. The one they call One Sister."

"Right in front of—of One Sister."

"Who is with you?"

"The taxi—I came in a taxi."

"*Oh*, so you still have some money?"

"For the taxi, yes."

"Okay, I'm coming."

Shakira sighed. "Thank you. See you soon."

"I think I should just take you back to the hotel." The driver shook his head. "This place is a famous brothel. I know this area." He frowned. "Let me see the piece of paper with the address." Shakira gave it to him. He pointed at the address. "See the way the address is written. After the number and street name, what is this?"

Shakira read aloud: "Ask for One Sister."

"Everyone knows it once you enter this street." He pointed at a two-story building. "Ah, here she comes, from inside the brothel."

Shakira took a deep breath to summon courage. A brothel. A woman about in her thirties dressed in a simple knee-length gown, and holding two phones in one hand, and another to her ear, walked across and around the debris to the taxi.

"Shakira?"

She nodded. Shakira opened the door and, seeing how filthy the ground was, exclaimed, "The ground is muddy! Can you move away to somewhere better?"

"Are you sure you want to follow this woman," the driver muttered under his breath. "She's a prostitute. Do you know her from somewhere? This is a terribly bad place!"

She shuddered. "She's a friend's sister."

The driver shrugged and moved a little forward. The ground wasn't all clean but at least not as wet. Shakira paid his fare and got out with her empty suitcase and handbag.

Glory chewed gum noisily. "Welcome. How was the journey?"

Glory had a slim stature and a fairer skin color than Florence's. Shakira didn't see a resemblance although Mo had told her they were sisters. It could mean anything in the African context, though. She hesitated, and Glory arched an eyebrow. Quickly, she reminded herself of her mission and followed her host.

"It went well; a little long for me."

The taxi slowly pulled away, and for a moment Shakira wished she could go with him. Inside the One Sister building was a reception area, with a young woman behind the counter. Glory waved at her and took a staircase. Rooms lined both sides of a corridor with tiled floor, much like a hotel. The wall was stained with peeling paint. The doors were wooden gloss-painted with gold-plated fancy numbering. Glory's was number eleven.

She opened it, and they both walked in. The thick stench of body sweat, and cheap perfume filled Shakira with nausea. She held in the bile and observed her environment. The curtains were open, and she caught a glimpse of the filthy street she'd just come from.

Glory's furniture was cheap and old, limited to a couch, two chairs, a double bed, and a table in the center of the room. A flat-screen TV unit was mounted on the wall. She switched it on, and the room filled with hip-hop music from a music channel.

"So how is everything? Please sit down."

Her warmth convinced Shakira she was right to stay. "I wish to go to Efayaw tomorrow."

Glory sighed. "This is the weekend and I am so busy. We can go to Efayaw on Monday."

"No, I won't—"

"You don't even have money to pay me to take you there. You said everything is gone?"

There was an edge to Glory's tone, which reminded Shakira of the taxi driver's suggestion.

"Yes." She nodded. "But I can give you my word. I promise—"

"Promise! Promises don't pay my bill here. I have to work," she snapped. "We will go on Monday; otherwise, you can give me two hundred thousand to take you there tomorrow."

Shakira gasped. Did she make such a huge amount on a weekend? "I don't have so much."

"Then let me work." Glory squeezed her nose. "Today is Friday. Customers are many."

"What do you do?" She probably shouldn't have asked. "I mean—do—you have to go out?"

"I work here in my room. You may just wait in the corridor until my clients leave."

Shakira glanced at the rumpled sheets on the bed. Coupled with the reek of body heat when she walked in, she thought Glory must have been "working" when she called in the morning.

"I need some clothes."

"*Huh*! With no money? What is this?"

She opened her bag and brought out a bundle. "I have some nairas."

Glory pursed her lips. "*Hmm*. How much?"

"Enough. I can get simple clothes worth ten to fifteen dollars each, I hope."

She wanted to tell Glory she changed a thousand but held back. The hungry look on Glory's face spoke volumes. Her money would be all gone if she trusted this one.

"There are shops down the street. We can walk there now."

"Thank you."

Shakira was glad to buy five simple dresses at the equivalent of about thirty dollars each. She bought underwear she found too cheap for her taste, and at ludicrous amounts, wondering if they were supposed to be this expensive or whether Glory had a pact with the shop owner.

A rough-looking Asian was at the reception desk when they returned. Glory motioned to him with her head, and he followed them upstairs. At her door, she clicked her tongue. "Drop your things inside and wait for me outside."

The Asian followed Glory in. When she realized what was about to take place, a wave of nausea overwhelmed Shakira and she could have thrown up the sumptuous meal she had that morning.

She held on to her bags and waited outside. In her heart of hearts, she wished this experience away. She should have waited on Interpol to do its job. Coming to Nigeria was a huge mistake. Why was she so impulsive? Did her daughters' deaths rob her of all reason?

She leaned against the discolored wall and fought tears. Maybe she deserved this. To be punished for taking up a job instead of looking after her babies herself. This would never have happened if she'd been home with her kids. But Deon's real estate business was going down. They needed the extra cash, though he never agreed with her.

A door down the corridor opened, and Shakira startled. A drunken dark-skinned man stumbled out into the corridor, the loud laughter of a woman trailing him. He headed toward her, and she pressed her back against the wall.

She held her breath until after the drunk staggered past with a mumbled greeting.

About an hour later, the Asian opened the door and stepped out. He walked away without a word. Shakira struggled with the decision to stay or go inside. She couldn't bear the stench, which would only be stronger in the room. Her stomach rumbled with hunger, and she wondered when she might eat next. But as it was, she had to bear with Glory until she got to Efayaw.

A phone rang, and it took a minute to realize it was her new phone. "Hello?"

"This is Detective Dauda from Airport Area Command. Ms. Smith?"

"Hello, detective."

"How are you?"

He hadn't paid her hotel bill, even knowing she had been robbed. But this thought had no authenticity. He didn't owe her, after all. "I'm fine."

"I checked at the hotel and was told you left."

She had to make up a quick story. "Yes, I—I'm with my friend's sister."

"Are you sure you're alright?"

Shouldn't she have a police officer take her to Efayaw? He might better understand her plight, and she'd be safer.

"Yes. Thank you."

"If you need any assistance at any time, call me."

"Thank you." She hung up. Could she rely on the policeman? He'd shown a noteworthy level of concern.

She faced Glory. "Are you coming in or not? I cooked dinner."

"Yes, thank you."

Chapter Fourteen

Monday couldn't come fast enough. Glory made Shakira pay for accommodation and food. She endured several men coming in and out of the room and ate rice all weekend because it was the only edible thing Glory offered.

Finally, she woke up from the couch she'd insisted sleeping on, all stiff and sore, but excited. Today she would get on to the real reason she had to put herself through this hell.

Glory left early to get some supplies and returned midmorning. "I have a problem." She dropped a bag of medical supplements on the center table. "I can't travel today. Some people came in early this morning. From the ships."

Shakira frowned. "I don't understand."

"I'm going to have visitors. These guys have a lot of money, and we are few. I can't leave today. Maybe tomorrow or next. Because those guys may be around for a week."

"A week!" She couldn't stand another day in this disgusting mess.

"I'm not saying it will take a week. But I can't travel today. We'll go tomorrow."

Shakira swallowed. One more day. She let out a long breath. "Okay."

"Good." Glory removed packets of noodles from a drawer. "They will soon be here. We have to be ready."

After a tasteless meal of noodles, Glory made her help tidy the room. They changed the sheets and sprayed air freshener. It helped a little.

"They may come in back-to-back, or more than one at a time," Glory said. "I'll just take a shower now." She walked into her bathroom and shouted, "These guys will pay top dollar."

Shakira held her waist. The room did look some better. She thought of what to do if they came more than one at a time. She hoped Glory didn't expect her to participate in an orgy. In the last couple of days, she'd counted at least ten men, most of them Asian. Dirty, scruffy-looking, smelly men she couldn't imagine standing close to, let alone share a bed or body with. What sort of life was this? Mo never told her Glory was a soiled bird.

Glory soon re-entered the bedroom and popped two capsules from a bottle she'd brought from the bathroom. She opened another bottle and drank all the liquid. Her eyes rolled back, and she let out a sigh of relief. For a moment, she stood swaying, and then she laughed.

"Good to go, girl."

Shakira cleared her throat. "I'll, um, wait outside."

"You go ahead."

She wished she could go for a walk but feared the streets. The few times she'd gone out with Glory, she'd come to a blunt realization. She was in the worst of the ghettos she'd ever visited in her life. Mo's neighborhood didn't begin to come close. Besides the people, the filth on the streets measured to none she knew. She carried the only stool in the room, and with one last look at Glory's stoned face, stepped out.

The corridor was narrow, and she had to sit sideways so as not to obstruct the flow of human traffic. The whole floor seemed to be busy. Girls walked up and down in a hurry, calling out to one another.

Soon a well-dressed woman walked up the stairs and shouted, "They are here!"

Girls from different rooms yelped and squealed. No sound came from Glory's room. Maybe she was too high to speak.

Shakira folded her hands in her lap and blinked several times. The woman returned downstairs, and two dark-complexioned, muscled men walked up. They came to her. One lifted her from the stool by her arm.

Shakira's heart pumped fast, as if it would pop out her throat. "No, not me. Glory—she's inside."

"Oh." He arched his eyebrow and without a word opened the door. Both men entered and closed it with a soft thud, but it sounded like thunder in Shakira's ears.

On their heels, more men came up the stairs and went into other rooms. Shakira shook so badly she wondered if she could walk. She willed her legs to move and went downstairs. To her amazement, the small reception area buzzed with men of all ages and sizes.

The well-dressed woman she saw earlier stood behind the counter with the receptionist and allocated rooms. One by one, the men dispersed. There were so many. No wonder Glory felt she needed to be drugged to accommodate them all.

Shakira walked to the door. She'd have to find a place to sit and wait. For how long? She clutched her bag to her chest. A man pulled her back.

She flinched. "I'm not—"

"You're coming with me." He wore a dark-colored T-shirt and jeans, and his hand wrapped around her upper arm. She wasn't taller than his shoulder.

"No, I'm a visitor here. I'm not—"

He frowned and bared his teeth. "I already paid for you. What's wrong?"

"I'm not one of the girls."

He dragged her along toward the stairs. "You're in room sixteen, are you not?"

The well-dressed lady called out, "She's in room sixteen! Don't mind her!"

Shakira struggled against the firm grip on her arm. "Please. I am just a visitor. I don't live here."

He pulled her up the stairs. "But I paid for you, $100 for the whole day. Don't be a rat." He sniffed her. "I like your hair."

A sob escaped her lips. "Please. I can give you—Glory. She's beautiful and ready for you. In room eleven."

She couldn't believe she uttered such a despicable thing. The man knew the room because they were numbered. He must have been here before. He didn't answer her and opened the door. He tossed her inside where Glory was sandwiched between two other men.

Against her better judgment, Shakira threw up on the hunk who brought her in. He swore and dealt her a dirty slap. She screamed. He pulled off his messed-up T-shirt, and she took the opportunity to run out of the room.

She didn't stop till she was out in the open street. Such horrible people. How could the woman take money for her? She walked down the road so she would not be in front of the brothel and entered a small shop she'd bought groceries from with Glory.

"A bottle of soda, please," she panted. "Cold one."

The shop owner gave her a bottle, and she put it to her mouth till it was nearly half gone. Then she got her phone and dialed the police detective.

He found her at the shop almost five hours later. What time was it? Early evening? She was tired and frustrated and resigned to the fact that she would have to go back to Glory.

"The traffic today is insane," Detective Dauda said. "Sorry I am this late."

"Thanks for coming." She held her bag close. "I have to get my suitcase."

"Okay."

"It's with—my friend's sister." With night fast approaching, she couldn't get into the building alone. "I don't feel safe there. I—they—"

"We'll go inside together." He led her to his car, an old model Toyota Corolla. "You know the room?"

She nodded. She dreaded what she'd see but felt instant relief when the detective tucked a handgun in his waist.

Glory was asleep when she knocked and entered the room. A man snored beside her. It didn't matter. Detective Dauda stood by the door, his hand on his gun, and she tiptoed inside and picked up her stuff.

She didn't breathe until at the reception, when the girl shrugged and apologized. "Sorry for what happened earlier. Madam used everybody. Even I had to work."

Shakira had nothing to say to her. She quickened her steps and left the building. The traffic was thick again, and she wondered if Lagos had a road free of cars, or at least fewer ones.

"Does your friend know the kind of work her sister does? Where she sent you to?"

Now the question had come, Shakira had a second thought. She'd wanted so badly to come to Africa to find Florence, yet the people she trusted to help betrayed her. She knew they took more than was necessary to get her a visa, a thousand dollars, but she expected them to at least lead her right. She'd had faith in them.

Mo must have known Glory's type of work. They'd lived together before she got lucky and left the country. Their plan dawned on her through the drive away. Mo knew she would have a lot of money. Glory had been so disappointed her suitcase was gone and made her spend the little money she had left.

"I think she knew."

"You need to investigate people before you follow their lead." He sighed. "You are lucky they didn't drug you. We have cases where girls are abducted by pimps, drugged, and converted to prostitutes."

"Oh dear."

She feared for her life. Justice for her babies seemed to come at an unimaginably high price.

"What are you here for, anyway?"

She decided to be truthful with him. If he was another wrong lead, then God help her to not get killed in this jungle. To go back home would be her best option.

"Sorry about your loss." He stole a glance at her. "I can't promise any help. Efayaw is in another political zone, and I don't think I know any officer I could refer you to."

"I need to go and look for her."

"And then what? Arrest her?"

"I can lead Interpol to her."

Detective Dauda shook his head. "Does Interpol know you're here?"

"No." He couldn't sway her, but her voice lowered as she was forced to evaluate her actions.

"Who knows where you are?"

"My husband does." She couldn't let him know only Mo and Sean knew her whereabouts.

He pulled up at the parking lot of the hotel, and she gasped. "I don't have any more money. Glory—she—"

"You don't have money."

"No. Only about five thousand nairas, and it's not enough for a night here."

"Hmm." He switched off the ignition and faced her. "I think it will be best to take you to your embassy. I'm sure—"

"No. No, please. I don't want to go back home. Not yet. Now I'm here. I came a long way." She sobbed. "I need to find the woman. I—"

He was quiet for a while. "Listen, Nigeria is nothing like your country. You have come to the wrong side of the world, and I'm putting it mildly."

She sniffed and shook her head. Everything back home was gone. She had nowhere left to turn unless she returned with the killer of her babies.

"If the university community had brought you here, or an organization, or even a church, it would be different. You would have enjoyed Nigeria. But to come here like this—the best thing you should do is to go back home."

She grabbed his hand. "You're a policeman. Can you help me? Take me to Efayaw? I promise you it's all I need now. Once I get there, I will find my way."

He snickered. "With only five thousand naira? You don't know what you're talking about."

He put the car in gear and drove. She didn't dare ask what his plan was. She quietly prayed he would not take her to the embassy. After another hour or so, he drove through a gated estate. Most of the houses were lit, but there was a mixture of bungalows and story buildings.

Detective Dauda stopped in front of one of the houses. "A friend of mine lives here with his sisters. I will ask them to let you stay with them tonight while I think of who could take you to Efayaw tomorrow. But I warn you. Where you want to go is not anywhere like America."

"Thank you."

All she needed were little mercies.

"My friend, Dele Thomson, is a teacher in his thirties who works for a small private primary school in the neighborhood," Dauda said. "His sisters, Bessie and Tami, work for the government. They're not rich, but they are comfortable. Upward mobile."

The sitting room they walked into was cozy and nicely furnished with two cream leather sofas, a center table, and a Persian rug. The curtains were gold and beige. A huge bean bag with African print patchwork lay on the floor beside the wall, where a forty-inch TV hung. Multicolored throw pillows were scattered on the sofas with three more on the floor.

A sweet aroma much like cinnamon wafted to Shakira's nostrils, and she took a deep breath. This was more like home than anything she'd experienced in a while.

Dauda made the introductions, and the siblings offered seats. Bessie, the older, picked up the throw pillows and took them inside. Tami served sodas and biscuits on a tray.

After some idle talk, Dauda explained why he was there.

"Wow," Bessie said. "We have only one bedroom. We girls share it while Dele sleeps in the parlor."

Dauda scratched his head. "Oh. I never knew how many rooms you had."

"Well, we can all sleep in the parlor," Dele said. "And our guest takes the room. For only one night, right?"

Bessie shook her head. "It's not appropriate."

Tami shrugged. "We'll manage. *Shey*, it's just for a night."

Dauda left as soon as the slightest agreement was reached, and Shakira was shown the room.

The bedroom was large enough to accommodate two single ladies with a wall-to-wall wardrobe on one side. A mirror hung atop a big chest of drawers whose top doubled as a dresser for the ladies' cosmetics. The bed was king-size, neatly made, and pushed against the wall.

A full-length mirror hung on the back of the door. Shakira stared at herself for a whole minute. Her dress was shabby though she just bought it. She dragged her hand down her tear-streaked face. She was a shadow of herself, and the journey had not even begun.

Dele knocked on the door. "Dinner is served."

"Just a minute, thank you."

She debated if it was safe to leave her handbag in the room and decided to. If any of her new hosts stole anything from her, she would know. She took her phone though. Who knew who would call? Her contacts here were limited to three people, and she doubted Glory would call. Still.

Dinner consisted of fries with egg sauce. The sauce was quite spicy, but Shakira was too hungry to complain. She drank extra water. After the meal, Dele got her to talk about America. He repeatedly made mention of the opportunities available and asked several questions on the businesses, education, and prospects.

Bessie stood after about an hour. "There's work tomorrow."

She didn't seem altogether friendly, but Shakira was grateful to escape Dele's excessive chat.

Chapter Fifteen

The ladies were gone by the time Shakira woke up the following morning. She used the bathroom and prepared for the day before she stepped out of the room.

Dele Thomson sat against the dining table and made notes in a small book. He beamed when she walked in. "Ah, good morning. Hope you slept well."

She yawned. "I guess I did. I'm waking up so late and wondering why."

He laughed and his eyes twinkled. "My sisters said you didn't even turn over when they went in to prepare for work."

"Oh dear." She covered her mouth. "I was quite tired yesterday." She let out a long breath. "Aren't you going to work as well?"

"I teach in the neighborhood. Besides, someone had to be home when you woke." She checked her watch subconsciously. She knew from earlier on it was already past eight.

"I'm so sorry."

"It's okay. Glad we were able to accommodate you." He stood. "Breakfast?"

"I would appreciate it, thank you."

"The sauce from last night remains. You can have it with bread and tea."

She hated the sauce. "Uh, do you have—any coffee?"

He laughed. "Oh, I forgot you Americans like coffee more than tea." He walked into the kitchen. "I'll check."

It didn't feel right to be served by him, but his sisters had told her the previous evening it was not the Nigerian style to allow a guest to serve herself, so she couldn't do more than sit and wait. She wanted to discuss her plans. Detective Dauda had not made any commitment to take her. For all she knew, he may have dumped her and run off.

Dele placed a tray of food in front of her. "My dream is to live in the United States."

"I've never lived anywhere else." Shakira shook her head. "Thank you."

"It's okay." He sighed. "I have never even met an American before. I watch your movies, and I tell myself, I belong in the US of A."

"Oh, the movies don't tell all the truth about us."

His eyes widened. "Are you serious?"

She hated decaffeinated coffee, which was available, but preferred it to tea any day. "Yes. It's all make-believe."

"Then Hollywood is perfect, because I believe everything I watch." He laughed. "Wow, unbelievable."

The sauce tasted even spicier than the previous night, and she drank two cups of coffee before she could finish a slice of bread. He didn't seem to notice her plight.

"I want to visit California and New York." He gazed at her. "Are you from there?"

"No, I'm from Houston, Texas."

"Ah! Texas. Cowboys!" He drummed his feet against the floor. "Do you live on a ranch?"

"Oh no." She stirred her third cup of coffee. "I live in a block. We have apartments and condos, and I live in one."

His excitement was contagious. "You live in a city?"

"Well, suburb of a city. Houston."

"Ah, I would like to visit Houston too. And Texas city." He chuckled. "Now I have an American friend. Your coming here is a blessing."

She wanted to tell him there was no place like "Texas" as a city or town, but a state with cities like Houston in it, but she had more pressing concerns.

"I need your help." She put down her coffee and leaned toward him. "I must get to Efayaw, and I have no idea how to get there."

"Efayaw. I don't know where it is." He frowned. "Which state is it?"

Shakira's chest tightened. "Cross River, I believe."

"Ah. It's so far from here. What do you want to do there?"

Shakira poured out her heart. When she was through, Dele drew his brows together and glared at her.

"You want to do the impossible." He shook his head. "Cross River, ah. Those are militants. I hate to sound negative, but you would never find anybody in Cross River. They have rivers all over the place, and small villages under the rivers."

How can a village be under a river? Shakira wondered. "I thought you said you didn't know Efayaw."

"I don't, but if it's in Cross River state, then I know about it." He stood and shoved his hands in his pockets. "Why don't you just let your government handle this?"

"I've waited over a year for my government."

He shrugged. "America always catches offenders. Even if it takes fifty years. I used to watch this program on TV called cold file or something like that. They always catch those wicked people." He chuckled. "I used to ask myself, why do the crime when you know they will still catch—"

She stood too. "I can't wait fifty years. And America has some notorious unsolved cases." She drew in her breath. "Besides, I can't go on with my life. I don't want to live until she's found!"

"Ah." He paced. "I don't know what you can do. Maybe you should talk to Detective Dauda. At least he's on the police force."

She walked to him and touched his arm. "Please, all I need is to get there. You can leave me in Efayaw—"

He growled. "You wouldn't survive one day alone. Even if you have a million dollars. The people there are greedy, and they will rip you off."

"I don't care."

"How sure are you the woman is in Efayaw, anyway? There are a thousand and one hiding places in Cross River, not to speak of Nigeria as a whole. Many holes a car can't reach. This is not America, my dear!"

After a number of questions and negative predictions, he agreed to find out how to get to Efayaw but made no promises.

His sisters returned late in the evening.

Bessie spoke first. "You're still here?" She scowled at Dele. "I thought your friend said—"

"Detective Dauda was busy today. He couldn't come for her."

Tami frowned. "So? We sleep on the floor again tonight?"

Dele smirked. "Hey, let's be nice to a stranger. She's stranded."

Tami scoffed. "Who's being nasty? It's bad enough I pay the bills around here and you do nothing. Now your friend brings a lady to stay with you. It's like we don't exist in our own house!"

Shakira bit hard on her lower lip. The ladies hadn't been altogether nasty yesterday, but this was beyond rude.

"I'll take her out tomorrow. And you didn't have to rub it in that you pay the bills. I buy groceries."

Tami raised her voice. "Once in two months more like."

Bessie stood in the middle of the room. "Enough, please." She lowered her voice and addressed Shakira. "We mean no offense, but you've come at a bad time."

"Let me tell this big, good-for-nothing—"

"Tami, enough!" Bessie snapped, then nodded at Shakira. "You can sleep in the bedroom. The rest of us will sleep in here."

Dele worked his throat for a second. "Tami, remember you still owe me a thousand bucks for your boyfriend's taxi fare I paid last month."

Tami grabbed her bag, took out a rumpled note, and threw it at Dele. She stomped into the bedroom.

"That's a new low, Dele," Bessie hissed and followed her sister.

A few minutes of silence ensued while Dele straightened the note and folded it into his pocket.

Shakira released her lower lip from the clutches of her teeth. "I'm sorry to cause you so much—trouble."

Dele shrugged. "It was bound to happen anyway. She's been grouchy for days."

"Hope she'll be okay."

"Her boyfriend broke up with her. I'm tired of staying here anyway. We can leave tomorrow morning. For Efayaw."

"Seriously?"

"I know where you get transportation east. We can get a bus or something."

Her throat went dry. "Thank you so much."

"You'd better rest. We don't know what tomorrow holds." He stretched out on one of the two sofas and closed his eyes.

Her heart weighed heavily as she straightened out on the other sofa. No way was she going to sleep alone on the bed the sisters so generously relinquished the previous night.

She closed her eyes though she didn't sleep. The sisters moved into the sitting room moments later and mumbled to each other, but neither "woke" her to go into the room. Better for everyone.

Dele wanted to use her to escape his issues, but what did it matter? He would take advantage of her as much as she'd do to him. She closed her eyes. Tomorrow. Finally, she would get to Efayaw and face the beginning of the end. Thoughts, doubts, and fear of the future prevented her from a good night's sleep.

Chapter Sixteen

ele called Dauda the following morning after breakfast, and he picked them up and took them to the bus station. The detective paid the fares because Dele was broke.

"I don't know what you're thinking." Dauda spoke in the local Yoruba language while Shakira stared blankly at them. "You should let us take her to her embassy."

Dele scratched his head. "When I get to Efayaw, I will know what to do."

"It's not too late now."

"I want to help her." Dele glanced over her to the rickety bus they'd use for the ten-hour journey. Dauda was right. "But also, I have nothing here."

"Your teaching job—"

"Can't even pay the electricity bill. I need a change too. I don't know where this will take me, but it can't be much worse than living with my cranky little sisters." He realized he was shouting when Shakira cleared her throat beside him. A few eyes darted toward him in the busy station. "Last night Tami challenged me."

"I told you to leave them before."

"And go where? If I could I would have. Am I not leaving now?"

"Hmm, leaving now, you say. This is a foolish thing to do. You risk your life and hers."

"This might be crazy." He stared at the ground. Nothing had ever worked for him, and he was done with this place. "But I'm going ahead. I have nothing to lose."

"Do they know your plan? I mean the girls?"

"I left a note for Bessie." Dele sighed. "Don't you see this is an opportunity for me? You know how bad things have been with my sisters. You know how long I've tried to do something else." He stole a glance at Shakira. "America. This is my chance to leave this country."

"Don't bother because you can't convince me." Dauda shoved his hand in his jacket pocket and pulled out a piece of paper. "I got a name of an officer for you. His last post was Efayaw Area Command. He may have been transferred out."

Dele collected the paper. "Thank you for this. If he's not there, at least someone who knows him will be."

Dauda rocked on his heels. "You'll call me if you get into any trouble."

Dele sighed. "I will." He hugged his friend and stepped back. He spoke English for Shakira's benefit. "We need to get in the bus."

Dauda stepped back as well. "Sure." He avoided her gaze till she spoke.

"I didn't understand what you discussed but I have an idea. It can't be worse than where I've been." She swallowed. "Thank you for everything." Dauda frowned, his concern etched in his forehead and dark eyes.

Dele was used to traveling in the fourteen-seater buses, but Shakira complained that the seats were too straight and the leg space tight.

"How long did you say the trip is again?"

Dele watched as she adjusted and readjusted her legs. "I don't know how good the roads are—but let's prepare for ten hours."

"Ten hours!" She bent her neck. "Will there be stops?"

"Maybe one. Or two. I don't know."

She kept quiet afterward. They'd had to leave early to get into the first or second buses, so they didn't have breakfast. Dele wasn't in the mood to answer her many questions. He was hungry and angry with his life. Nothing he'd ever done had panned out, and on this journey, he wanted to reflect. She was American. And despite her tale, she had come to the wrong side of life. She should have left her government to deal with the tragedy of her daughters' deaths. But she was here, in his neck of the jungle. What mattered most was how she would be of benefit to him and his future.

He bought two canned drinks and a loaf of bread for breakfast, and after everyone settled into the ride and the driver hit the road, he handed her a drink and shared the bread with her.

The journey lasted more than twelve hours. Shakira could have sworn she wouldn't last half the time. Her legs were numb, and her feet swollen. The wonky bus surprisingly never broke down, but the road was bad most of the way. She had never seen a highway in such a deplorable state. Didn't the government ever fix them? It surprised her how calm and quiet the other passengers took the ride. Some even chatted through hours of slow-driving and pothole-dodging. Maybe they were used to it. She wasn't.

Dele slept part of the time.

The bus stopped once in Benin City. The passengers got off to stretch, use the restrooms, and get a bite to eat. The driver refilled his tank at the gas station.

Shakira couldn't understand the layout at the stop. There was a store at the station, but she couldn't buy anything except biscuits. The store was dirty, and she wasn't sure it was wise to eat there.

Dele offered her the option of eating in a kiosk along the road where most of the passengers went, but she refused. In the end, she bought another can of Coke and more biscuits.

Night had descended when the bus stopped at the evening market in Efayaw. People disembarked with shouts and murmurs of "Thank you, Lord" and "Glory be to God."

Dele collected their bags while she tried to make her feet move on the littered ground. Mixed odors in the air made it impossible for her to detect the differences. They trekked through rows of dirty stalls with wares displayed without tags. Sellers called to them in a language that sounded harsh to her ears.

Finally, they left the filthy market behind.

When Dele said nothing to her, she was forced to ask, "Where to next?"

He seemed affable. In the near-pitch darkness, he sounded amused, and she wondered why. "I want to find the police station. The driver gave directions, but I'm afraid we have to walk." His gaze roamed to her swollen feet. "We don't have enough cash."

"How far is it?"

"Around the corner," he said.

It ended up being a ten-minute walk. The police station was a ramshackle solid block building of dirty and peeled blue and yellow paint. The officers behind the counter addressed the visitors with a disregard Shakira found unprofessional. Dele asked for the name on the paper Dauda gave him and was told the man worked at another station in town. Well, not bad, but she couldn't take another step from where they were even if she tried.

The officers refused to give a number for the name they had, so Dele said he would return the following day. They should call the man and inform him of his proposed visit at a given time.

A different language was spoken by the men in uniform.

She tapped Dele. "Do you understand this language?"

He shook his head. "*Abeg*, can I see you outside?" He addressed the youngest of the three officers.

Once outside, Dele pulled out a five-hundred-naira note and pressed it into the man's hand. "I need accommodation. We're new in town and can't afford a hotel."

"Where are you coming from, *sef*?"

"Lagos. It's why we want to see Sergeant Gabriel. It is important."

The young officer shared a curious look between them. "You can sleep in my room. I'm on night duty today. But you will add five hundred, oh."

"Aha, officer. How much is a hotel room then? I gave you five hundred already."

"Okay, add two. Two or nothing."

Dele glanced at Shakira. "Give me two hundred."

She removed the last bundle in her bag. It was nearly depleted with only ten five-hundred-naira notes left. He handed a note to the officer, who returned three hundred naira to him.

"Come with me. The house is just down the road."

Shakira dreaded what she would experience before they got to their destination. The fenced compound had a bungalow covered in blue dawn, a beautiful African flower. They walked to the back of the house where the walls exposed mud, cement plastering and three doors. The young officer opened one with his key.

Stale air mixed with spoiled food accosted her. She waited a second to catch her breath. The men entered, and the officer switched on a small yellow bulb.

"I'll be back around six. Then you can look for accommodation."

Dele nodded. "Thank you."

The officer made to leave. Dele cleared his throat. "Sorry, I didn't get your name."

"Corporal Osuji."

"Okay. Thanks."

He stopped at the door. "There's a little rice in the pot."

Dele arched an eyebrow. "Oh, so kind of you."

When he left, Shakira sat on a white plastic chair, the only one in the room. A double bed was pushed against the wall. Despite the stale smells, the room appeared clean, the bed made. A small corner was dedicated to crockery. A twin kerosene stove, much like the one she'd seen used in the 1960s back home, was against the wall, with two medium pots on it.

Dele leaned against the wall and stared at her. Several thoughts went through her mind. Why had she brought herself to this situation? Stuck in a strange country with a man she knew nothing about. A man running from his shadow. His sisters couldn't live with him, but she agreed to travel across the country with him. Her death wish became apparent to anyone who cared to take a look at her. If she died, what would he do with her body?

From her peripheral view, she noticed he followed her gaze as she took in her accommodation for the night. She had nothing to say. As this journey progressed, she fought harder to push her doubts away. What must he think of her, though? A woman on an impossible mission without support from her people? How pathetic she must look to him, and anyone else!

When her eyes lingered on the kitchen corner, he walked over there and opened the pots.

"There's rice and beef stew. You must be hungry."

She opened her mouth to speak but words failed her. Instead, a sob escaped, and she covered her mouth to stop it.

He came and squatted in front of her, drew her into a hug. It had been so long since anyone had shown her such affection. She melted into it and allowed her emotions to explode.

When she stopped weeping, he cupped her face. "You'll be fine. I'll take care of you." He wiped her damp cheeks. "Now, you eat some rice and get some sleep. You look drained."

"I'm not hungry, thank you."

"You're not eating because you're hungry. It's for strength."

She laughed. "No. I don't want food. Sleep, yes."

Chapter Seventeen

Shakira leaned into the soft massage. His hands were deft and skilled. They touched all the right places too. Everywhere her muscles were knotted, his soft knead relaxed them. She moaned at the sweet pain from the crook of her neck, to her shoulders, to her waist. The dream was the best she'd had since—what a sweet dream. Deon must be repentant. Surely, he now realized she was right to do what she did. Leaving home made him come to his senses.

His hands roamed over her soft buttock cheeks to her thighs.

"Ah, ah."

"You'll be fine, dear," the deep male voice murmured.

Something was off. This wasn't a dream. Deon wasn't here. She jerked away and opened her eyes. She twisted to her side and faced a bare-chested Dele.

"What are you doing?!"

His eyes gleamed with lust. The dim yellow light was still on, and she could figure him out at once. She sat up.

"Get away from me!"

"I thought a massage would—"

Thankfully he hadn't undressed her. She jumped off the bed and ran to the door. "Don't you ever touch me again!"

He stood. "Where are you going?" Only his shirt had come off.

She breathed hard. "Wherever I can."

"Listen to me." He folded his arms across his muscled chest. "I am your only help and protection here. And I don't plan to harm you. For your information, they eat visitors in some parts of this country."

She gasped. He nodded. "Yes, they do. And you don't want to find out on your own if these people here do." He grew bold and walked toward her. "I can't speak their language as you may have noticed. So, all we have is each other." He stopped in front of her. "Trust me."

She couldn't. He had touched her inappropriately. She was too frozen to move. What had she gotten herself into? "I am a married woman," she whispered.

He chuckled. "I know. But your husband is not here."

Whatever did he mean? "It doesn't make any difference to me."

He pulled her. "Come to bed. It's about midnight. You need to sleep."

She snapped her hand out of his, and he laughed. He'd succeeded in scaring her with talk about possible cannibalism around here. She was stuck with him in this room in this strange land. But whatever he planned against her, she would not help him succeed.

She walked back and lay on one side of the bed. He took the other side and maintained a small space between them.

———

Dele woke to the woman cuddled in his arms. At some time in the night, she must have rolled over, and he instinctively drew her close for warmth. He disentangled himself, careful not to wake her up. He didn't want to scare her away till she achieved his purpose—his ticket to America.

She was soft and supple, and he wondered what kind of man would let his wife go to a strange country alone. All her money stolen, and he hadn't heard her call or contact her family. If not for her accent, and her passport, which he'd spied while she slept in his sister's house, he might have thought she was a con. Answers about her life would come out sooner or later. This was his one chance, and he had no plans of blowing it.

For now, he needed money. From the little he'd seen here, there weren't many opportunities. Schools were almost halfway through second term, so the possibilities of getting a teaching job were nil. He was never good at sales, so there was no question of getting involved in a business. They also needed accommodation. He hated this room, and it would be better if they had two rooms.

Dele had never taken such a bold step like this, to leave his comfort zone and dare something different. He couldn't believe this was happening now.

Shakira moved toward him once more, and he got up before she wrapped herself around him. He checked his watch, seeing it was close to six. He reckoned Osuji would soon get home. They needed to get cleaned up and ready for the day.

Only one door led outside. The bathroom must be somewhere in the compound, shared with other tenants. Dele hated the idea but needed to use it. And Shakira would too when she awoke.

He went on to inspect and find a bathroom. He smelled it before he found it. Unacceptable for Shakira's use; he wouldn't use it himself.

He needed to think of something.

Shakira's American accent could open many doors, but what lies would he need to tell to access important places and people? He had to get her plans straight again. This woman she was after, how did she plan to get her arrested?

Osuji stood outside his door and knocked.

"Good morning, Corporal." Dele walked up behind the policeman. "You're on time."

Osuji spun round. "Good morning, sir. I thought you'd be inside."

"I went to look for the bathroom."

"Oh. You find it?"

Dele shrugged. "Yes, but I doubt my—"

"I know. I know. I was even pitying your wife. How is she taking all this?"

His wife? Dele sighed. "What do you suggest?"

"Let me speak with my landlord's wife to see if you can use her own. She used to like American people."

"How did you know she is American?"

Osuji laughed. "Aha, the whole town now knows the American has arrived."

Was this a good or bad development? Dele hated to weigh the pros and cons. First, he hoped they'd get a clean bathroom this morning.

"Please tell your landlord my—wife—is not awake yet."

"Okay. Let me check." Osuji walked around the house the way they'd come the night before.

Dele entered the room and tapped Shakira's feet. "Wake up."

She opened her eyes and for a moment was lost, then she rose and groaned. "Good morning."

He sat beside her feet. "The bathrooms are in a terrible state, so the corporal wants to speak to the landlord, in the main house, I presume. We may be allowed to use theirs."

She smoothed her hair away from her face. "Oh my."

"Another thing, he thinks you're my wife. It may help our stay here."

She swallowed hard.

"I'm sorry you misunderstood me in the night. My intentions are most honorable. But being husband and wife gives us an advantage. I'd like to keep the pretense going for a while."

She bit down on her lips. Her light brown eyes narrowed. Dele waited for her to comment, and when she didn't, stood.

"You may also want to know *the whole town knows the American has arrived*. Those were Osuji's exact words."

"Oh my, no! She'd know I'm around and run again."

He folded his arms across his chest. "I also think I should know the full story about this woman you're after."

"She—worked for me—watched over my two babies. She—killed them. They are dead because of her. My two daughters."

Dele thought he had never seen eyes so void of emotion.

Chapter Eighteen

The main house was a sprawling bungalow. The formal room had a staleness Shakira could not understand. The furniture may be expensive but old with gold frames on the wooden casings covered with rich brown and straw velvet. The floor, carpeted wall to wall, needed a good vacuuming, but the brown color probably concealed more dirt and the stench it gave off.

A young woman walked into the room to welcome them. "Our mommy will be with you soon. She doesn't normally wake up so early." She clasped her hands as though nervous. "Welcome to our house."

"Thank you," Dele said. He dropped their luggage by the side of the couch and took a seat. "Shaki, come."

She didn't like the name. It felt too familiar, a false intimacy, hinting at a closer relationship than there was. No one had ever called her Shaki. She stepped beside him with a soft smile.

"Thank you."

"Excuse me." The young lady curtsied and left.

"Please don't call me Shaki," she murmured.

"It's a native name to Nigerians. Mostly Muslim, though. I thought you were one when I heard your name."

She never knew this. There seemed to be a lot she had no idea about before coming here. Nigerians had cannibals in some parts, maybe all parts, and her name was a Muslim name. Would this help or hinder her?

"All the same." She sighed. "Are we going to ask for accommodation here?"

"Relax, I'll handle everything, Mrs. Thomson."

She gasped. "I am not! Don't you—"

He got up. "Good morning, madam."

She hadn't heard anyone come in. She sucked in her breath and faced a rotund woman in her middle age, wrapped in a dressing gown.

She stood. "Good morning, ma'am."

"Oh, good morning, our American visitors. You are so welcome."

"Thank you. My name is Dele Thomson. My wife is Shakira."

"Oh, you are welcome. Sit down. Please."

"Thank you." Dele held out his hand, and she took it, sitting at the same time.

The woman sat on one of the single chairs facing them. "My daughter told me one of our tenants brought you."

"Yes, madam. We got here late last night."

Shakira noticed a slight change in Dele's accent. He now sounded like a male version of Florence. The mere thought made her tremble. The fake accent must be for a reason; she decided to ask him about it later.

"I heard so."

Dele continued. "We are missionaries. Um, I am a Nigerian, though I have lived all my life in the United States."

"Ah, welcome back home. Are you from Efayaw?"

Dele laughed. "No, not at all. I am from Lagos. But we believe the Lord led us here. In fact, my wife had a dream two years ago. She has never been in Nigeria."

"And I thought Shakira is a Muslim. Like Shakirat?"

"No, we are missionaries." He took her hand. "Do you want to share the dream, darling?"

Shakira cleared her throat. She had never been good at acting, and Deon said she was the worst liar on the globe.

"I saw the house. The flower on the wall and fence," she stammered. "The colors, the layout, everything." She didn't know what more to say.

"Go on, dear." Dele squeezed her hand. "Besides the blue flowers."

"I believe I heard the Lord saying we should come here."

Dele interrupted. "She heard the word *Efayaw* and at first thought God was telling her He would show her *a far yard*. But it wasn't so. We spent weeks praying about it until our pastor told us it sounded like Efayaw to him. So, we had to come here to confirm what we felt we heard from the Lord."

He was such a good liar; she shuddered. "Oh yes."

"We thank the Lord! We need more of our dear Father in our town!" The woman bought it hook, line, and sinker. "I am so happy. Out of all the houses in this town, God showed you ours. This is amazing."

"I saw the house. I saw the flowers, the blue dawn flower. I told my husband, this is the place." Shakira nodded. "I am so sure."

"God be praised. Hallelujah!" Their host clapped. "My husband has traveled to Aba for business, but he will be back tomorrow."

Dele sat forward. "We need a place to stay, please. If you don't mind. We are fasting and we would like to—to pray for a while."

"Not a problem at all. My daughter will prepare the guest room. I will also tell our pastor you are here."

"Thank you, madam."

She raised her voice. "Cordi! Cordilia!"

The young lady ran in. "Yes, Mommy."

"Please prepare the guest room for our guests. They are fasting. But by evening, maybe you break your fast and have something to eat? Possibly soup with vegetables or a potato? I don't know what Americans eat." She rubbed her plump hands. "I will invite our pastor over."

Dele nodded. "Anything you offer us. Thank you so much, madam. The Lord bless you."

The guest room had cross-ventilation, and Shakira gulped in as much fresh air as she could. It wasn't big and the double bed sagged. The one good feeling she had about the bathroom being en suite soon wore off—as the shower had no water pressure, though she got to use water fetched in a bucket.

After her bath, she dressed quickly and sat on the soft mattress to wait for Dele. He had said a lot of things she needed to clarify. He had no right to turn her into a missionary. She didn't know the first thing about being one. She hadn't been in church since her wedding. What was she supposed to say, and how could he declare a fast when her stomach had been complaining about hunger all night?

She sat up when he walked into the room clothed. At least he had some decorum.

"I want to discuss what happened out there with you." She breathed in to calm down. "I don't know the first thing about being a missionary."

He leaned against the wall. "You didn't do too badly."

"Well, her pastor will be here in the evening, and I don't know what tests he will put us through. I am not a good liar."

He snickered. "You are convincing, though."

"Listen to me! I am not going to go through with this!"

"Let me do the talking then."

She flew to her feet and clenched her teeth so hard it hurt. "I didn't come here to play missionary! I came here to find a killer. And you cannot derail me from this."

He stared at her till her breathing became normal. "Well, go ahead with your plan. Go out there and find the killer."

As though he was what he pretended to be, he opened his bag and brought out a Bible. Shakira hated his indifference.

"How dare you make light of such an enormous task? You are not here because you want to be. I asked you to come here, and you must do what I need done."

She knew she was overboard but didn't know how to get him to stop his foolish game and face the problem. Her problem.

"Dele! Are you listening?" She glared at him, but he only flipped to the next page. She kicked the book out of his hand. "Listen to me. I am not a missionary."

He picked up the Bible and continued reading. Rage filled her. She flung his bag at him. It hit him in the face. He pushed the bag aside and gave her his back.

No matter what, she needed to get him to cooperate before anything else. Being in a strange country, and with a strange man, the reality of her situation bore down on her.

She sank to her knees and wept. How did she hope to get through this without help?

He got to his feet and reached for her handbag.

"What are you doing?"

He opened the bag and rummaged through. Shakira lunged at him and tried to get her bag.

"What do you want with my stuff?"

"I'm looking for your phone." He sighed. "I'm calling your husband. You are out of line."

Chapter Nineteen

The meeting with Pastor Goodwill went better than envisaged. The man of God did most of the talking about his ministry and spiritual influence.

After her outburst earlier in the day, Shakira seemed subdued, which made the atmosphere surreal. She clasped her hands between her knees and stared at the floor during most of the meeting.

As Dele promised, he answered the few questions the pastor had about their mission.

"We have a meeting this evening at our church," Pastor Goodwill said. "The brethren will be glad to receive you, if you can share a word or two with them."

Shakira bit her lower lip. She had no idea what one would say. Dele concurred. "We would love to encourage and exhort the brethren."

Pastor Goodwill laughed. Shakira noted with amusement his potbelly clad in the traditional shirt and trousers. She liked the outfit and wondered for a moment if this would look good on Deon. It dawned on her how much she missed him. What if he'd agreed to come on this mission with her? She'd never bothered about her roots, though many of her friends in college had imagined her being from one African country or the other. It seemed to make some sense to her. Despite the shock of the last few days since her arrival, she could see a beautiful culture of respect, and the clothing was something she would consider buying when her problems were solved.

"We are going to have a great time this night. The people will gather tomorrow evening as well," Pastor Goodwill said, smiling. "Evangelist Dele, would you say we organize a seven-day crusade or so? The harvest will be amazing."

Shakira cleared her throat. "We should pray about it."

Dele shrugged. "The Lord is good all the time. We—yes, pastor. A seven-day crusade will go a long way to help us establish our missions."

"What is the name of your church in the States again?" Pastor Goodwill said. "I'm sorry, I didn't get the name from your host this morning."

"We didn't tell her, actually," Dele said. "We are itinerant missionaries."

Shakira swallowed.

Pastor Goodwill nodded. "Oh, indeed?"

"Though we have worked with several international ministers." Dele mentioned two of the prominent televangelists she had seen on air, and Pastor Goodwill's smile broadened.

Dele nodded. "I can get pictures from our last missions. You'll be able to see these mighty men of God working with us and serving Christ. Humble leaders and generals."

Pastor Goodwill beamed. "We are blessed to have you." He leaped to his feet. "I want you to prepare now. I will take you to the church."

Dele stood. "Darling, we shouldn't take long. Will you have a shower first?"

"I suggest you both have a shower. It will be a long evening." Pastor Goodwill rubbed his hands together. "We are so glad to have you in our little London."

Little London? Shakira wondered why the pastor would even as much as think this rundown little town was anywhere close. For the first time, she really noticed him. He could be somewhere in his mid-forties and wore gold necklaces, one of which had a big cross pendant. There was a bracelet at his wrist and a heavy gold ring on each of his fourth fingers.

After a much-needed cold bath, because the weather was in the 80s Fahrenheit (something she had to get used to), Shakira sat on the bed, contemplating the night ahead.

Dele returned dressed and ready to go.

"I don't think I can do this. I have never preached before." She sighed. "I don't know how to pray. I don't even know a single scripture, except—" She shook her head.

He arched an eyebrow. "Except?"

She gazed at him. "Something I learned in Sunday school a long time ago."

"It's a good start." He walked over and sat beside her. "You see, this is Nigeria. Half of what you say will not be remembered. They will say this is a great service, we have American missionaries in our midst. That is what people will remember."

It was all nonsense. "But what will I say? I have no clue. No—"

"Relax, Shakira. Take a few deep breaths and recite the scripture you remember."

She shuddered. "How do you know so much about the church and God?"

He laughed. "This is Nigeria. There are churches everywhere. Everyone is religious. Even if you don't know anything about God, your neighbor likely goes to a church where the leader's face is all over the media. Or you have a church in the shop next to your house and you hear all the preaching."

She frowned. Yes, she'd seen many buildings with religious signposts and wondered if they were all churches indeed. Some of the names seemed repetitive and others were rundown shacks she couldn't imagine to be places of worship.

It had not piqued her interest to inquire about those places because they couldn't be dedicated to God's worship in her opinion. Like turning a manger into a temple.

Dele's words were dubious, and she challenged them. "So, you preach though you don't believe a word of it? You pretend to be a holy person, even though you're not?" The mere thought revolted her integrity.

"I am here to help you. I don't have to be a pretender except you came here without your husband or family's consent, joined up with a prostitute, and got into a lot of trouble, and I am just being a good Samaritan to you." He stood. "Now, I think you should have a few minutes to yourself to prepare. A long night, according to the man of God." He chuckled and strode out of the room.

She hated his attitude. When he'd found her phone was dead, he'd proceeded to charge the battery and copied out all the numbers he assumed could be her husband's because she'd saved his number by his name and hadn't told Dele what her husband's name was. He must have gotten through because he said nothing more to her. She'd fought him with all her might, which proved to her he was stronger. Deon told her all the time that her physical strength was limited, especially since she wasn't trained to fight. Dele had held both her hands in his left while he copied the numbers with his right. She felt all the vulnerability attributed to her situation. It dawned on her that he could do whatever he wished with her.

When he was done, he had tossed her on the bed and walked out of the room. She'd wept till he returned almost an hour later to inform her he told their host he called off the fast and they would have breakfast, a welcome change.

She glared at the Bible he left on the bed. What did she know about the Word of God? Next to nothing.

"Jesus loves me this I know, for the Bible tells me so." The words from a song she sang during her childhood days danced through her mind.

Her family had gone to church on only a few occasions. Most of those times were when her maternal grandma came for a visit from Tennessee. She loved wearing her floral dresses with swirling skirts and singing with the other children. After Grandma Bea died when Shakira was in her early teens, church had been remanded to Easter and Christmas. Sometimes on Sunday after Thanksgiving.

Shakira didn't think she was worthy of this book. She'd had little to do with it for a long while.

"He should have called us explorers or something." She pressed her lips together. "Grandma Bea would never approve." She covered her mouth to suppress a sob. "Forgive me."

Dele returned later. "All set?"

She hadn't had the nerve to open the Bible. She nodded.

"Good. I understand the pastor invited some of his friends for the service. Don't be surprised if we get other invites to other churches."

"I won't be surprised if we get caught and thrown out of town like common criminals."

He chuckled. "This is Nigeria."

The ride to the church was a five-minute drive in Pastor Goodwill's '90s model Mercedes Benz C200, driven by a young man. Shakira noticed a little more about Efayaw. The town seemed to be lined along one narrow road inundated with deep potholes. The houses, shops, businesses, and banks all lined the main street in no organized pattern.

The church, situated somewhere off the main street, was a small building under construction on a large expanse of land. Pastor Goodwill stood in front of the building in a religious robe, looking fresh and ready for a great service. Shakira cursed her simple knee-length dress and brown sandals when she saw how well-dressed everyone was. Dele's shirt and trousers fitted better than her outfit.

"I hope I am not dressed inappropriately," she whispered, jumpy.

"You are an American," he murmured as though that settled it.

"Our American friends!" Pastor Goodwill raised his hands in the air and tottered toward them.

There was something funny about the way he walked. Shakira found him interesting to watch for different reasons. His accent seemed to be different from earlier in the day too. Like it now had a foreign tang.

They exited the vehicle, and the pastor hugged them together.

"I want you to see our facility," he said. "You work with the government of your country, yes?"

Shakira opened her mouth to educate the pastor. Where she came from the State Department did not sanction Christian missions because of separation of church and state, but Dele spoke first.

He nodded. "On this mission, yes."

"We want you to know we have churches and sister ministries in virtually every state of this country. In case you need to go to other parts, or you have other missionaries coming to Nigeria."

"We will remember your kindness, pastor," Dele said.

Pastor Goodwill had a few buildings on the property that Shakira found misplaced in this town where everything was old and rusty. He crossed the yard toward another building.

"This is our international training institute." His pride could not be hidden. "You are our first American visitors."

The structure was not painted outside. Inside was sparsely furnished with artwork of the second coming and some scriptural quotes. The roofing looked new but the paint on the walls peeled. The floor was not covered, and part of the screen was damaged. It reminded Shakira of the roads with potholes.

"The painting is beautiful." She pointed at the one with angels in the clouds. "This must cost a fortune."

"We have a gifted brother who does all this for us." Goodwill nodded. "I will make sure he gets some for you. When do you hope to leave?"

"We are here for another month or two, at least," Dele said as if he had documentation to back up his claim. His ability to lie continued to amaze her.

Pastor Goodwill expressed delight and rubbed his ringed hands together. "Great. Come and see the school."

Chapter Twenty

"**I** remember in my Sunday school we were taught great Bible stories. And these stories have kept me in awe of the wonders of God." Shakira stared above the heads of the people in the small hall. Her heart thudded in her chest. The expectant looks she saw in the eyes of the members made her feel rotten.

The accommodation was not large enough for the congregation, and many stood against the walls, notepad and pen in hand.

"Love Him and serve Him always. He is the only God who can save you." She wished she could believe those words. "God bless you."

The rousing applause stunned Shakira. What had she said? The pastors and elders stood and clapped until she took her seat. Dele squeezed her hand.

Pastor Goodwill took the podium and spoke at length about the "Great Commission" and the need for brethren to rally round and support the missionaries from America. Later he gave a sermon, and at the end of the service, announced the seven-day crusade. The audience screamed in excitement, and the drummer and keyboardist played loud, rousing tunes.

After service, all the elders waited to meet with Mr. & Mrs. Thomson. Dele spoke on behalf of the couple.

"We are overwhelmed by your welcome and believe it is God who has led us here. Honestly, we came here with only our personal items, not knowing what would happen. But because we serve a God who never lies, we are thankful for everything."

He walked over to Pastor Goodwill and whispered in his ear. They deliberated for a few seconds, and then Dele went back to take his seat.

Shakira refused eye contact with the twenty or so leaders of the church. She was ashamed and sure they would be able to see right through her. But what if they didn't? These people were so trusting and caring. They didn't deserve to be treated like this.

Dele took his seat beside her.

Pastor Goodwill took over the address. "Evangelist Dele has requested our prayers and support as they intend to begin their work without further delay. They do not have private accommodation, but we have offered to give them a two-bedroom apartment within the church complex at the new residential area." The leaders shouted and clapped. "Also, we hope to raise an offering for them." He exchanged glances with a woman Shakira assumed was his wife, who sat on the seat next to his. "At the service tomorrow?"

The leaders deliberated among themselves, mumbling, and afterward the woman said, "Day after. S o we can announce tomorrow for people to prepare."

Shakira couldn't take it. She didn't deserve to have an offering raised for her. Not when she couldn't even quote a simple scripture or remember any she'd been taught as a child. Besides, she was angry with God, if He existed at all. He watched Florence Odu murder two innocent children.

She raised her hand, and through a sob, said, "No, this is too much." Her emotions overwhelmed her, and she covered her face and wept.

Dele gathered her into his arms. The leaders clapped more, mistaking her emotions for humility or perhaps something else.

"We will do more, Lady Evangelist," Pastor Goodwill said. "Jesus admonished His disciples to wipe the dust from their feet against any town they are rejected in." He raised his voice. "But we cannot reject servants of God. Hallelujah!"

The hosts, in a convoy of four cars, led her and Dele back to the house where they'd stayed earlier, and their bags were collected. Then they went back to the church premises not quite five minutes' drive away and were taken through a gate with a banner in front.

Shakira couldn't read what was written on it. "What is on the gate?"

Dele shrugged. "Something about a housing project." He arched his eyebrow. "Why do you ask?"

"Just wondering."

Vast land, with some grass overgrown in parts and pavement on others, surrounded one house. Shakira thought it was too much space with bushes all around. She had lived the last six years in an apartment building after she got married to Deon. Before then, she'd been with her parents in a dense residential area.

She whispered, "Will we be alone in all this place?"

"I'm coming here just as you are, Shakira."

Dele's curt reply shut her up. She clasped her hands in her lap and thought of all the reasons she was here, and only one made sense to her. To fight for justice. But she doubted her actions. The events that brought her to this point in her life seemed more obvious to her. She must have made a mistake. Being in this place, with this man, wasn't what she ought to have done. Many brave women had taken action in their moment of distress, but this couldn't be seen as heroic or wise. Her new consistence was inconsistency of the highest order.

She decided right then she had to go back. It wasn't too late to return home. She would plead with Deon and agree to go on the tropical vacation with him. Anything else but here.

The group alighted from their vehicles, and the lead pastor walked to the front of a newly built bungalow. Two huge halogen lamps hung on poles lit the immediate environment of the house.

Pastor Goodwill stood on the porch. "This building is the first in our housing estate project, and we are most honored to allow you to be the first to use it. Please manage it for us tonight, man of God." He motioned to one of the elders. "Please ensure it is properly furnished tomorrow." The man nodded vigorously.

Dele cleared his throat, and for a moment Shakira thought he would cry. "We are so blessed, sir." He raised his hands high above his head. "As we make use of this provision, every plan and project on this land will be fully accomplished!" The group chorused "amen." "I give this place six months, and it will be developed!" The chorus this time was resounding. "Amen!"

Dele shook the pastor's hand and nudged Shakira to do the same.

One of the younger ministers opened the front door. "We have cleaned everywhere and brought dinner as well."

"God bless you," Pastor Goodwill mumbled.

Shakira walked in behind Dele to a large sitting area with just a sofa and a center table.

"We will bring in more furniture tomorrow by God's grace. But a room is prepared and ready." Pastor Goodwill nodded at his elders once more, as though trying to make sure some previous incident didn't get repeated.

One of the other ministers carried in their luggage, and Shakira followed him. The man dropped the bags, bowed, and left her. She inspected the clean room, with the bed made. One bed. She made a note to force her fake husband to sleep on the couch. She wasn't going to embarrass herself by cuddling into him again like she did the night before.

How much longer before she got back home? She stared at her fingers, and tears she thought were spent dropped on them. She lowered herself to the bed, a thudding she had come to acquaint herself with starting in her chest, but she dozed off and startled when Dele tapped her shoulder.

"I was calling you. We wanted to pray before they left."

She sat up. "Have they gone?"

"Yes." He started to unbutton his shirt and at the same time check the softness of the king-size mattress. "Good mattress," he said.

"You're not sleeping here."

A strange silence ensued. She refused to break it or look at him, and after a long moment, Dele cleared his throat.

"Hear this, woman. I did not come here to suffer. I know you may not have met me in a great place, but I wasn't on the run from my family."

She burst out, "I wasn't on the run. And not from my family."

"Well, it's not important what you are running from or to. We are here now. The good people of this town have done well to welcome us. We have food and shelter, and we are treated like royalty. If you are not grateful, I am. And I am not about to mess things up. It is genius to pretend to be man and wife. And it's working out well."

"I will not share a bed with you, either." She stood. "If you will not use the couch, I will."

"Sorry, you're too late. A lady from the church is using it. She's been detailed to wait on us."

Chapter Twenty-One

Shakira didn't sleep much at night, and her restlessness affected him just as much. Dele Thomson, thirty-six years old, graduate of environmental science from a prestigious university, first-class student, and best in his department, hadn't earned more than the equivalent of $200 a month in all his eight years after graduation. His story wasn't much different from that of many men and women he knew.

A few like Dauda had people in positions of power who'd helped them secure employment in government service. His sisters, he knew without being told, had slept their way into the jobs they had.

He sat on the edge of the bed and stared at Shakira's curled-up figure. She didn't know what she had. A citizen of a first-world country, with everything at her beck and call? Who had not lost a child before? He'd watched a building in his neighborhood collapse, taking all four children in a family. She was privileged. Yet she now gave him an attitude. Did she even imagine what he'd been through? Did she know how he fought through university to get a degree top of his class, only to graduate and be forced to teach primary school children social studies, a job that paid near-nothing, and one he hated with his life?

The first opportunity he had to leave his country would be the only one because he would take it.

Shakira stirred again and whimpered. She'd done so all through the night, and several times he'd been tempted to either wake her up or cuddle her. The latter she would fight.

Here he was now, living a fake existence. With Shakira's current instability, she might blow everything up in their faces. He imagined she'd break down and confess everything sooner rather than later, and he couldn't let that happen.

Two good things were in view for him at the moment: the church would raise enough money for him to take and run off with. He'd seen it happen several times, and though he never thought he could do it, fate had dropped the opportunity in his lap. Depending on how much the church donated, he could return to Lagos, get a small house, and invest in a business. His main problem in life would thus be addressed.

A second good thing would be to win Shakira's heart, marry her, and return to America with her. Or convince her to help him get a visa. Once he left the shores of Nigeria, heaven would be the limit for him.

Two good things, and he wasn't ready to let Shakira mess either up for him. If he played his cards well, he may even get both.

However, he needed to strategize. She had to play along. He needed her in every step of this plan. With the way she got emotional yesterday, he had to find a way to calm her down. She was his ticket to a better life, and he couldn't miss this one opportunity.

He tapped her leg when she shuddered from her sleep. It was close to daylight, and he wanted to have this conversation before the lady in the sitting room awoke.

"Shakira." He tapped her again. "Babe."

She roused and for a moment lost track of her environment. He observed this happen to her every morning since she slept in the same room with him, and he didn't like it at all. She had to be coordinated at all times, with no warning.

"Wake up. We need to talk."

She scooted to the head of the bed and glared at him. She obviously didn't like being disturbed, but this was important.

"What is happening now, believe me, is not normal. I've never tried to deceive anyone to believe I'm someone I'm not."

She yawned. "Me neither."

"So I want you to understand I'm not some fraud. And you can't think of me in such a way."

"Why are we having this conversation? What time is it?"

Dele checked his cell phone, though he knew. "It's 4 a.m. Too early to wake up, but we need to talk."

She pressed her lips together. "I need to use the bathroom."

He waved her toward it. Her attitude needed to improve. They could potentially make a lot of money from these people without extra effort. He also had to keep in mind that she wasn't here for money, so he'd make sure she understood she needed it for her search. Nigeria wasn't like America or any other country. There was no textbook description to help her find the woman responsible for her children's death.

She returned and resumed her seat. "Okay. I'm listening."

"As I was saying, we are both in this situation not because we want to defraud anyone, but you have to play along. First, you need the money, and second, it is a good undercover for you to find the woman you came for."

"And what's in this for you."

"We're not talking about me."

She sneered. "But you are going to benefit a lot from this. It's your only reason for doing it."

"You think I know about this church before I followed you here?" He glared. "You think I do this every once in a while?"

"I don't know you."

He raised his voice. "Oh, but you were willing for me to bring you here. I see." He took in a deep breath. He couldn't afford to lose his temper. "At least you know I brought you here. Now listen to me."

He waited for her to make a comment, and when she didn't, continued speaking in a controlled tone.

"I am a Lagos boy. All my life, I have struggled and fought for everything." He swallowed. "My parents didn't give me much more than their tissue." He closed his eyes to let the nasty detail sink in. "I fought for everything I have. You met my sisters. They live in a nice house because Bessie is sleeping with her boss."

He stole a glance, but she only flinched.

"Yes. There are many people in this country who get by. I am one of them. I have never defrauded anyone, but what we are doing now is not a big deal." His lies did nothing to his conscience.

She gasped. "This is a church."

"Yes!" Dele said forcefully. "And it is nothing new. I have been in churches where people steal from others and the church itself. All these pastors you see around, how many serve God faithfully? Look at this church. Look at the pastor. Why do you think he's doing all these projects, and why do you think he's being so nice to us? You think he cares about us?" He smirked. "He's using us to raise more money. Soon he will have a private jet and live in a mansion." He shook his head. "I don't feel a twinge of guilt for deceiving this pastor."

He paused and breathed in. "Now you need to continue to play along. I have attended many of these churches. All they need to hear is your American accent. You don't need to be a great preacher. Pick a scripture from the New Testament and read it over and over again. Explain what it means to you. Many of these people can't discern anything."

"Then what happens to us?"

"We need money to find your woman—"

"She's not my woman!"

"Right. The woman. We find her, we return to Lagos. You go back to America, and—" he winked—"you take me with you, or I have made enough money to go by myself." He threw up his hands. "It's a win-win."

She took her time in responding. "Well, maybe for you. I have made up my mind. It was a big mistake to come here." Her throat worked up an effort to continue. "I regret everything *ar* done up till now." She switched to the hard accent she used when she wanted to sound tough. "*Ar* miss *ma* husband." Tears trickled down her cheeks, and she brushed them away. "He don't deserve the way *ar* treated 'im." She sniffed and seemed to take control of her slipping accent. "I'm going back. I'll tell the good pastor everything, and I'm *outta* here."

"Not on your life!"

Chapter Twenty-Two

Dele jumped to his feet, and Shakira recoiled. What did he mean to do to her? She had told him her decision to give up on finding Florence, and he could never imagine how tough the choice had been for her.

To have come this far only to give up was defeat on a personal level. She didn't even know what she would return to. Would Deon be willing to forgive and forget? Could she? She would submit herself to a mental health facility because, on her own, she couldn't bounce back, and she hoped to God she could get pregnant again. *Move on*; Fraser's words resounded. She had to.

"You can't. Can't decide to go back home. Not now."

He paced like a caged animal, his eyes wide. She didn't care what he may think was at stake for him. She started all this, and she had to bring it to an end. She didn't foresee a deception this huge, and if it was normal in Nigeria, it was criminal in America. She was desperate for justice, but not this much. She may not have had a deep religious upbringing, but she had a conscience.

She sighed. "I have, Dele, and you can't change my mind. I miss my husband."

"Let's call him then. Call him every day. I will recharge your phone every day. You can't go back."

"I can. And I will. It was wrong of me to come here in the first place. And it is wrong of me to pretend to be what I am not."

"What about your search? Will you just give up on it?"

She choked. "Yes, in the way I took it up. I will let law enforcement find the woman. My babies will never return, but my home, my family—I had a life, and I want to go back to it." She folded her arms in resignation. "I'm sorry, Dele. I apologize for bringing you here, and I would do anything to correct my mistake. But I went too far."

"So you will let the killer of your daughters go free? Probably return to America to kill more babies?"

His words hit below the belt, but she understood what he was trying to do, and she couldn't fall for it. It was obvious he didn't have a good life in his country, and he may never have defrauded anyone before, but to jump at the opportunity without regret spoke of the kind of person he was. Desperate didn't begin to describe it, and she shuddered. Her father had always warned her about such people.

"They could kill you, Shakira. Stay away from them."

It occurred to her she may have put herself in harm's way by expressing her feelings.

"It hurts beyond reason," she stammered. "Especially when I don't know if she'll ever be found."

"Exactly." He moved to her side of the bed and squatted. "Look at it this way. You are helping to get justice for your babies. At the same time, you are not hurting a fly by presenting yourself as a missionary. See all the churches in this country? It is a billion-dollar cow, and those men in collars are milking the life out of their members." He took her damp hands in his. "Should we bet? Just in one or two nights, this small church will present half a million naira to us."

Shakira considered his handsome face. The tilt of his lips made her feel insecure. What did he mean when he said he was a Lagos boy? Back in her home country, statements like this had meaning. Places in the country could be good or bad, and depicted a spirit. What did Lagos represent? Good or bad?

She withdrew her hands from his and clasped them in her lap. "I don't think they have so much money."

"Exactly. They don't. But those pastors will make widows sell the property their husbands left for them. Listen, this is just like ripping off a thief. You have done no wrong."

She shuddered. This man was more evil than she thought. It convinced her how urgently she needed to get away from him.

"You have to stay, Shakira. At least till we have enough." He straightened. "If you are no longer interested in catching the criminal you came for, fine. But you stay till I am ready to leave." He stomped out of the room.

She stared at her shaking hands. She was convinced more than ever she had to leave. She slid between the sheets and closed her eyes. Praying had never been a part of her family culture, especially not since Grandma Bea, but Shakira sucked in her breath and muttered the one prayer she could remember. *Our Father, who is in heaven, hallowed be Your name, Your kingdom come...*

The lady from the church was awake and in the kitchen. Dele couldn't remember her name.

She half-turned when he walked in, and curtseyed. "Good morning, sir."

He raised his hand the way he saw men of God do. "Good morning, daughter of Zion. How was your night?"

"Fine, sir. We thank God."

"Please, I need cold water for my wife. She had a rough night, you know. I think the environment is just not good for her."

She opened a small fridge and placed a bottle of water on a tray, with a glass. "So sorry about this, sir."

"What's your name, again?"

"Veronica."

"Sister Veronica. Hmm. Please, I will ask you not to disturb us. I'd like my wife to try and sleep. Maybe the water will help. Then I want to spend the morning praying."

"Yes, sir." She carried the tray.

"No, let me have it." He took it from her. "Thank you."

"What about breakfast?"

"I will let you know if we will have some or not, but if there's a thermal flask, you can have hot water available for tea, or rather, coffee."

"Yes, sir."

"Thank you."

He left her and returned to the room. Shakira was back in her fetal position, and her eyes were closed, but he guessed she wasn't asleep. Her desire to return home had caught him unawares. They needed to plan the next few days or weeks, make sure they told the same lies.

To reduce the complications of their situation, they were childless for the sake of their ministry. There were other little details he wanted to tidy up as well, like his family history. Who knew, there may be one inquisitive person, someone who had genuine interest in serving God, or had the gift of discernment. Such people needed to be given the right answer. Instead, he had to make her stay.

How did he plan to achieve his purpose now that she seemed to have suddenly realized how foolish she was to embark on such a senseless venture alone?

He wasn't a difficult or violent person. In his sisters' words, he was laid-back and unmotivated. He had never laid a hand on a woman, but he'd seen fear in Shakira's eyes, much as he hated to admit it. He didn't want her to be afraid of him, but he couldn't afford to let her leave either.

He placed the tray of water on a table in the room and sat. He needed to think and act. Whatever happened, Shakira could not buckle now when things may just as well begin to work for his good.

First he had to restrain her, physically, if need be. He locked the door and put the key in his pocket. It should not get to such, and he couldn't afford an outburst of any kind. He searched and found her handbag just under the bed, at the edge. Stealing glances at her, he dragged the bag as quietly as he could to his side and removed the little money she had left, along with her passport.

In the same way, he returned the bag to its previous position. Her cell phone was on the floor beside the bag. He removed the battery and sim and kept it. He put the stolen stuff in his jeans pockets and knelt against the bed. He'd told Veronica he wanted some time to pray, and he meant it.

Chapter Twenty-Three

leep caught up with Shakira all the same, and she came awake about three hours later. She attributed it to fatigue. She was anxious and sad, and her roommate offered no comfort. She sat up and stared at him for a few seconds, then rushed to use the bathroom.

When she returned, he was still in the kneeling position, his hands clasped on his forehead, which shook with a fast left-to-right movement. She couldn't make sense of anything he was saying because he spoke another language. Was he praying in his local dialect?

After her resolve to return home, she felt lighter than she'd been in all the months since her tragedy struck. The stress of fighting back lifted, and she stifled a giggle. She missed her tacos and strawberries. She didn't belong here.

No need to waste any more time. Home was what she longed for. She picked up her cell phone from the floor and flung it in her bag. Since Dele didn't seem interested in her final decision, and would probably ignore her till she left, she figured she'd have to talk to the pastor herself. He should be more sympathetic and would be grateful she didn't deceive him into taking all the money from his poor congregants.

Shakira took her bath and wore one of her simple dresses. Judging from the strenuous journey from Lagos, she knew she couldn't leave Efayaw immediately. The following morning, however, would be good.

Dele continued to mumble and spurt out inaudible words on his knees, and she considered leaving a note for him out of respect. She tore a sheet off her notepad and scribbled an excuse, which she placed on the open Bible in front of him before she picked up her bag and luggage.

"Goodbye," she muttered, and opened the door.

At first, she thought the hinge was hooked. Then she realized the handle didn't budge. The door was locked. Her reaction was slow as she tried to process what could be wrong. Earlier, Dele had walked through this door without difficulty. Could they have been locked in after he returned? Did he know about it?

She stared at his ridiculous profile, muttering gibberish and shaking his head copiously.

"Dele! The door is not opening."

He didn't respond. She opened her bag to check the time and noticed her phone was off. Something was wrong because her battery had been charged before she went to sleep. She switched it on, but it wouldn't boot up.

"Dele. Dele!"

He stopped shaking. "Yes?"

"The door is not opening, and I need to leave."

His tone was even. "As you can see, I am praying. I will call the church to let them know there's a problem with the door when I'm finished."

"When will this be?"

He shrugged. "As the Lord leads me." He promptly resumed the theatrics.

Shakira took in several deep breaths. She could wait him out. If she had the pastor's phone number, she would call by herself, but she didn't. To take her mind off his annoying rambling, she took her cell phone from her bag, remembered it was off, and proceeded to charge the battery.

Nigeria's electricity sucked. There hadn't been once since she arrived that it wasn't out for several hours a day, so she made sure her battery was full when there was power. She plugged the charger and discovered the battery wasn't even in the phone. No one had to tell her what this was about. She never took her battery out.

She tapped Dele. "Give back my battery and open the door. Now."

Dele stopped his noise and narrowed his eyes. "Oh, you figured it out."

Warning bells rang in her ears. "How dare you! You think you can stop me, get away with this crime?"

"I may not stop you, but I can pause you." He corked his neck. "And I have right now." He pulled the key and her battery out of his pocket. She reached out to take them, but he withdrew just in time. "Not so, my dear."

"What do you want?"

"I need you to stay."

She clasped her hand over her mouth to curb her sob. "You've kidnapped me."

"Kidnapped?" He chuckled. "What a word to describe our situation." He lifted himself off the floor. "You arrested me and took me away from my home."

"How?" she cried. "You had no home. You were just looking for who to hang your senseless life onto."

"And I found you."

She sniffed. "You won't get away with this. You think you're smart—"

"I am smart."

She moved around to stand right in front of him. "Give me the key. And my battery." When he folded his arms across his chest, she screeched, "Give me!"

"Lower your voice, Mrs. Thomson. We have company in the house." He breathed in. "And you don't want to upset her."

"I don't care who gets upset. Let me out!"

"Screaming at me will not solve your problem. You see, Nigerians may be anything to Americans, but we are also believers. We believe most things we are told." He leaned against the wall and studied her. "Especially when it comes to your people and your weird diseases." He rubbed his hands. "I will tell them you have a mental problem. It comes on you every now and then. They will believe it's why I had to lock the door, so you won't run into the streets. They will feel sorry for me and be extra sympathetic."

She moaned. Her situation became clear. This man was a sociopath. From anger and pain at her loss, she now felt helpless. She thought of the many movies she'd seen and how a desperate woman would end up in the bunker of some deranged "nice" man's house.

She shuddered. "You're not going to hurt me, please."

"I won't. Unless you are not ready to deal."

Chapter Twenty-Four

Dele made her understand the consequences of her dilemma. *They won't believe you. No one will. Your story is a hard sell, Shakira, dump it. With such a tale, most people will think you're crazy, babe.*

On and on he went about the tight corner she pushed herself into. She hated the way he called her "babe" and wanted to understand his problem about her dilemma but couldn't.

"This is my main problem. This is not America. Not even close. Nigeria is like a graveyard. Nothing is happening, yet my best opportunity is right here." He paced. "How will I convince you otherwise? I am not a bad person, and I mean no harm." He sighed. "But this is my chance. I finally got my chance!"

With tears in her eyes, she asked what he needed her to do.

"The plan is simple. Play along. Read your Bible, pray every day." His singsong tone rankled. "Then we'll be fine. I will not hurt you. I have sisters about your age."

She remembered how little he thought of his sisters, and trembled.

"But listen well, Shakira, if you speak to anyone about our plan, I'll hurt you. The American embassy is far from here, and you may not be lucky a second time to find a police officer as good as Dauda."

He'd said so earlier, and for him to repeat this meant he was not joking around. She would be free of him soon, but she didn't want to get hurt before she was free. She now had a new focus: to be free to return home. It wasn't as difficult as what brought her all the way here. As long as she didn't derail from Dele's plan, she could be free in a few days.

"Now, let's plan today."

The door was still locked, and her seized property was still in his custody. She lowered herself to the bed, afraid her knees would not hold, with her hands folded on her lap, and her back straight like a school child about to be given the riot act.

"The pastor comes to see us soon. Since we now have an agreement to do this together, we will not give him an audience. Helps with the suspense. Now," he rubbed his hands, "tonight is going to be big. We will both preach. I will give you a scripture to read and prepare a short message on. Tonight they will take an offering for us, so we must pray for the people. Have you seen how praying is done before?"

She shook her head. Her heart beat faster. This was worse than being with Glory in the brothel or visiting Mo in the ghetto in Houston. It couldn't be compared to any form of fear she'd ever experienced.

"You place your hand on the forehead. Don't push. You can mumble. Say God bless you, or anything at all."

She closed her eyes. God would never forgive her for this. She was doomed to hell.

"Are you listening, Shakira?"

She nodded.

"After the prayers, we will close the service. I can do this. We will ask for the money raised if they don't give it to us straight up."

"When you have the money, can I leave? Go back to Lagos, and to my home?"

"It depends on how much they give us."

How could he? Her eyes popped open. "You said you'd be fine once you had the money."

"If the money is enough, we leave together. You can go back to your country—"

"How much do you expect?"

"Enough." He glared at her, and she returned his gaze. "And you don't need to ask me how much because I don't know."

She jerked her face away from him. He was worse than any criminal she ever knew. There was no justification for what he did and made her agree to.

"Listen to me, Shakira. I'm not going to go over this with you anymore. Play your part and you will be fine." He went back on his knees and scribbled on the piece of paper she'd left for him. "Study this scripture."

She didn't remember having a Bible when she left home, but now they both held one each. She wondered what lies he told to get them because he didn't have money to buy the Bibles. This was the worst kind of fraud. She doubted she'd ever come to terms with it.

Shakira stared at what he'd written on the paper: 1 Peter 3:11. She had no clue where it was in the Bible and had to go to the contents page.

She sat on her side of the bed and read the verse over and over again. Why would he choose such a verse? It meant nothing to her. She didn't want to ask him what he thought of it, so she read the whole chapter to get a better understanding.

Each scripture seemed to jar her. She heard voices at the back of her mind, asserting her, encouraging her to focus on God and let Him touch her. The Bible in her hand burned and sweat broke out all over her body.

Dele continued to shake and mumble on his knees. He didn't notice something was happening to her. She slid to her knees and clutched her stomach. Her life played out before her and tears dropped from her eyes to the floor. Was she having an encounter? And if she was, shouldn't she face her fears and tell the truth? It would take only a few days if the money was enough.

She didn't want any money. She only wanted to do right. She sobbed for a long time. When she had thought she was hungry for food it passed.

Now there was a new hunger in her and an anger against what Dele was putting her through.

She begged God's forgiveness and healing of all her anger against Him, her husband, and even Florence Odu. It was time to move on.

At peace with herself, she clutched the Bible to her chest and waited for Dele to be done. She decided she would not share any more of her fears or faith. Once he got the money he needed, and she was back in Lagos, she would send a message to Detective Dauda and report everything. The policeman would know what to do about his friend's fraudulent activities.

Sometime later in the day, Dele opened the door and asked the lady from the church to serve food. Shakira overheard him tell her they just finished praying and wanted to break their fast. All well, she thought. Since she had read from the Bible, she hadn't been hungry.

They were served pepper soup, which was so hot and spicy she couldn't take more than a sip. Then a dish of stir-fried rice was served. But it didn't taste as spicy as she assumed, and she ate enough to fill her stomach.

After the meal, Dele asked, "Would you like to freshen up? They should be here to pick us up in an hour or so."

She shook her head. "No, thanks."

He started to say something, but his phone rang, and he picked it up. She realized after a few words exchanged that it was his detective friend, but they spoke his local language, and she didn't understand a word of it. The conversation was intense by the sound of Dele's voice, and several times he paused for long minutes.

Finally, he hung up.

"Shakira, it's Detective Dauda." He rubbed the back of his neck. "Things have changed a little bit. I told him what we are doing now, and he said we must continue, like undercover. The police in Lagos have information on your—the woman, Florence Odu. She's headed to Efayaw and will be here any moment now."

Chapter Twenty-Five

*D*ele watched Shakira's mouth drop open and her eyes dilate. She didn't say anything for a few seconds whereas he'd thought she would be happy at the news. For him, it wasn't good for his plans. He wanted out as fast as possible.

Once when he was so desperate to travel out of the country, an immigration lawyer had told him he could get an American visa if he paid half a million naira. Though some other people had told him it was the most unpredictable visa to get, he had been willing to risk it, if only he had the money. At the time, he couldn't even boast of one percent of the fee. Now he had hope. If the church raised enough money, he may not need Shakira for his escape to fulfill his American dream.

"What are you thinking?"

Her throat worked up and down for a second, and she frowned. Why was it so difficult for her to respond? This was what she left her husband and family for. Was she so averse to pretending to be a missionary that finding the murderer of her children would not change her mind? He'd not thought she was such a religious person.

She cleared her throat. "I want to go home."

He gasped. "You don't want to find the woman who murdered your kids anymore?"

She moved her lips, but words didn't come out, and he understood. The news made her emotional.

"Don't worry, you'll be alright."

He would have given her a pat or a hug, but he didn't think she would appreciate it. Even when he noticed tears had clouded her eyes, he didn't offer any more comfort.

"I'll prepare myself for the evening." He walked to the bathroom door but stopped short. "I think you should see this as a good thing. The hand of God. I don't like the idea of being here longer than necessary, but I wanted to help you. It's why I agreed to bring you here."

"Did you say you told Dauda what we're doing?"

He rolled his eyes. What was her issue with this exactly? "Yes."

"We're pretending to be missionaries?"

"I told him we decided to go undercover."

"One lie after the other," she mumbled.

"Well, he thought it was brilliant. He even suggested he might mention me to his superiors. To get a job."

She raised her chin. "Good for you."

"Your snotty attitude does not work in this country. Count yourself blessed to meet people like me." He grabbed the door of the bathroom.

There was a knock on the door. Veronica called from the other side. "Excuse me, sir. The car is here from the church."

"Oh! I didn't know it was time so soon. Please give us five minutes. Thanks."

"Yes, sir."

He glared at Shakira. "Get ready."

Dele moved back to the wardrobe where their bags were and changed his clothes. Shakira remained seated as though she weren't coming with him. When he was set, he strolled to the door.

"Will you get ready?"

"I am ready." She picked up her bag and dragged in a deep breath. "Can I have my passport and the other stuff you took? At least now we know I'm not leaving till all this is over."

"Then you shouldn't worry about it." He stepped out of the room and slammed the door.

Two young men waited in the sitting room, standing almost at attention. Veronica was with them, carrying a covered basket and her bag.

"She'll be here in a second. Good evening, brothers."

They chorused, "Good evening, sir."

Dele felt good to the bottom of his stomach. Even though this was all a sham, no one had ever waited on him. One of the brothers collected his Bible and cell phone just as Shakira stepped into the room.

Veronica handed over the basket to the other brother and insisted on taking her bag. The group moved out to the car and arrived at the church to meet the worship in session.

The couple were led to the pastor's office where they were received with warmth and eagerness by a room full of leaders. Everyone seemed to want a touch, and the ladies hugged Shakira.

Dele noticed the way she flinched each time someone came close or touched her and contemplated bringing up her "mental" problem. He pulled Pastor Goodwill aside.

"We got some disturbing news from home, so my wife is a bit concerned."

Pastor Goodwill frowned. "We're so sorry to hear about this. Will she be able to preach?"

Dele nodded. "I believe so. You may have just noticed she's a bit withdrawn."

The pastor affirmed with a nod of his head. "I was wondering too. Though Sister Veronica told me you fasted and prayed all day, so I assumed that was the reason why."

Dele made a point to remember that the lady in the house with them could be a spy. He had to be careful around her so she would not overhear some of his discussions with Shakira.

He pulled her closer in an intimate way. "Dear, pastor is worried you won't be able to preach tonight. Because of the news, the phone call."

She shook her head and would have agreed, but he cut short whatever she had in mind to say.

"But I dismissed it. You are a strong woman, and God gave you a message for us tonight."

He knew the way the minds of people worked. If the American woman did not preach, there may not be enough donation. They needed to hear her.

"I believe so," she mumbled.

"Great! Pastor, whenever you are ready, we are."

He took Shakira by the elbow and ushered her to the packed hall. It was a good sign. The more the merrier. He would preach his heart out tonight. Mimic everything he had ever joked about preachers. Every gimmick he could imagine would be put into absolute force. This was his one chance, and he wasn't about to bungle it.

Chapter Twenty-Six

ele counted the notes in denominations. Some were so dirty and rumpled, Shakira wondered if they would be good to spend. The counter didn't seem to notice, though. He'd made her help in sorting the money and straightening the bills out, but she complained that she was tired and wanted to rest. She wasn't in the least interested in how much it was, as long as the money reached Dele's mark.

Shakira lay on her side of the bed and stared at the man she had to share her life with for the time being. He had made her think he was kind, but the dark side he now revealed to her scared her more than anything else. She didn't know herself anymore. Tragedy, many had said, was good and could make a person strong, but not her. She had degenerated beyond being suicidal. She couldn't even recognize who this Shakira Smith was.

"It looks like it will be a little more than two hundred." Dele glanced in her direction. "Though I'm not done yet."

"Is it enough?"

He snarled. "Far from not enough."

She gusted out a breath she may have been holding since he seized her passport and phone battery. It had to be enough. She was tired and lonely and frightened. All the fight had gone out of her. She couldn't make any decent decisions about her life. Instead of running into her support system, her husband and her family, she had run from it and flung her life into a jungle of strangers who cared nothing for her or her future.

If I die here, where will I be buried?

The thought had been on her mind from the moment she landed at the airport and with every turn of events became a more realistic question. Probably the American embassy would claim her body. But how? She'd refused to check in with the embassy.

"Thank God," she mumbled. "It will be good to have enough."

He paused counting. "You still want to leave even though the woman you came for is close by?"

She thought about this. It would be good to see Florence apprehended. But at what cost? A person so evil being so close made her shudder. Why was she headed to Efayaw? Did she know Shakira was in town? And a threat? Or was she still running? Glory and Mo made her believe Florence was already here, or had they sent her on a wild goose chase?

Her decision to go back home and give up at this rate came from a deep conviction she couldn't explain. Maybe it was the deceit of the church, the yearning she saw in the eyes of the faithful...so much expectation.

And reading the Bible, preparing a message, had done something to her. She couldn't explain it even if she tried, but the Word of God had cut through her conscience like a sharp knife. The voice of reason had tormented her into submission.

She shook her head. "I don't want to stay one day extra."

He shrugged. "Well, Dauda said he was worried for you, and so he called a former colleague who now works at Interpol and your story came up to be true."

So they thought she had lied? Who in their normal thinking would take up such a journey on a lie? She couldn't imagine any reason someone like her would leave everything and come to such a country.

"I hope she gets arrested." She sucked in her breath. "But I am no longer going to be in the middle of it. I will head back home and pray the police are successful."

"I thought you were a brave woman, but I must agree with you. Coming here was quite risky, and it's better you return home."

She could weep for the softening in his eyes and the lowering of his voice. He pitied her.

She didn't want any of it. Not from him. "I think you should finish counting so we know." She pointed at the cash laid out in between them on the bed.

He nodded and finished up. "Two hundred and seventy-three thousand naira! Hallelujah! Wow." He laughed. "This is wonderful. And there were some pledges. But I don't care for those." He arched an eyebrow. "Are you sure we should leave with this? Tomorrow?"

She stifled a giggle. "Yes. Please." His joy was contagious, and she couldn't help but be affected by it.

"No problem. I won't even tell Dauda we're leaving. So here's the plan." He leaned toward her. "I will take two hundred, and we can use the seventy-three for our travel and any other expenses. Early tomorrow morning, we will tell Veronica we're going for a prayer walk. We will not take any of our stuff. Nothing is important. Right?"

"Right." She lost everything important on her first day.

"The bus station is not far from here. We go there and get a taxi to Calabar. Calabar is not far. We fly out from there." His eyes twinkled with pleasure. "Is the plan good?"

She nodded. "It is." Particularly, the part where they would fly to Lagos made her pleased. She couldn't imagine the stress of riding on a rickety bus back to Lagos. "How long is the flight from—from—"

"Calabar to Lagos?" He shrugged. "One hour."

"Ah." She clapped. "Great."

"Yeah." He packed the money and put it in a plastic bag. "If we leave here before six, we should be in Lagos before twelve, unless there's no morning flight."

"I may need some money to change my ticket to Houston."

He rubbed his hands together. "Shouldn't be a problem. Can't be more than two hundred dollars."

"I don't think so."

He kept the bag of money under the bed and lay on his back, staring up at the ceiling. She didn't care about what was on his mind. She could only smell freedom and see her home again. She needed therapy, but more importantly, Deon's forgiveness.

"I will find you when I come to Houston," Dele said. "Before the end of this year."

Shakira thought she didn't want to be found by him once she separated herself tomorrow, but she had to play along. If he asked for an address, she had several. Least of all, she would give him Mo's in the ghetto, where he belonged with other criminals like him.

Chapter Twenty-Seven

It wasn't quite morning, and Shakira imagined she must be dreaming, but the hand pulling at her nightgown seemed too real, and she hadn't been having a dream. She opened her eyes and screamed at the sight of several men carrying machetes.

Dele stirred beside her, and she realized he wasn't awake yet. The one who had pulled at her gestured to Dele.

"Wake him."

She tapped her fake husband. "Dele, wake up."

He grunted. "Yes?"

Her scream ought to have got him up, or maybe it had only been in her head. "Wake up, please. Wake up," she sobbed.

Her voice must have alarmed him. He moaned and startled when he opened his eyes and saw they had company.

"The blood of Jehu!"

"Shut up, man of God," the leader said. "Where is the money?"

Shakira gasped. Their faces were not covered, which meant they knew they would not be recognized. What an irony! To think they were being robbed of money they'd defrauded from the church.

"The money, sir, it is the seed of the people of God. The expectation—"

The leader slapped Dele. "I will ask you one more time, or my boys will make a feast of your American wife while you watch. And then we will search the house, and if we find the money, we will kill her. And her blood will be on your head."

His menacing words tore through every bone in Shakira's body. "Please, give them the money. Please."

She willed herself to look at the armed robbers. There were six of them. She shuddered. This wasn't just a random operation; they had insider information. They knew she wasn't a Nigerian, and they also believed Dele was truly a Christian preacher. What sort of a country was this, where people had no fear for the things of God? Growing up back home, the priest was respected by everyone in the community.

Dele rolled off the bed and put his hand under the bed. He came up with the bag of money and threw it at the leader, who threw it at one of the boys.

"Ah, may the Lord have mercy on your soul."

"Where's the remaining? And the dollars?"

Shakira cried, "Thieves took all the dollars in Lagos. Please, we don't have any more."

The irony was not lost on the leader. He smirked at his fellow crooks. "Go." He called to Dele. "God save you. Now, if I hear a pin, I'll come right back and finish you all."

Dele moaned. "You need to turn your life around."

The criminal didn't wait. He slammed the door after him. Shakira hugged her shaking body, wondering what next and grateful they hadn't carried out their threat. What could she have done to stop them?

Dele was shaking too. He walked to the door and pressed his ear to it, his hand on the handle, and she could see how his hands trembled. Those thieves hadn't spent more than ten minutes, but Shakira doubted she would ever forget them.

She couldn't react now. She pressed her lips together to control her nerves, but it didn't work. Veronica screamed from the parlor, and Dele closed his eyes. He remained rooted to the ground, though the distress in the lady's voice was raw.

"Maybe she needs help," Shakira whispered.

Dele shook his head. "You don't think I'm going out there to face those terrorists."

Shakira sobbed. Was this what the good Samaritan would do? Leave a helpless woman at the mercy of six men drunk on power and probably high on weed?

"She needs help." She pushed Dele out of the way and opened the door.

It wasn't the smartest thing to do, but nothing else came to her mind. Veronica lay tied to one of the sofas, and to Shakira's relief, none of the evil men were in sight. She untied the lady, who pulled her into a hug, trembling uncontrollably and sobbing aloud. In comforting another, Shakira found strength and consolation. No matter what, the dreaded men were gone, and no one was visibly hurt. It could have escalated dangerously and quickly.

"Did they hurt you? Did they touch you?"

Her urgent inquiry was answered by a firm shake of Veronica's head and sniffs. She heard the door open and jumped. It was Dele, who approached with caution.

"Are they gone?"

Shakira nodded. To think this was supposed to be the man in the house. He let out a heavy sigh and slumped against the wall.

"I forgot how vicious the thieves in these areas are."

His words made her furious beyond her expectation. She screeched, "You knew there were thieves around here?"

Veronica stifled a sob, and Dele sneered. "How was I supposed to know we would be attacked on the premises of the church or in such a place as this?" He touched his fingers to his temple. "Please, what time is it?" He asked no one in particular.

"It's about 4 a.m. I just woke up for my early morning prayers when they barged in." Veronica drew in a ragged deep breath. Still shaken, Shakira believed she only answered from her subconscious. "Pastor needs to post policemen here before they kidnap her."

Shakira shuddered. "Kidnap? Who?"

"You." Veronica sat up straight. "Thank God they didn't take you with them."

Shakira peered at Dele. "They. Kidnap?"

The lazy loll of his head made her want to scream. Her hands shook uncontrollably. She needed to leave now. Had to get out before things got worse.

But how?

"Don't get yourself all worked up, dear." Dele sighed. "God is our shield and defender."

She wondered why he spoke with the endearment, and it took a moment to remember they were part of an act.

"Don't you dare call me your dear! Do you think you can continue with this act the way things are?" She pushed him. "I am leaving this place and now. If you like, go to hell and back trying to stop me."

He grabbed her by the waist before she could breeze past him. "Oh no, she's having an attack. Nervous breakdown."

Chapter Twenty-Eight

A doctor had a drip set on Shakira's arm and told Dele she would soon sleep it off. "It's quite normal for one to have these symptoms in cases of extreme panic attack."

"Thank you, doctor." He stared at Shakira, who blinked several times. "I was afraid she would lapse into a full-blown mental attack."

The doctor, a man in his fifties, or perhaps a little older, nodded. "Thank God it didn't degenerate. Try and be here when she wakes up to reassure her."

"I will, doctor. Thank you."

He walked with the doctor out of the guest room. Pastor Goodwill had put them in his house after Veronica called him to come to their aid. Dele had struggled to control Shakira for several minutes without success as she pushed him off and threw things around the house. When a side stool hit the wooden entrance door and splintered the cheap wood, Veronica called for help.

"I have spoken to Pastor Goodwill. Our land is not so safe. He must get armed protection for you both." The doctor clasped his hands. "How long will you be here?"

"I don't know now. With this, she might just want us to return home right away."

"I guess it will be the best thing."

Dele sighed. "Thanks again, sir."

They shook hands, and the doctor left. Dele sat on the only chair in the room and cursed every evil that ever existed.

He had been so elated, sure he'd be in Lagos now, talking to an immigration lawyer. His sisters might have been awful a lot, but he knew they would find money to help him get out of the country if he told them he had part of the money needed. America was the dream, and he planned to get there. Why would God deliver an American woman into his hands, when he wasn't even praying for it? It wasn't just a coincidence. This was what his pastor in Lagos called the hand of God. He would not lose focus.

With no money, he needed a new plan. Shakira had to cooperate and stay back a little longer. It was the only way they could get more easy money. Foul words sprang to his lips against the robbers who had taken more than money from him in the early hours of the morning. They had taken hope.

There was a soft knock, and the door opened. Pastor Goodwill walked in with a crease on his forehead.

"Doctor said she was sleeping."

The two men watched Shakira, whose eyes were open but drowsy.

"She will wake soon."

Pastor Goodwill sat. "I'm so sorry about your experience. We have sent the seven curses to the thieves. They will not run far."

Dele stifled a chuckle. "Seven curses?"

"Yes. We have what is called the seven curses prayer. The vicious prayer attacks every area of a culprit's life."

"We are asked to pray for those who despitefully use us, man of God."

"The Bible also says we should suffer not a witch to live."

Dele deferred. "You are the great man of God. We are just missionaries."

"Doctor said you might be leaving soon."

Dele sighed. "Yes, pastor. Once she's fit to travel, I think the best thing is to leave."

He hated to think it, but with the little display of hysteria, Shakira may not be controlled next time. He may not get any money to pursue his dream, but he'd rather leave Efayaw with a good name. He knew people around here could be vicious, and he wasn't about to be a victim.

"The devil is a liar! No. No, sir." Pastor Goodwill paced. "I have spoken to Sister Veronica. Her brother is in the army. We will get the army to come here and follow you about."

Dele smirked. "Will it work? The armed robbery shook my wife up. She has never experienced anything like this."

"I can imagine. But we thank God for His mercy." The pastor sighed. "We have made a police report. They will catch all of them. Dead or alive."

"I pray so."

"I'm not sure your wife can preach this evening."

"Not at all."

"And you, sir?"

Dele arched his eyebrow. "We must preach in season and out of season."

Pastor Goodwill clapped. "Glory be to God. I told the police you cannot give any statement and would rather not see anyone, so they are talking to Veronica."

"She was rather shaken up."

"Yes. We just thank God they did not hurt anyone."

"The money they took can be replaced."

Pastor Goodwill nodded. "By the grace and mercy of God." He studied Shakira, whose eyes were closed. "The devil has been put to shame. All of this was to frustrate your mission, but he has failed."

"Indeed."

"I will excuse you now. We will serve lunch at about three and leave for church at five."

"Okay, man of God."

At the door, Pastor Goodwill clasped his hands. "Thanks again for the powerful service last night."

Dele nodded. Shakira had spoken with passion and tears in her eyes. He had never heard any message so moving. He was almost convinced.

After Pastor Goodwill left, Dele walked over to the bed and pored over Shakira. She breathed evenly and seemed at peace. The best thing was to let her go. He had been at this brink before. His pastor called it a "near-success syndrome." Several times in his life, he'd been so close to getting something he wanted so much, then something would go wrong and he'd lose it.

He could never forgive himself if Shakira stayed back against her wishes and got kidnapped or killed. A lot about her life remained hidden from him, and he would love to meet her husband and give him a punch on his face for allowing her to come on her own, but that might never happen.

Once she woke up, he would make a new plan with her. He'd ask Pastor Goodwill for some money, and they would leave the following morning. If America was in his destiny, it would come to pass sometime.

Chapter Twenty-Nine

The first time Shakira came awake, she was alone. She pulled at the cord attached to her hand, and it came off the hook on a stand. For several confused moments she struggled but finally got the needle out of her hand.

Drained from the exertion, she lay back and closed her eyes. She woke up later to find Dele at her bedside. She stared at him without feeling.

"Good afternoon, dear. You've been asleep forever."

"Where am I?"

"Pastor Goodwill brought us to his house. It's safer here, and he has a military escort for us now."

Shakira gasped. "Why am I—a military escort?"

He patted her hand. "You were hysterical. A doctor was brought to calm you—" He stared at her hand. "You pulled off the drip?"

She followed his gaze. "What drip?"

"The doctor wanted you to rest." He sat on the bed close to her. "I think he just gave you some stuff to calm you."

She shot up straight. "I don't need any rest. I have to get out of here."

"Considering the circumstances, there's no way to leave without money."

She swung her feet off the bed. "I will ask the pastor to give me money. I am not going to continue to—"

"You'd better cool yourself down. This is Nigeria. The moment they suspect you are fake, they'll throw you out and not give you a cent."

"You keep saying things like this, and I am not impressed. I'd rather let them throw me out. I'll call the embassy. I'll call my—give me my passport and my phone battery." She raised her voice. "Now!"

Dele rubbed his neck. "I'm sorry, Shakira. I kept it in the money bag."

"You what?!" she screamed. "My—oh my gosh. Oh my gosh." She slid to the floor. "What am I going to do? I will never go back home. I'm stuck here, dear God, help me!"

Pastor Goodwill knocked and called out, "We're set, man of God."

"I'm sorry." Dele walked to the door and opened it. "My wife is having another attack."

Pastor Goodwill hurried over to Shakira and laid a hand on her shoulder. While she wailed and puked on the floor, he prayed over her.

Dele called on one of the young women he realized lived in the pastor's house. "I need some sand, please. My wife is sick."

The girl ran out and came back with a pan full of dry sand. She rushed into the room and poured it on the floor, over the mess.

"I'm so sorry," Shakira moaned. "I'm so sorry."

Dele helped her back onto the bed.

Pastor Goodwill sighed. "We understand why you can't be in church. I will just preach a simple message and dismiss the members."

Dele shook his head. "I'm not sure we shouldn't just leave tomorrow, pastor."

"No, please." He glanced at Shakira. "She'll be alright. We will ensure she is."

"I know, but when she becomes like this, believe me, it usually gets worse." Dele closed his eyes, and when he opened them there were tears. "This has been a huge hindrance to our ministry, yet God keeps pushing us to go into all the world."

Pastor Goodwill held Dele's shoulders. "If you go back home now, you have allowed the enemy to defeat you. You mustn't. You can't." He waved at Shakira. "See how God used your wife yesterday? The presence was thick!"

"I know, pastor." Dele rubbed his temple. "She gets this sick—aww, I don't know." He sighed. "We will pray about this, and if it is God's will, we'll stay."

"Please." Pastor Goodwill shook Dele's shoulder. "Please, sir."

After he was gone, Dele looked at Shakira. "You want him to know you're not a missionary, fine. Go ahead and tell him, but I'm not going to tolerate your hysteria any longer."

Shakira snapped. "I'm not hysterical!"

"Try and convince yourself." He moved to the other side of the bed and sat. "The doctor comes to check on you in the evening. Do whatever you like. I'll just tell them you're stark raving mad."

She realized her panic may get her into more trouble, but she needed to reach her embassy as soon as possible. If she could get use of the internet, she didn't even need money. Her country would get her out.

She took calming breaths. "I'm sorry. I won't lose control again."

"You shouldn't." He bent over and studied something on the floor. "Oh, wow."

"What?" She followed his gaze and saw his cell phone.

"Dauda's man is here. I just saw his text message."

Shakira sat up. "What does it mean?"

She had her own ideas. Whoever this man was knew who she was and why she was here. She planned to tell him the truth and request his help to contact her embassy.

Dele stood. "I'll go and fetch him from where he is." He tipped his head to one side and studied her. "Stay here. And even if you want to go home tomorrow, there still must be a meeting with this guy."

Her voice thinned from her internal ache and external exhaustion. "Who is he?"

Dele shrugged and read his text message again. "A police officer. Dauda's former colleague who now works in Interpol."

"Interpol!" She jolted. "You mean they have finally found her? For the Interpol to come instead of total strangers? From the normal police?"

"Listen, Shakira, this jumpy you is not good. I know you've been through a lot, and you're anxious to return to your family, but it's just a matter of days now. Relax and let things just roll by you."

She nodded, not because she agreed but because she wanted him to believe she was alright.

"Good." He stood. "I'll soon be back. And we will discuss the next plans with this man."

"What are the next plans?"

"You want to return to America. We were robbed so we don't have any money, and your passport was taken as well, so he has to facilitate your return."

She slumped. "Thank you," she said hoarsely. "Thank you."

"See you later."

She closed her eyes and daydreamed of a night in Deon's arms.

Chapter Thirty

The Interpol officer was young and suave, against Shakira's expectation. He spoke well too and reassured her of his desire to help in every way within seconds of introducing himself with a warm handshake.

Shakira had insisted on having the meeting in the guest room, for the sake of privacy, though Dele told her no one was in the house.

"I'm glad you're here, inspector." She shook his hand. "Please sit."

"I've brought Inspector Joshua up to speed on our situation," Dele said. He sat on the edge of the bed, and the officer took the only seat. "He understands our plight."

"However, Ms. Shakira, I need you to answer a few questions for me." Joshua sat forward and removed his phone from his pocket. "Permit me to record this." He arched his eyebrow for a second but fiddled with the phone without waiting for her consent. "Yes, we can start." He introduced himself and mentioned the location, with the people in attendance.

Joshua was convincing. He also knew more about the case than Shakira imagined. Fraser's assurances resounded in her brain. When she'd thought

Interpol had given up, this man just proved her wrong, and everyone right. Justice would be served, and for the first time since the worst day of her life, she thought she could go home and sleep well.

After what seemed like an hour of continuous questioning, Joshua stood. Shakira thought it was over, but his next question almost threw her off balance.

"How did this Nigerian woman kill your daughters?"

Shakira stammered, "She—bathtub. Drowned."

"I'm sorry for your loss. And I assure you again, we will find her. We are so close now."

Shakira croaked out a "Thank you."

Joshua closed the interview and put his phone back in his pocket. "There is information that this woman came into this area last night. We contacted members of her family, who until now denied knowledge of her whereabouts." He narrowed his eyes. "But through one of our informants, we've gotten one of her relatives to help us."

"I appreciate this."

"You've been through a lot, dear." Dele squeezed her hand. "So, inspector, what is next in the plan?"

"This will determine how we progress," Joshua said. He took out his phone again and pressed it for a bit. "She's here, and so are we."

Shakira studied him. He wore a simple dress shirt and black slacks with sneakers and hung a set of earpieces around his neck. He couldn't be older than thirty-five and had smooth, dark good looks. Somewhere in her mind, she thought he was the first handsome Nigerian she had met.

"You have a team?" she asked. Shakira didn't think it was an appropriate question, but Joshua's smile made her feel welcome to it.

"A large team. Florence Odu has been on the Most Wanted list of Interpol for a year or more."

Shakira gasped. "Is she so dangerous?"

Joshua nodded. "It makes her dangerous. We have reason to believe she used someone else's identity in the States, though this is still under investigation as well."

"I wondered how she could have gotten the green card too," Shakira said.

"A Mrs. Florence Odu was a nurse in the state of Texas. She came into the country with a valid study permit. She was brilliant and worked for years after she graduated. She went missing sometime five years ago."

Dele's mouth fell open. "Is it possible this woman we're looking for killed her?"

"We don't think this woman is in on it. There is a ring of fraudsters and identity forgers, some still in hiding, that we have worked with the governments of different countries to burst. We believe Florence, the real one, may have fallen into mischief under them. Her identity was sold to this woman."

"Oh my gosh." Shakira thought she would puke again. Sweat broke out on her forehead. "The poor woman was living her American dream."

"And she's just taken out." Dele snapped his finger. "Just like that."

"What took us time to find this criminal who babysat for you was the mixed-up identities. We were following the real owner of the name for several months. I believe it gave our real target enough time to cover her tracks."

"So bold of her." Dele clicked his tongue. "She sure thinks she can hide in this country."

"She thought so. And considering the fact that no one was on her trail until a couple of months ago, she thought she had gotten away."

Dele moaned. "You have her picture? Who knows, I may bump into her."

Shakira didn't want to look at it.

"I do. But I want you to see something more." Joshua brought out three pictures from his wallet. "Look at these three pictures." He put them on the bed, and Shakira reluctantly peeked.

Two of them were a little old and rumpled.

She muttered, "Florence Odu."

"Which one? There are two different women there."

Dele's eyes widened. "They look so alike."

"Yes. Almost the same age too." He put the pictures away. "You see, the identity forgers are so good. They sell to people who are alike. They cost high too."

Shakira touched her hand to her pounding chest. "The woman—how would she have been able to pay?"

"People do whatever to get what they want. This stolen identity could have cost five to ten thousand, or more—"

Dele gasped. "Dollars?"

"Yes. They are advised not to take up jobs where background checks will be done, and they won't use credit cards or open bank accounts."

"Goodness," Shakira said. "She came a lot cheaper than most we found. We killed our babies just because we wanted to cut costs."

The two men were quiet as she sobbed. They mumbled words of comfort, but she didn't stop crying until she felt she could.

"Many of these people stay out of trouble. They make the money they need and return to their countries, so they are never found. Sometimes the identity fraudsters get the identification back and sell to someone else—depends on the terms of the sale."

Dele rubbed his forehead. "Wow, the woman—this woman on the run—must be so dangerous."

"We prefer to call them desperate, which rates them higher than dangerous. It means they can act on impulse and do anything. They cannot be predicted."

"It makes sense for Shakira to go back home without delay."

Joshua squatted right before her, and for a moment she thought he would take her hands, but he didn't.

"Not yet, please. We need you to be here, Shakira. We have made arrangements for everything you need. To be here and remain. We have cause to believe she's followed you here."

Chapter Thirty-One

ele jumped to his feet, surprising all of them. "No way." He shoved his hands in his pockets. "Do you know what Shakira's been through? Being here alone is enough risk, and she has to go back to her family."

Joshua didn't seem fazed. "We have men and women working undercover, watching her. What she's been through, as you say, is because she was on her own."

Dele threw his hands up in the air. "She's been with me, and we are still not safe."

"You have no training whatsoever to protect her. How can she be safe with you?"

Dele flailed his hand at Shakira. "Say something. Are you going to let them tie you down here till forever? This is your chance to return home. You shouldn't have come in the first place."

Joshua raised his eyebrows. "Dele, why do you want to compromise the investigation? We know what you tried to do while here. I may have to remove you from this discussion, you know."

"She has a right to her decision."

"And she knows." Joshua held his hands loosely at his back. "Shakira?"

She cleared her throat, not sure her voice would come out either way. "What do I need to do?"

"Shakira, you don't know how long this will take," Dele said. "They are not even sure the evil woman is here. And you heard him, a desperate woman will do anything to get away. You can't agree to this plan of theirs. They turn you into their bait! How can you even consider this?"

Joshua let him finish. "You will simply continue being a missionary here."

Dele shook his head. "I'm not going to play the game and hang out here. If the criminal comes as they think she will, we'll be in the line of her fire."

"And it's not your problem, Dele. I have made adequate plans for you to return to Lagos. In fact, we have different plots in place for Shakira which may or may not include you."

Dele frowned at her. "I can't believe you now want to continue with this. Yesterday you were full of hysteria about leaving this country."

"I just want to know the plan." Her voice was so thin she didn't recognize it.

"We will send Dele back to Lagos. You will be safe here, and we will let you know what to do."

"But, with Dele gone, what will be the story? What will you tell the church?"

Joshua sneered. "This is Nigeria. We have a plot in place."

Dele hissed. "Of course, I am not going anywhere."

"You are, unless you are willing to cooperate with us." Joshua took his seat and brought out his phone. "Now, I need you both to tell me what your decision is."

Shakira swallowed. She'd not seen this coming. Another total stranger with a good look and lots of words. She wished she could get a reference for him from someone like Fraser.

Dele stared at her. "Can we discuss this first?"

Joshua's expression remained the same. "Discuss what?"

Shakira twisted her fingers in her lap. Her heart raced so hard she felt she was having another panic attack, yet she knew she had to stay coordinated. Trusting her life into the hands of a stranger with a badge in this country could mean anything. Though she hadn't gotten any bad treatment from anyone in uniform, for her the plot only thickened. Her best option was to leave the country, count her losses, and pick up whatever was left of her life.

On the other hand, she could help capture this woman who was a criminal, and probably a part of a dangerous ring of fraudsters. If only she could affirm Joshua. He had come in gentle and forbearing, explaining many things. His soothing words had diminished her fears. He won her confidence. Now she realized he'd planned to. The way his gaze remained straight, expecting her to succumb, terrified her. He wasn't the cajoling man who walked into her room an hour earlier. This was a nut-cracking, hard officer trained to apprehend mean criminals. She had never felt so confused and conflicted in her life. One minute she was so sure she was done, but the next something new came up and she wasn't sure anymore.

"I'd like to talk with Shakira."

"You can go on. I'm listening."

"Dele." She breathed in. "I am going to work with Interpol and Inspector Joshua. There's nothing to discuss."

"You will stay here and allow yourself to be the lure for the criminal woman?"

"I will do whatever is necessary." She clenched her fists. "What's the plan? I'm ready."

Joshua formed a steeple with his fingertips. "I will ask you for the last time, Dele, are you staying or returning to Lagos?"

Dele stammered, "This is not—will the force pay my transportation back? Armed robbers attacked us yesterday and took everything."

Joshua smirked. "Like you had anything coming here. Yes, the police force will foot the bill for your return to Lagos, first thing tomorrow morning."

Dele breathed hard, his teeth gritted, eyes narrowed, all directed at her. Her resolve must have shown on her face as she returned his gaze because he slouched and shrugged.

"I came here to help. I will."

Joshua stopped the recording again and put his cell phone away. "Good. Let's get to the plan."

Chapter Thirty-Two

Inspector Joshua reminded Shakira of Jorgeian Fraser, perhaps because they worked in the same organization. He was composed and had a team ready to work at his whim. She trusted him a little more when the following morning he picked her up from the pastor's house and took her to a neat neighborhood in the heart of town, a neighborhood called GRA, Government Reserved Area.

The compound was made up of a one-story building with a short driveway and a garage.

"You will live downstairs." He opened the front door. "It's a three-bed and two-bath."

"Thank you." Shakira assessed the room. "Will I live alone?"

She didn't want to, and Dele was nowhere in sight. He would be a better housemate than no one at all. Joshua had taken him away the day before, and some part of her had felt guilt. He would have been living his mediocre life in Lagos if she hadn't asked him to bring her to Cross River state. On the other hand, she found his dishonesty appalling. His plan to turn her into a money bag made her glad it was over. He could be anywhere for all she cared. He had fulfilled his purpose in her search. She really wanted to be done with him. Why were her emotions so erratic? She wished she could be as assertive as she used to be.

"You will not live alone. One of my officers will serve as your housekeeper. She is trained. Her name is Runo."

They stood in a small sitting area with full upholstery furnishing, a television mounted on the wall, and a wall unit air conditioner. The curtains and Persian rug matched with blue and navy blends. The room was clean and smelled fresh. Homely. Shakira's stomach knotted. It passed too much for what she could take as hers. A place to keep.

"Good to know," she whispered.

Joshua walked toward the connecting door. "Come with me. I'll show you your room."

She followed him. There were many questions in her mind. She'd only been told the basic plan to have her work in the church school as a missionary, with the hope the woman who murdered her children would show up to the bait. This wasn't a plan her country would approve of because it put her in the line of the criminal's fire, but she agreed to it.

Just the day before she hadn't wanted to be a part of the investigation anymore. With her newfound conviction, she only wanted to go back home and reconcile with her family, but it seemed Joshua and his team would have none of it. She knew she could refuse to be a bait, yet a part of her yearned for it.

Joshua stopped in front of a door and opened it. The room, like the parlor, smelled rose-fresh. A king-size bed was made with brown and pink sheets and covers with four fluffy pillows. The floor tiles matched beige and brown curtains. A petite woman wearing a frock walked out from what Shakira discovered was the bathroom with a towel thrown across her arm.

She nodded. "Inspector Joshua, Shakira, welcome."

"This is Runo, your housekeeper," Joshua introduced. "Her room is connected to yours."

Shakira extended her hand. "I'm pleased to meet you, Runo." The two women shook hands.

Joshua sighed. "I will leave you here. We may not meet again unless something happens. Otherwise, I wish you the best."

Without any delay, he walked out. Shakira stared after him. He had been so brisk in his approach she didn't know he would leave. Again, thrust on a total stranger. It seemed to be her new-normal lifestyle.

"You'll be fine, Shakira. I have your profile, and I know what you have been through," Runo said. "We'll make sure no harm comes to you."

Her soft voice drew Shakira in, and she noted the other woman's features for the first time. They could be in the same age bracket, and Runo, though shorter, was fit. Her slim body had the defined muscle tone only those with military and paramilitary training could boast of. Her dark-chocolate-colored skin stretched firm and spotless under the simple gown she wore. Perhaps because of her job, her features were rather taut, but she may look pretty if she relaxed a bit.

"Thank you." Shakira swallowed. "Uh, you said *we*. Who else is here?" Joshua made it clear he was gone unless something came up.

"Dele is here too. He's in the third room."

Shakira huffed. "Dele? I thought he was returned to Lagos."

Runo smirked. "It was a debate, but Joshua accepted in the end. He thinks an extra person around you will make a difference."

"What will—is he here as—what?"

Runo put the towel on the foot of the bed. "Your husband. Only in public, of course." She checked around the room. "I think everything is set. If you need me, or anything at all, call. Or here." She walked to the head of the bed and lifted one of the pillows. "There's a small thing here. Feel it."

Shakira moved closer to see what she was about. She put her hand where Runo's had been. "I feel it."

"Don't press. If you do, three police stations will respond, and it will light up the compound. Whoever got you to press the nub will not leave without being caught."

"Makes me feel better." In her heart, though, Shakira didn't believe any good would come from all this. "Thank you. "Um, who lives upstairs?"

"We use it as an operations office for now."

"Oh. Okay."

"Tomorrow morning you will start work at the church's primary school. You have some teaching experience, don't you?"

"I do. With special-needs kids."

Runo shrugged. "Okay. Once I'm done with lunch, I'll take you to a hairdresser's, and we can give you a little makeover."

"Oh."

Shakira didn't expect any special treats. She laughed in her soul.

Chapter Thirty-Three

Dele was lounging on the couch reading an old magazine he found in the house when Shakira and Runo returned from their outing. Shakira's new hairstyle brought out her beauty, and for the first time, he found himself attracted to her without prejudice. The plaited hairdo with extensions whirled around her head with twists and bends that terminated at the crown, rolled into a donut. It highlighted her light skin and strong forehead. She was so pretty with a sharp nose, delicate full lips, and slim bone structure. Her face makeover emphasized her brown eyes and shaped eyebrows.

He wanted to tell her how beautiful she was but didn't think it was a good idea after Joshua belittled him and asked that he be returned in the morning.

In truth, the new plan worked well without him. Church members would be told he had to leave for Lagos to attend to urgent family matters. The police force had enough men and women on the team, but he felt defeated on a personal level to have to be returned, thrown out like a sack of bad potatoes. Therefore, he agreed to all their terms. He would stay in the house with Shakira and the tough undercover policewoman, Runo. He would sleep in a separate room and make no unnecessary contact with Shakira, unless in public. And he agreed not to be paid a cent for whatever his stay was worth.

However, he would be fed and accommodated for the period and transported back to Lagos when due. He got a few new additions to his wardrobe too. To cooperate was the only thing to do to save face under the circumstances he found himself in. He hoped to improve his reputation, if with no one else, with Shakira at least. She was still his only passport to a better life in America.

"Your hair is beautiful," he said before he could stop himself.

The policewoman arched an eyebrow. "We're seeing the principal of the school in an hour."

He shrugged. "Okay."

Shakira smirked. "You're not expected to come with us, Dele."

He took note of the smooth way she ignored his compliment. He addressed Runo. "As her husband, I shouldn't be left out."

"Yes, but we already made an excuse for you. You are spending the day praying today." He raised his hand to protest, but Runo continued. "You are still upset about the armed robbery. Remember the story about your strong desire to return to Lagos?"

His jaw dropped. "Shakira?"

She shrugged. "The police are in charge now, Dele. And I like it this way."

He raised his chin. "Indeed. You like it this way. So what am I supposed to be doing while you're away?"

Runo chuckled. "Praying, man of God. You started this plot, and it is working so well." She spoke to Shakira. "Wear one of the new dresses in your wardrobe and a flat shoe. With your hair done, you don't have to cover it."

Shakira nodded and Runo walked off in the direction of the kitchen.

He swallowed hard. "Is this how things will be now between us?"

"I am not holding you hostage here, Dele. You can return to Lagos anytime you want."

"You mean you're done with me!" He snapped his fingers. "Finished? After I left my family, risked my life to come here with you?"

"What do you want? Money? I will ask Runo to get some money—"

He flew to his feet. "Don't insult me, Shakira. What money? Because you witnessed the way my sisters talked? You think I am helpless? I am a Lagos boy, never forget."

Runo walked into the parlor. "Is there a problem?"

Dele brushed past her and out of the room with a grunt. "No."

———————

"Don't mind him. He's just one of them. Never-do-goods," Runo said. "Go get ready for the school."

She didn't wait for Shakira's response but returned to the kitchen. Shakira entered her room and checked out her new look. She liked her new hair and touched it. Many Africans back home wore the same style, but she'd never had the courage to try it out. Beyond the fear of the pain brought while making it, no one ever told her where to get it done.

To her surprise, her wardrobe was full of lovely things. The clothes Runo spoke about had been purchased in her absence, but she found them close enough to her style. A simple chambray striped midi dress caught her fancy, and she wore it with a flat black shoe. She stared at the beautiful woman reflected in the mirror, and tears filled her eyes. She was attractive again, with her face made up and the nice clothes.

Runo oohed when she stepped out into the parlor.

"This missionary looks good."

Shakira blinked. "Well, thank you."

"I'm sure Dele will be salivating over you, fuming too." She lowered her voice and giggled. "Silly guy."

Shakira liked her, though she found the joke about Dele distasteful. "I hope he gets over it." She rolled her eyes.

The cop raised her voice. "Let's get going. Schools close at three here, and I'd like you to take a sneak peek at the students." She raised it even louder. "Dele, you're home alone. Some food is in the flask in the kitchen." She lowered her voice. "If you're hungry. Let's go, dear."

Runo mothered everyone around, and Shakira couldn't decide if this was part of the undercover act or the woman would sooner or later become overbearing. Whatever the case, she chose to play along and draw strength from her newfound love for God and His Word.

The school premises sat just behind the uncompleted church building. Two blocks of unpainted cement-plastered rows of four classrooms each made up the entire school. The principal's office at the end of one of the blocks also consisted of the school store and sick bay. A total mess if Shakira had ever seen one.

Mrs. Ogah, the principal, welcomed Shakira with a hug. "Please excuse our office. We are trying to move the library and store to another place." She curtsied, displaying a huge gap on her front teeth. "I was at the service. God bless you for ministering so to us."

Shakira flushed. "Thanks, ma'am."

"We are so blessed to have you here. It is just great the way God works because our Primary Two teacher just got married and moved to Abuja with her husband." She busied herself with some documents. "These are some of the class books for you. I'm sure you'll pick up fast even if you haven't taught the class before."

"What grade is Primary Two?"

"Hmm, I think it should be Grade Two," she said. "I remember in those days my mother told me all the grading system. The children are between five and six years old."

"Grade One. But it's fine, I can teach them." Shakira swallowed. Leila would be close to five now if she were alive.

Mrs. Ogah stood. "Let me take you to the class."

She carried a bunch of notebooks and textbooks. Shakira and Runo followed her.

The class had small desks and accommodated about twenty children. They made a lot of noise while a young lady in her late teens clapped to get their attention.

"Class greet," the lady shouted.

The children stood and chorused, "Good afternoon, Mrs. Ogah. And may God bless you, ma!"

Shakira fought tears.

Chapter Thirty-Four

The kids, oblivious to her plight, continued with their greeting while Shakira fought to keep her control.

"Good afternoon, first aunty, and may God bless you, ma."

"Good afternoon, second aunty, and may God bless you, ma."

She wanted to laugh at the pitch of their tiny voices and how stereotyped they all sounded. There could be ten aunties and they would greet each one by one.

Mrs. Ogah didn't notice her little emotional moment though Runo did but didn't do anything about it. Perhaps because of her position as a mere servant.

"Good afternoon, children. You may have your seats."

The children screamed, "Thank you, Mrs. Ogah."

It took another few minutes before their chatter stopped and the principal introduced their new teacher.

"This is Ms. Shakira. And she will be our teacher. Children, welcome Ms. Shakira."

They hopped on their feet with as much energy as they could muster and screamed at the top of their voices, "Welcome, Ms. Shakira. And may God bless you, ma."

Shakira stood before them, unable to control her tears any longer. She didn't know what it meant in the Nigerian context, but the children clapped, following the principal and the lady in the class.

She sniffed. "I'm so happy to be here with you all." She dragged in a deep breath, but it didn't help stem her tears.

Mrs. Ogah walked over and hugged her. "We are happy to have you here too."

Shakira nodded and took a moment to curb her emotions. When she knew she could, she inhaled. She didn't mean to, and never planned to, but thoughts of Leila formed words.

"My daughter would have been about your age now. She was three when—she died." She choked. "It is such a pleasure to be here with you. I love you all."

The children shouted and clapped. The school bell rang, signifying close of the day, and the children jumped around. The lady, later introduced to Shakira as Rose, the class assistant, calmed the kids and led everyone through the closing prayers. Shakira stood aside, her heart thudding as the class dismissed. They picked up their school bags, pushing and shoving, and ran out onto the playground between the school and the church building.

"They will be so blessed by your ministry," Mrs. Ogah said. "I can see you have passion for children."

"I pray so." It would be hard not to get emotional around them. "I will give my best."

The principal patted her back. "I believe so." She dropped the books in her hand on the teacher's desk. "Rose will assist if you need anything, and you can walk to my office anytime for anything."

Shakira nodded. "Thank you, ma'am."

After the older woman was gone, Shakira sat on the chair behind her desk, a rickety white plastic seat she wasn't sure would hold long.

"What time are we supposed to close?"

Though her question was directed at no one in particular, Runo answered. "Your closing time is four, but we can go now, and you resume in the morning. Seven."

Shakira nodded. "I prefer to close today at the normal time."

"I will hang around then."

Runo walked out before she could respond. Rose picked up toys and educational posters and rearranged the chairs and desks. The classroom wasn't painted, but nice pictures graced the walls. Obvious changes needed to be done, but Shakira figured she wasn't the one to suggest it.

She pulled the books and files dumped on the desk closer and opened them one after the other. The teacher's notebook took much of her attention as she familiarized herself with the curriculum. It was downright different from what was done back home. There was a lot of coursework with little application, and she wondered if she had the right to change anything.

"I'm here for just a bit anyway," she mumbled.

The teacher's notebook aside, she opened the class register. Twenty-three students were listed altogether, but she knew there weren't so many in the class earlier. Many of their names were impossible to pronounce, and she called them out, mumbling to herself till Rose laughed.

"Aunty, don't worry, you will soon get used to the names."

"I do hope so." Shakira tittered. "Some look easy though. *Ee-sign*. Is this *Ee-sign*?"

Rose strolled over and checked it out. "*Essien*. You call it like this, *Ay-see-en*."

"Oh, will do. The kids will love hearing their names from me." She wiped sweat off her face with trembling fingers. "I'm sure I will enjoy teaching them."

"Yes, ma."

Rose returned to her work, and Shakira found a new notebook. She removed a pen from her bag and wrote the date on the first page. From the curriculum, the children were taught more than ten subjects. She proceeded to join them together and at the end had only five. This way the students would learn better.

An hour passed without realization, and she gazed up from her work when Runo walked in.

"I'm sorry, I got carried away."

Runo shrugged. "It's better for you to be busy."

On the ride home, with another policeman, Eddy, as her driver, Runo made conversation.

"Your husband called our office in Lagos."

"Deon?" Shakira gasped. "He did?"

"Yes. We gave him a number to call. You will speak with him tonight."

"Thank you."

Her heart rate sped up. She so wanted Deon's love and forgiveness again. What tragedy she had experienced could never be forgotten, but with the Comforter by her side always guiding her every thought, she could face her life again. If the criminal responsible for her daughters' murder was never found, she would at least thank God for bringing her here to find Him. Thus settled, she wanted her husband again.

"He will call a secured line, but still you are not to disclose your location or anything about the plan. He knows you are in Nigeria, but not where."

She murmured, "Yes."

Runo's voice hardened. "You are in a safe place and the police are taking care of you. He doesn't need any more information."

Shakira couldn't think straight. All she could do was wait for Deon's call, hear his voice, and tell him she loved him. She wanted to do whatever he wished. The selfish woman who jeopardized everything in her life to feed her grief was gone. This new Shakira was a giving one with the ability to do anything through Christ who gave her strength. She would share her new-found faith with her husband one day, but first she needed to regain his trust.

Chapter Thirty-Five

"Deon, my love."

His voice wasn't clear. "Shakira. Fraser told me they found you."

She gave a shaky laugh. "Was I lost?"

He sounded hesitant, or maybe the connection or her nerves made it seem so. "You were, Shakira. I searched all I could. No one would help, but Fraser promised to update me weekly."

"Dear Fraser. He's committed, isn't he?"

"I was told the search is near an—"

"I can't talk about it. We can't. The line could be tapped."

He inhaled. "You're right. I guess I can't ask when you're coming home either."

The call was on speaker, with Eddy and Runo listening in. She glanced at both officers. Runo shook her head.

"I don't know, darling. But I can't wait."

It was the truth, and it made her emotional. Why had she needed to come this far away to realize how much she loved her husband? Though she may not be able to discuss the case, it gave her sweet relief that she could at least be sincere with him about her desire to come back home to him.

The flatness of his voice broke her. "If it will ever happen."

"Oh, Deon." She sucked in her breath, but the sobs escaped all the same. "I'm so sorry."

He made a guttural sound, and soon his cries were louder than hers. She heard rather than saw Eddy a moment before he took the receiver from her.

"You need to say goodbye," he whispered.

Shakira sucked in her breath and through hiccups told Deon she had to hang up.

"They told me I may not call for a while. I agree you are in safe hands and should do whatever—"

Runo snapped, "Say goodbye, Shakira."

Shakira wheezed. Her eyes accused Runo and Eddy as she succumbed to a quick farewell and hung up. It seemed a good call, but she knew she had to talk to Deon again soon. Everything she might have done in the past would somehow haunt her now. She didn't expect Deon to hop back on the soul train and dance all night long with her. She had work to do.

"Can I write to him? Send an email?"

Runo took the cell phone from her limp hand. "We'll discuss it and let you know."

It was late. Nigerian time said some minutes to midnight, which meant Deon was home after work as well.

She stood. "I'm tired. It was a long day."

Eddy waved her off and spoke to Runo. The two understood a language she didn't, and they delved into it. She returned to her room, where she'd paced for hours waiting for Deon's call, and changed into a soft cotton nightgown, part of her new wardrobe. Whoever did the shopping knew how to stock a woman's closet.

She slid between her cool sheets and succumbed to tearful night worship and prayer.

The following day dawned with her having a fresh mind and a desire to work and earn a living again. Her circumstances were weird. She wasn't even given a contract for her job, and she wondered how much Mrs. Ogah knew about her besides being a missionary. Did the principal know she was someone else, a lie? All she was sure of was the order not to speak about her identity with anyone. She would bury her head in her work as a teacher and preach in Pastor Goodwill's church when given the go-ahead.

After the call from Deon, she had a new assurance that she had not lost her marriage. He may never forget she left him, but she hoped he would forgive it and let her be the woman he once loved and married. Even better. She refused to judge him by the coldness she heard in his voice and attributed it to the long-distance call. She would pray him into loving her again.

The first full day in the class got Shakira so occupied with knowing her students better that she didn't know when it was time for break. The bell rang, and the children screamed with excitement as they rushed to their bags to get their lunch packs.

Shakira beckoned to Rose. "Do they leave the class during break time?" *Where would they sit to eat?* She hadn't noticed a cafeteria or hall besides the main church.

"They eat in class. But you can go for lunch. I will watch them."

Shakira shook her head. "No, thanks. I will eat my lunch here as well."

"Can I go for lunch then?"

"Yes, please."

Rose nodded. "Thank you, ma. I'll be back in ten minutes."

"Okay."

Rose picked up her handbag and exited.

"Alright. Settle down to your lunch," Shakira said, raising her voice. "I don't want to get mad at you now."

The kids obeyed at once, perhaps because she was new.

Runo walked to her desk. "Joshua is here. I'm meeting with him in the principal's office if you need me."

"Yeah. Sure."

The cop left, and Shakira bent to take out the sandwich she'd packed for her. To give credit to the hard woman, she could cook. Her food wasn't as spicy as some Shakira had eaten in Nigeria, and it tasted nice.

"I'd advise you to go back home so you won't need any of them police people."

Shakira snapped her head up and came face-to-face with Florence Odu, or whatever her name was. Right in front of her desk, wearing one of the uniforms the two school cleaners wore. To her chagrin, the criminal wasn't recognizable at first. But Shakira knew the voice.

She gulped. "Florence?"

"I didn't kill your babies. They drowned while I was busy."

Shakira could scream, but she considered the class, the little children in her care, unaware of the evil lurking.

"How could you?" she said in a harsh whisper. "Come here? Meet me somewhere else; let's talk."

The woman headed toward the classroom exit. "Go back home!"

Chapter Thirty-Six

The evil woman passed through the door a moment before Shakira realized what just happened. She leaped to her feet, toppling her chair, and ran to the principal's office. It didn't occur to her to knock. She threw the door open and, panting, pointed at the door.

Joshua, Runo, and Eddy stood in a near-circle, deep in discussion. All stopped short when she barged in.

"She came. Just now." Shakira fought sobs. "Just now."

Runo stepped toward her. "Florence? Where?"

"My class." Her fear transferred to anger, and she swatted tears off her cheeks. "Dressed like the janitor."

Runo left the room in a flash followed by Eddy. Joshua dragged a chair closer and made her sit. He didn't say anything until his colleagues returned half an hour later, and then he took out his cell phone.

"She's gone. No one saw anything." Runo stood with legs wide apart, her hands locked behind her back. "What did she say to you?"

Shakira had had time to calm down a bit while the officers checked out her report. "She said she didn't kill the babies and that I should go home."

"What did you tell her?"

"I asked why she would come here to the school. I invited her to let us meet to talk. She only walked away. She didn't stay even five minutes."

Runo snapped. "Why didn't you raise alarm?"

"The kids were having—"

"Runo!" Joshua retorted.

The female officer moved back. "One of the kids confirmed the same thing. She was straightening Shakira's chair when we entered the class. Rose said she wasn't in the class when this happened."

"She slipped in a minute after Rose left for lunch."

Eddy folded his arms. "You said she wore the blue cleaners' uniform?"

Shakira nodded. "She must have been watching for a while. I didn't recognize her at first. She appeared different."

Joshua leaned against the wall. "Different in what way?"

"I couldn't remember her so well, but I thought she was dark. This person is light-skinned. She wore heavy makeup."

"Did she cover her hair?"

"Yes. The same blue scarf of the janitor's uniform."

Joshua formed a steeple with his fingers. "You should know the reason why I am here, Shakira." He exchanged a brief glance between Eddy and Runo. "Dele called me early this morning. After you left for work. A woman came by the house."

Shakira's heart dropped to her stomach. "Oh, no. She knows where I stay now."

Runo found her voice. "We have reason to believe she does. And she may not be alone."

"Should I stop coming here? My presence may endanger the lives of the children."

"Today was too close for comfort, and we don't know if she's armed." Joshua arched an eyebrow. "You handled her well, and if she returns—"

Runo cut in. "It's too dangerous to keep her here."

Joshua showed the first sign of frustration when he rubbed the back of his neck. "Do you have an alternative? If we send her away, the criminals will leave the area."

"They may as well kill her and leave the area. Or just simply leave. What is her presence here doing for anyone other than put them under pressure and her, all of us, at risk?"

"Your argument is good, Runo." Eddy shrugged. "But you haven't suggested any other plan."

Shakira closed her eyes for a moment. "I want to stay. At least being here drew her out of hiding. It's worth something."

"It is dangerous, and we knew this from the start," Eddy said softly. "It's a risk we were all willing to take."

"She's not fit to roam the streets in any country. I know now. And I want her to be caught."

Runo threw her hands up. "My point is this. What if she was armed? She'd walk into the class, shoot Shakira, and walk right out."

Eddy glared at her. "What do you suggest we do?"

"Send this woman back to her country and continue with our investigations."

"No, please. This is the closest we may ever get to capturing her." Shakira held Runo's gaze. "Please. I want to stay."

"I agree, Joshua. Runo. We've combed these areas and never found her. Is it a coincidence she made an appearance now Shakira is here? I don't think so."

Joshua nodded. "If she leaves, the criminal will go back into her hole."

Runo snapped, "And we follow her in."

"It's a good plan. It is obvious she considers Shakira's presence here a threat. She may also think Dele is just a friend, and Runo is a servant." Eddy sighed. "Good job so far. Let's hang on a little more."

The officers decided to add one or two more undercover agents to the team who would work in the town as craftsmen, commoners who could get word around. There were several already, but with Florence making an appearance, the hunt had changed and more tact was needed.

Shakira couldn't remain in the school, though. Shortly after the meeting with the officers ended, she excused herself and asked to be taken back to the house. The little girl Runo spoke to in the class, Kem, walked to her when she told Rose she had to leave and picked up her bag.

"Aunty Shakira, sorry the woman scared you."

Shakira shuddered. "Thank you, dear." She couldn't remember her name and made it a point to ask Rose.

"The other aunty said she will catch her for you and punish her."

"She did?"

Kem nodded. "She asked me to tell her what the woman said. I heard everything. I didn't eat my lunch. I was looking at her."

"Thanks for watching over me. Now go back to your seat. Good girl."

Kem hesitated. "Okay, Aunty Shakira." She hugged her teacher to the latter's surprise and bounced back to her front row seat. "Will you come back tomorrow?"

Shakira swallowed several times, overwhelmed by the little girl's concern. "Yes, dear."

Runo met with her right outside the class and followed her back to the accommodation.

Chapter Thirty-Seven

Rain fell all through the night, adding to Shakira's fear and frustration. Florence Odu's words rang in her brain, and the menace on the woman's face got her heart thumping time and again. She was so petrified during the night, coupled with heavy thunder strikes, that she couldn't find the courage to use the bathroom, though she was told new security details had been fixed in the house, including a CCTV camera. She hated the intrusion on her privacy but knew it was necessary.

Runo knocked on her door close to seven, and when she didn't respond, opened the door. She was cuddled under the duvet, afraid, though the policewoman announced her entry.

"It's time to leave for work."

Shakira moaned. "I didn't get any sleep last night."

Runo walked to the curtain and peeped out. "Me neither."

"There was a thunderstorm." Shakira drew herself up against the headboard. "I kept hearing the door slamming. Like she was back."

Runo closed the curtain. "Perfectly normal." She strode to the bed and stared at Shakira with her arms akimbo. "You opted to do this. You gotta get out of bed." At the door, she murmured, "Ten minutes tops, madam."

Shakira rolled her eyes after the woman was gone. She was a remarkable undercover officer considering how well she fit the subservient housekeeper role in public. At home, she was a vixen, a hard cop who did her job with blunt detachment.

It took less than ten minutes for her to be ready and in the parlor. Dele was pacing the room, his jaw clamped, when she came in.

"I told her you shouldn't go to the school today."

She sighed. "I guess they know better."

"I didn't sleep. Did they tell you the woman came here while you were at work?"

His open distress caught her interest. It seemed the police officers didn't update him on the drama back in the school, and she couldn't either.

"They did." She bit her lower lip. "But I have to go to work."

"She will trail you from here and find you there. To be frank with you, I think it's time to leave this country. Since she's come out of hiding, she will make mistakes and be caught in no time."

Runo cleared her throat. Neither had known when she walked in. She marched to the door. "Let's go."

Shakira nodded. "See you later, Dele. And thank you for being here."

If he hadn't been home, no one would have known the woman had come earlier. The new security devices in the house would not have been fixed, and her life may have been in more danger. Dele was making his presence useful.

"I'm coming with you."

Until then, she didn't notice he was dressed to go out. She expected Runo to object but the latter shrugged.

"Shouldn't someone be in the house?"

"I don't want to be home when she returns. She picked the locks and entered the house. Can you imagine how I felt?" He went to stand beside Runo. "I don't mind sitting outside the school. Or in the church till you're done."

Shakira wanted to laugh at how scared he was, but she knew it would be inappropriate. If the police were okay with it, she was too.

School went on without incident, and afterwards, the rest of the evening too. Runo and Eddy sat in the parlor and scanned through the CCTV recordings of the day and saw nothing unusual. For hours later, they analyzed the case in coded terms and out of boredom, Shakira went to bed.

She could not sleep even after a drink of the local chocolate beverage. Instead she read her Bible and began to pray for her family and the school. She'd been told the town was on the border of two countries with one of the most porous boundaries. Children from neighboring Bakassi schooled here, and this meant it was quite easy to move in and out of Nigeria.

"I commit the country into your hands too," she murmured. "Help them to build better institutions so evil will not continue to thrive here."

Dele knocked. "Shakira. Shakira, are you awake?"

She paused. "Yes."

"One of the students has had an accident. You are wanted. The pastor is here."

She snatched her robe and opened the door. "Where's Runo?"

"They are checking the surroundings. She asked me to call you."

"Does she agree I follow the pastor?"

Dele lowered his voice. "They think we are missionaries, Shakira. It's good for the ploy."

"Give me a minute." She closed the door. "Tell Pastor Goodwill I'll be out in a second."

She wore the pretty black and white polka-dot dress she'd removed to get into bed and flat slippers rather than her low-heeled pumps.

She smoothed her hair with her hand and opened the door. "I'm ready."

"You look beautiful." He reached for her hand, but she ducked. "We're married," he whispered.

"Not in an emergency." She stomped off, and he followed her.

Pastor Goodwill's defeated slouch against the wall spoke volumes, and Shakira shuddered at the mere thought of the magnitude of the accident. What was she to do? How did one pray for the sick?

It was close to midnight, and Runo insisted they ride in their car as against Pastor Goodwill's suggestion to ride together.

The parents of the child sat on the bare floor at the altar in the church, praying. The child had been laid out under the huge cross on the wall. Some members paced the length and breadth, shouting and singing.

Shakira didn't think the child was alive from the strange angle her neck lay. On the ride to the church, Runo had told her the girl slipped and fell from the top of a tree, and probably broke her neck. They rushed her to the church instead of the clinic. She'd suggested the hospital.

Runo had muttered. "My thoughts too, but let's get there first."

"Please, pray. Woman of God, pastor. Please." The child's father went on his knees when they approached the altar. "She's not talking."

His broken voice rang a bell in her mind, and Shakira thought she would pass out. She remembered another time and place. Two little girls, their lives cut off by a senseless act she was yet to understand. The lost look on the mother's face mirrored the fear and hopelessness she now lived with.

Dele took charge, and she was grateful because she couldn't find words. "She will talk. Let's form a circle, and everyone begin to call her forth in the name of the mighty God we serve." He motioned to the father as they formed a semicircle around the mother and child. "What's her name?"

The hoarse voice responded as from a distance. "Kemini. But we call her Kem."

Chapter Thirty-Eight

Kem, the bright, vigilant, and thoughtful child Shakira just got to know, was buried in the early hours of the following day. They didn't sleep through the night as they prayed to no avail. At about 5 a.m., Pastor Goodwill surrendered to the will of the Almighty and encouraged Kem's parents to lay her to rest.

A small coffin was purchased from a local carpenter, and the women of the church rallied around Kem's mother to give the little girl a bath and clothe her in a new dress brought by a neighbor who sold children's clothes in the market.

Shakira was too exhausted to do anything but stare. Several times she wanted to reach out to Kem's mother but feared she would make things worse as she couldn't trust her emotions to hold out. She understood just what this mother was thinking. The initial feeling of finality and despair, and then hope against hope. In this case, though, it had all happened as an accident no one could prevent.

According to her father, Kem climbed the tree every day. It was assumed the previous night's rain might have caused the trunk to be more slippery than usual, and being so small, she wasn't so experienced in tree climbing. The time of night was another issue Shakira wondered about. If it happened in the States, the parents would be held accountable for negligence. Whoever let a five-year-old climb a tree at ten in the night?

The men alone went to bury Kem while the women sat with her mother in Pastor Goodwill's home. People from the church and school trooped in and out offering condolences. Shakira, with Runo beside her, sat in a corner, too distraught to do anything more.

Pastor Goodwill's wife, a small woman who seemed relegated to the background most times, prepared a meal of spicy coconut rice and encouraged visitors to eat.

The men returned an hour later, and Pastor Goodwill raised a song. From one to another, the group of about twenty people continued singing praises for another hour or so.

Pastor Goodwill waved his hands and brought the singing to an end. "I want to call our missionary, and a wonderful woman of God, who was Kem's last teacher, Mrs. Shakira Dele Thomson."

Shakira Smith, she thought before she realized everyone expected her to come forward. She stared at Pastor Goodwill, who beckoned her.

"We need a word from you, madam. Please exhort us."

Shakira walked to the front of the room, and Dele followed her. His presence contributed to her confidence level, and she heaved a heavy sigh. Everybody went quiet, waiting on her to speak.

"Not too long ago, I was in a room like this, mourning the death of my daughters." She swallowed. "Leila was just three, and Latoya, eighteen months. I didn't think I could survive." She locked her gaze on Kem's parents. "It was a double-murder, and the person who did it was on the run."

Dele took her hand in his. "Our lives were sold out to the gospel, and it was in it that we found our succor." He stole a glance at her. "We refused to get carried away by our fear and anger and submitted instead to the will of God. It's the reason why we are here today."

Shakira glowered at the floor. She'd almost slipped out of her reality, being a missionary and not a sickened mother searching for closure. She ought to be grateful to him for bailing her out, but she wasn't. Maybe later she would sit with Kem's mother and tell the truth. She didn't want to be undercover all the time. She just wanted to be a grieved mother offering comfort to another.

"Kem has gone to be with the Lord. The Lord gives and the Lord takes. Blessed be the name of the Lord." Dele raised his hand, with hers still locked in it. "We give Him all the glory and the praise." He brought down their hands. "We will not mourn like unbelievers. Kem has gone to rest from this weary world. She sits with the hosts of angels and urges us on." He eyed everyone in the room one by one. "It's now left for us to follow her example and live right for God."

Shakira cut into his harsh admonition. What did he know about a mother's loss? He was a con-man. "Kem was a loving, beautiful little girl. She would look out for you, always the mother to everyone in the class. She loved God and believed in Him, and we all should too."

A woman burst into tears, and for a while it rippled around the room. Shakira would later realize she didn't shed a single tear.

Dele lifted his voice in a worship song, and the others took it up. Pastor Goodwill prayed and dismissed the meeting. People moved around in circles talking, consoling one another.

Runo strode over to Shakira's side. "We should leave now."

"I wanted to talk privately with Kem's mom."

"We will arrange for you to visit when she returns to her house." Runo held her elbow. "You haven't slept for two days. I think you should rest. Say a few words to Kem's mother and tell her you'll be back."

Back in the house, Shakira slid out of the polka-dot dress and back under her duvet. She thought she would sleep right away, but the blank expression on the bereaved mother's face left a dull ache in her heart.

On hindsight, Kem's father never once stopped by his wife to console her. The man became a beehive of activities, probably to push away the reality of losing his precious daughter. It reminded her of how much one needed the love of their lives at these initial weak hours, when the terror was still fresh and you desperately wanted to believe it wasn't true. If she hadn't been there, she'd not know how much the woman needed her man.

Nothing anyone else said would make a difference. All the woman wanted was a cuddle. Her man's strong arms around her, telling her it would be alright, and he would be there for her.

The more she thought about it, the more she saw herself in the true light. Deon Smith had been the man she now considered the perfect lover in the time of grief. From the start he stood by her while she pushed him away and did everything to mourn alone.

She closed her eyes and hugged her pillow. She wanted her husband more than ever.

Chapter Thirty-Nine

ele nursed his infatuation but could do no more than be nice when Shakira let him near, which was rare. A week after Kem's death and burial, he escorted her to see the mother, and Shakira told the woman about her daughters. The two women had only this in common and the faith which kept them sane in the toughest times.

"I see her every day," Kem's mother said. "In my dreams."

On the way back, Shakira told Dele she was thankful she didn't see her daughters in any dreams.

She moaned. "I'd die each time."

He squeezed her hand. "You're a stronger woman now."

Except for this single time of togetherness, they had nothing more in common. He tried to break the wall, get to know her, but even the tight schedule Runo maintained gave room for little relaxation.

Three weeks later, with no word from anyone, and her continued inability to contact her husband got Shakira restless. She complained about everything from the clothes she initially loved, to the food, to the country as a whole.

Each night the trio watched local and international news till late, but Shakira wouldn't sleep until the early hours of the morning, many times pacing her room and talking aloud to herself. She buried herself in her work with the kids and at the church but never gave herself fully to it. Dele agitated over her, but besides this she didn't let him near her.

Joshua visited again, and they all knew there was news. It was the only reason he came around. He had dinner and herded everyone into the parlor. Eddy stood by the door and Runo by the window, positions Dele came to realize was for security purposes. He sat with Joshua and Shakira on different seats.

"We've gotten another passport for you, Shakira," Joshua announced. "There is bad news, though. Your visa expires in a few days."

Shakira's face lit up. "Well, I'm glad my passport—I have it. Can I have it?"

Joshua hesitated but handed the blue passport to her. Shakira flipped through like it was her lifeline.

Her head shot up. "I don't see the visa at all."

"We wanted a new one to be issued, otherwise immigration would have just duplicated the old one. You should have gotten a three-month single-entry visa, or sometimes, multiple-entry."

She gasped. "I was given one month. The man Mo connected me with said—what am I to do now?"

Joshua leaned forward, his hands steepled in what Dele believed must be a habit. "What man?"

"I got help. I paid a Nigerian man to process the visa for me. He's an immigration agent."

"Hmm. He cheated you." Joshua smirked. "Well, I have a form here for you to fill out. I'm going to apply for another three-month visa."

"I hope not to stay so long."

"Don't we all."

Dele arched an eyebrow. "What's the implication? If she's not issued a visa?"

His question seemed to imply some form of incompetence the police officers reacted to all at once with straightening and stiffening and, in the case of Runo, a hardened profile.

"My office is making this request. She's not here on vacation anymore as we all can see. An international criminal investigation has interest in her presence here." He handed Shakira a piece of paper. "Fill out this form. I'll need it back with your passport."

Shakira took the form and the pen offered and read through it.

"I'm thinking about something, with this new development," Dele said. "A few days to expire, and if it cannot be renewed—the woman she came for has been quiet all this while." Dele exhaled. "Is it possible she knows the visa will soon expire and decided to wait it out?"

Shakira's head snapped up. "I find your thoughts outrageous."

"We considered it. Only way is to have someone who will disrupt the process of renewal. This application is not going to pass through the normal route. You can relax, Dele." Joshua never made jokes, and still without a hint of mischief, he sneered. "Your wife is not leaving you."

Shakira paused in her writing, waited for any further comment, and when none came continued with her head bent over the form.

"I don't trust these people, and no matter what you think about my opinion, it should be checked out," Dele said.

Shakira lifted the form and pen, and after a quick look through, handed it to Joshua.

"I will hand-deliver this to my boss," Joshua said. "Your visa will be renewed by close of business tomorrow."

Shakira swallowed. "Thank you."

"As for the woman, she has gone back into her hole. One thing is sure: the next time she comes out, soldier ants are going to cover her up."

Shakira arched her neck. "I don't understand."

"You have nothing to worry about is all." Joshua headed for the door. "It will all soon be over, though. I assure you."

He exited with Eddy.

Runo switched on the television to watch the local news. They would end up with the international one before calling it a day.

Dele cleared his throat. "I think the woman knows about the theft. The passport being stolen. She must have planned it. Realizes the visa will soon expire and continues to lay low."

"It's a theory," Runo said.

"A credible one." Dele leaned toward Shakira's seat on his right side. "She came out to let you know she knows you're around. It's an audacity."

Shakira shuddered. "It's a scary one if it's true."

He got excited by his line of thought and reached out to hold her hand. "When she saw your visa would soon expire, she reckoned you'd go back before long."

Runo snickered. "People renew visas."

"Yes, but in our system, anything can happen. These are criminals."

Shakira took her hand out of his. "Well, Joshua is on it. Let's wait till he gets back to me."

She closed her eyes and succeeded in blocking him out.

Chapter Forty

The school didn't have a gym so time for sports and physical education was done on the playground. Shakira wore the comfortable pair of jogger pants she found in her wardrobe, and as she'd done each of the four weeks she'd been with the kids, ran around the perimeter twice, the children squealing with delight behind her.

She came to a stop, and her students formed two rows facing her. "Now stretch. All the way." She lifted her hands over her head and sideways. "Stretch, darlings." She laughed at their feeble attempt to copy her.

The smile froze on her face when she saw Joshua approach. It had been two days with no word from him. It had to be good news. The police officer never had an expression on his face.

"We run on the spot now." She imitated the exercise, and the children followed.

From the side of her eye, she noticed Runo chatting with Joshua. They both seemed engrossed in the discussion, and she struggled to concentrate. *If they need me, they'll call*, she thought.

"Now jump. Clap." She followed her own instruction. "And one, jump and clap. Two, jump and clap."

She counted to eight and walked over to Rose, who at the back of the rows joined in the movements. "Please take over."

Rose nodded and jogged to the front of the class. "Clap for me!" The children yelled and clapped. "Now, clap for yourself."

Shakira came up to Joshua and Runo. "I'm sorry I couldn't concentrate."

Runo folded her arms across her chest. "The visa expires tomorrow."

"Joshua was going to fix it." She shared a glance between the two. "Is there a problem?"

"There are complications with the process. The immigration boss is on leave, and the man serving in his stead is reluctant to work as fast as we require." Joshua pinched his nose. "There is one option."

Runo rolled her eyes. "Before you go into the option you speak of, I think Dele should be given a chance to know his options."

"Dele will play along."

Shakira inhaled. "What are you talking about?"

Joshua snickered. "Well, there are options. One is to call up someone in the immigration office and offer a bribe. Another is to get an agent and pay him a ridiculous fee to get your visa out in twenty-four hours."

Runo stared out at the children running and touching one another. Rose seemed to have gotten them into a frenzy. "I don't think we have much of a problem. After school we'll talk about this in the house."

"I am a child of God. I will not give a bribe."

"You don't have any money. Neither do I. And my office will not approve it." Joshua arched an eyebrow. "I don't have time, Runo."

"You'll just dump a plan on their laps without any consent?"

"I sent Eddy to bring Dele. We can discuss in the principal's office." Joshua started to walk back into the building, and the women followed him without any choice.

Shakira shouted, "What is Dele supposed to do?"

No one answered her. Eddy and Dele had just gotten into the office when the others arrived.

"Joshua?" Dele exclaimed. "Eddy refused to tell me anything. Do you have good news?"

"Depends on how you see it, Dele." Joshua recounted the situation. "I don't see any foul play, but still, there is any possibility."

Dele frowned. "Possibility of what? How far with the visa?"

"It's still not issued. And we don't want it to expire before something is done." Runo peeked around the room the way she did as a rule. "You may also be right about getting options."

Shakira snapped. "What are the options besides giving a bribe or getting an expensive agent?"

"I knew it," Dele swore under his breath. "Things don't go the way they should. For this woman to be hidden all this while. I knew it wouldn't be easy."

Eddy stared at him. "What are you talking about?"

"I don't take anything for granted. I may not be able to understand how all of this will end up, but a woman has been hiding for almost two years in this place—"

Runo sneered. "There are creeks all over this area, come on."

"So why can't police enter the creeks?" Dele shot back.

Joshua bared his teeth. "Maybe we should send you. You have such a good idea on how we should do our jobs."

Shakira massaged her temples. "Well, what is the last option?"

Joshua shoved his hands into his pockets. "Marry Dele."

Chapter Forty-One

"**I** will not!" Shakira cried after a moment of silence passed. "I am a married woman."

Eddy shrugged. "It's not a real wedding, is it?"

"It will be. Why else would I agree to such a crazy idea?" Dele hardened his tone. "Am I just a use-and-dump tool?"

Shakira's voice trembled. "If it means I return to my home tonight, then I will go. But I am not getting married to anyone in this country."

Dele stared at her. Did she understand what it meant to have a marriage certificate with her name on it? To be married to an American citizen? If she thought he didn't know what it meant then she had another think coming. This was his prize. Thanks to whoever made the visa difficult, and the thief who got her a one-month visa in the first place. He would be married to her, and she would file for his permit. Afterward, he could give her a divorce if she wanted.

Joshua cocked his head. "You do understand you are now the responsibility of the Nigerian Police Force. You can't return home unless we let you go." His gaze went blander than Dele had ever seen it. "Or you find your own way."

His words tensed the atmosphere. For a moment much like the one after Joshua announced the option, everyone went still.

Shakira drew in a shuddering breath. "I am an American citizen. You cannot force me to do what I don't want. And I don't recall signing any document handing my rights over to your police force." With this brief speech, she swung on her heels and stomped out of the room.

Runo followed, but Joshua blocked her exit. "Let her take a few minutes to fume."

Dele sighed. "There indeed is no other option, is there?"

Joshua scratched his neck. "There never was."

Dele gasped. "So why did you wait till this late hour to break the news? She will never trust you again."

Joshua paced. "You think she trusts any of us here? Let me tell you something, this is not the United States. There is no blueprint for anything, and whatever has a code has most likely been corrupted a long time ago." He glared at Dele. "Interpol has interest in this case. It's the only reason why I am here. Otherwise, lesser animals would have been trampled on for the greater ones. I know what is in this for you, why you continue to hang on. And I do not blame you. For you, it will soon be over. But the rest of us get on to the next case or sit on our butts and wait for the moving of the waters."

Runo rolled her eyes. "You make no sense to him. You have to win Shakira's confidence."

Dele snapped, "What if she insists she's not getting married to me? You can't force her."

"She can't leave here either. Florence Odu, or whatever her name is, showed up, so there's danger out there. Shakira will do whatever we want till we let her go." Joshua smirked. "She likes her new wardrobe too. I never thanked you, Runo."

Dele huffed. "You think this is a joke? You're playing with someone's life, and you make fun about it."

Joshua bit his lower lip. "Sue me."

The two men glared at each other for a long minute before Dele scowled. "If her visa expires tomorrow, I guess it's too late to use marriage to change anything."

"We will back-date the event.

Dele crossed his arms. "How convenient."

Runo strolled to the door. "I think she's had enough time to vent. And we need to get to the registry before the close of work."

Joshua made no move to stop her. "I know you, Dele Thomson. You've not held a job longer than a month in the last six years. You feed off your hustling sisters, and you'd started off your gimmick with Shakira Smith. Don't play saint here with me."

Dele bit out, "I'm not playing saint. You are supposed to enforce the law, but you are breaking it and flaunting it in our faces."

"What do you mean by breaking it? Do you know the law?"

Runo threw the door open. "Shakira is not here!"

Chapter Forty-Two

The men ran out without a second to digest the statement. Shakira had been on her own for less than ten minutes. A radio alert got the team on their toes. Everyone reported from their different locations within the town limits. It wasn't good news. No one had seen her.

To make matters worse, nobody saw her leave the principal's office. Classes were in session, so the corridors were bare. The two female janitors were in the storeroom, replenishing supplies, and the security man at the entrance of the school premises said he saw nothing. The church hall was empty too.

Dele followed the police officers back to the house, and they checked the recordings for the day. There was nothing unusual. No one had been to the house while they were away.

Joshua called his office and informed his supervisor of the new development. Afterward, he rubbed the back of his neck and paced the floor of the parlor.

"There's nothing we can do but wait."

Dele blew out a series of short breaths. "I can't believe this is happening. What happens with the marriage now?"

Runo clicked her tongue. "You're not worried about her safety but how to get yourself married to a woman? Do you think you'll be allowed to sleep with her?"

Dele stepped back as though stung. "You think that's what's on my mind? How dare you!"

Joshua spoke as though from a distance. "We just have to wait now."

Runo looked stunned. "What?"

"There's no report of her anywhere. The theory is she's been kidnapped, and we just have to wait till they contact us."

Dele slumped onto the sofa close by. "Hoping they will call. Hoping the people who have her are not her children's murderers and they have not killed her as well."

"Yes!" Joshua said stiffly. "We need to hope."

"I spoke about going into the creeks to find these criminals, but you gave me a saucy reply. See now?" Dele threw his hands up in the air. "If only you would listen to me. You know best, don't you? Where has it gotten any of us? Where is Shakira?"

The officers all busied themselves with their phones and ignored his ranting. It was already three hours since Shakira's disappearance and no word had come from any quarters. The school premises had been combed with no report. The idea that she might have left on her own was quickly dismissed because no one saw her leave through the bus terminals in town. She disappeared into thin air by some illusion.

"Pastor Goodwill has been alerted of the development." Runo spoke to no one in particular. "He's calling a meeting of the 'prayer warriors' in the church to hold a gathering and a prayer chain among the ministers."

Joshua sighed. It was the first time Dele ever saw him looking frazzled. "We're getting K-9 officers and their dogs in another six hours."

Runo arched an eyebrow. "From police headquarters?"

"Yeah. They've already been dispatched." Joshua blew out steam through his mouth. "We can comb the school premises with them."

Runo nodded. "Six hours. Hmm. Meanwhile, the staff at the school?"

"Are being interrogated."

Runo squeezed her nose. "Don't you think you should be there?"

Over the weeks Joshua had made it plain several times he didn't like being told what to do. Dele had not been able to determine who was boss between him and Runo. The lady sure could stand her ground. He spared Joshua a quick glance. The latter fiddled with his phone as though he'd not heard his female colleague.

"I'll go if you don't want to. We both can't leave the interrogation to those local boys." She walked to the door, and when Joshua continued to ignore her, left.

Eddy shifted from one foot to the other, waiting for instructions. Only one car had been available to the group here.

Joshua's attitude irritated Dele, and he blurted, "Is she going to drive or what?"

"How is this your problem, please?"

A call came into Joshua's phone, and he picked it up. He spoke for a short time and hung up. "We have two K-9 officers from Calabar. Let's go."

The three men got into the car and on the way picked up Runo, who was jogging to the police station several blocks away.

Two trained dogs were given Shakira's clothes and shoes to sniff, after which all went back to the school. The huge Alsatian dogs sniffed Shakira from her classroom to the playground and the principal's office. Out the door and down the corridor to the entrance of the church. Both dogs barked ferociously afterward, sniffing the length and breadth of the altar area, wagging their tails.

Dele marveled as the officers deliberated on the actions of the animals.

"She was last here. On the altar."

Dele cringed. "The criminals took her from the house of God? Is there no fear anymore?"

Joshua snickered. "We should pray for the old days when fire fell on the altar. And anyone who stole from the church would be consumed immediately." He narrowed his eyes, and Dele looked away.

"There are no signs of her from this point." One of the dog's handlers stood a few feet from the position of the pulpit. "She must have been covered and carried away." He surveyed the area. "Some form of struggle here." He bent and picked up a braided lock of hair extensions.

Runo took it from him. "This is Shakira's hair."

"She was removed at this point as you can see. Is there a door around here?"

"Behind the backdrop on the pulpit." Runo walked over to it and parted the satin material used to decorate the altar area. "It's usually locked except during service times. Leads to the pastor's office." She tried the lock. "It's locked now."

Joshua shouted, "Get Goodwill for me now!"

Chapter Forty-Three

Inside Pastor Goodwill's office, they discovered that a sliding window which led out had been cut and removed, replaced with a plastic flap for easy exit. It came across as something done by a workman, well planned and executed.

"An insider job." Joshua examined the damage. "Did you notice, pastor?"

Goodwill trembled. "No. I was here yesterday, and nothing was different. I mean, I didn't open the window, so I didn't suspect any change."

"When last did you open this window?"

"Maybe a few days ago. I don't use it because of the air conditioning in the office."

Joshua checked out other parts of the office. "Why didn't you come into the office today?"

The man of God bit his lip. "We have evening program. I come after school hours on service days."

For another hour, Joshua interrogated Goodwill. Voices of the prayer team members could be heard in a small conference room down the hall.

The policemen found a trail from the pastor's window, but it disappeared into an untarred road leading to the main street. It seemed Shakira had been taken in broad daylight under everyone's watch, yet no one had seen anything. Her abductors must have perfected the art of appearing and disappearing.

For the rest of the day, they continued to interrogate and search the area for any more clues but nothing came of it, and in the night Dele and the officers returned to the house, while the ones from Calabar went back with their trained dogs.

No one seemed interested in a simple meal of boiled white rice with corned beef tomato stew Runo prepared. They couldn't go to bed either, and all sat stoic in the parlor, waiting to hear something, anything.

"What happens to her visa now?"

He may sound insensitive, but he needed to know. When no one responded, Dele muttered, "Anyway, this is Nigeria. Anything can happen anytime."

He got up to leave the parlor, and his phone rang.

"Hello."

"Fifty million. Call back if you need your wife." The caller hung up.

Dele's mouth drooped. "Ah!"

Runo arched an eyebrow. "Who was it?"

"The kidnapper. They want fifty million."

The officers rushed to his side. Joshua took his phone from him and speed-dialed the number. A female voice came on and repeated the order. She hung up before he could respond. When he dialed the number again, it was switched off.

"They will start the hide and seek." He took a pen and pad from his back pocket and copied the number. Then he called a number on his phone and called out the number to the person on the other end. "They can trace this number in minutes."

Runo squeezed her eyes shut for a moment. "We need to start the strategizing. Who do they imagine will raise fifty million for Shakira? Her husband? Or the American embassy."

Eddy pointed at the TV. "Switch it on. Local and international news is airing it. Someone from HQ just called."

Runo ran to it, and they all gasped as a video of Shakira, tied to a chair, came on. Dele touched the screen as though to reach her and, overwhelmed by how frail and helpless she appeared, broke down.

Joshua cursed. "They made a video and posted it online!" His phone rang. "Yes?" he listened for a moment and hung up. "The number is an old one. Perhaps ten years old, and it hasn't been used in a while. Registered under the name of a gangster about five years ago. In Lagos."

Dele sniffed. "What do we do?"

"Nothing. HQ is going to take over negotiations. They are looping your number, Dele." He fiddled with his phone. "I need to sleep."

Dele never wondered where he spent the night, but it was not his business. Eddy followed Joshua out, and Runo sat on one of the single chairs. The newscaster had moved on to other updates.

"What are we going to do?"

Dele had never seen it before but Runo's voice cracked. "He thinks he's in control all the time. I should have followed her out." She wrung her hands. "I am responsible. First time Florence showed up was a failure on my part. They knew then I wasn't on top of my job."

"You know you shouldn't blame yourself for this. Joshua called you to the office and—"

Runo bent forward. "Wait a minute. Joshua." She wagged her index finger. "Joshua. Did he just say he's going to sleep?" She stood. "He was here on both occasions."

Dele gasped. "He said let her vent. He knew?"

"I'm going to find out now." Runo hurried off to her room.

Dele didn't think she'd return to give him any feedback. Even if Joshua was a bad cop, Runo would not want him to know. He switched off the TV and went to bed but couldn't sleep. He thought of Shakira bound hand and foot to a chair, videoed for the world to see. She had not said a word, and her face was void of emotion. Did she know her abductor? Was it the same woman who killed her children?

And Inspector Joshua. It was too coincidental that he had been in the school on the two occasions Shakira's life had been exposed. Runo's sole responsibility to protect her had been neglected for a few minutes on both instances because Joshua thought it alright. Somehow, he consoled himself, if Joshua indeed had anything to do with this abduction, he would ensure that Shakira was not harmed.

But in these cases, he knew too well things could easily go wrong.

Chapter Forty-Four

Veronica brought some fruit and a light breakfast to the house the following morning and was received by Dele. Her sultry eyes sucked him in, and he couldn't hold her gaze. Being so concerned touched him. No other member had reached out, though it was still a bit early to judge. Since things had changed with the accommodation arrangement, he and Shakira had only come across Veronica a few times and exchanged pleasantries. Like all other members of the church, she believed the couple were missionaries, and Runo a servant.

"Pastor told us what happened." She fidgeted. "I thought I would bring some food. I wasn't sure your housekeeper would be around."

The church had been swamped with police officers the previous day, and the evening service had to be canceled, so even if the pastor didn't make an announcement, news would have gone around.

Dele sighed. "Thank you, Veronica. God bless you."

Runo assumed her role with her hands clasped behind. "It's so kind of you. Though no one has been able to eat since yesterday."

Veronica opened her basket. "I know it will be difficult. I put in some fruits and goatmeat pepper soup. It helps when one does not have appetite."

"Thank you." Runo picked up the basket and left them alone.

"Please have a seat." Dele gestured and took one too. "I can't believe this is happening. Why would anyone kidnap a missionary? Where do they think we will get money from?"

"I'm so sorry, sir. Your eyes are swollen." She sighed. "I know it will be difficult, but you need to rest and eat."

He shook his head. "I am on a fast now. With my wife gone, my life is in shambles."

"Sir? Did you see the news last night? She's on the news."

He sobbed. "I saw it. Ah, it is pathetic how they treat a woman of God."

Veronica walked to him and patted his back. "It will be well, sir. She will be found."

Runo entered the room and cleared her throat. "I've washed the dishes."

"Thank you," Veronica said.

Runo placed the basket on the floor beside her and folded her arms across her chest. "We are just praying they will let her return."

"This time around, we need to leave," Dele said. "The land is rejecting our ministry, and the Bible says for such a place we must shake off the dust of this town from our sandals."

"No, sir. It is the work of evildoers, and we reject it. You don't have to leave. Your wife will be fine."

"We saw her on TV last night." Runo rubbed her hands together. "At least they did not beat her or anything."

Veronica clapped her hands and raised them up toward heaven. "Yes, they did not. And we thank God. People have continued to pray in the church."

Joshua entered the parlor with Eddy close behind. His gaze swept through the room.

Runo and Dele greeted the two officers, and they responded with curt nods.

Veronica picked up her basket and locked her gaze with Dele's. "I will bring something light for lunch."

Runo shook her head. "Won't be necessary. He told you he's on a fast."

"Oh, yes. Sorry I forgot." She sighed. "I have to go now. I will join the prayer meeting in the church." At the door, she murmured, "Stay safe, Pastor Dele."

When she was gone, Joshua leaned against the door. "Good news or bad? Which one first?"

Runo scowled. "Either, Joshua. We should go back to the school and see what is happening."

"I have been recalled to HQ in Abuja. I am to resume with immediate effect."

Runo shrugged. "I am happy for you. It's a promotion, right?"

Joshua grunted. "I don't know yet. The good news is—"

Dele blurted, "I thought this was the good news."

"For real?" Joshua scoffed. "All through the night, negotiations went on. Shakira will be released tonight if the process of the release is properly carried out." He rubbed his hands. "Sorry to say, I will not be here, so Runo you have to get it right. Or Shakira will be blown to smithereens."

Runo rolled her eyes. "What's the plan?"

"The money will be delivered to the church premises. Shakira will be strapped with a bomb and allowed to come in. Money must be dropped under the pastor's window half an hour before she shows up. She will pick up the money, take it to her abductors in their hiding place, and the bomb taken off—"

"No way!" Dele cried. "Nobody agrees to such a stupid plan."

Runo blinked. "How much?"

"They negotiated five million. The state government agreed to donate it." Joshua wiped sweat off his forehead though the sun was not up yet. "The time for all this is midnight. Tomorrow morning, you go to the registry and get her married. You all leave this town afterward. It's become too dangerous for her to be here."

Dele paced. "I said it from the start. Shakira is now roped into some grand criminal investigation. We should have gone back to Lagos."

Runo scratched her neck. "Why get married if she's leaving?"

"Leaving Efayaw, not Nigeria." Joshua steepled his fingers as was usual for him. "We believe her presence would continue to make the criminals take action, and in this they will make mistakes."

Dele grunted. "At least we will be in the middle of civilization. I will take Lagos any day."

Runo shrugged. "Anyway, I will get the rest of the picture from my supervisor."

Joshua snapped, "I am your supervisor. I will report the continued insubordination on your part, Inspector Runo. You may be of the same rank, but I got on this job three years earlier than you."

Runo waved him off. For a moment, Dele saw Joshua clench and unclench his fist and thought he would get physical, but the moment passed.

Runo spoke instead. "What time is your flight out?"

"Eddy will drop me off at the park," Joshua said. "I will be traveling by road."

"By road! Police is broke, huh?"

Dele would have done anything to capture the two faces before him: the defeated Inspector Joshua, humiliated before colleagues he felt superior to, and the smug little look Runo tried to hide but failed. Politics prevailed in every profession whether these two accepted it or not. He decided to focus his energy on the eventful day ahead.

Chapter Forty-Five

Eddy returned an hour later to drive Runo and Dele to the school. Class was not in session and the principal, some of the school officials, along with Pastor Goodwill and other ministers, were in the church hall. Prayer could be heard from the small conference room.

Runo spoke with two uniformed police officers for a while and then joined Dele and Eddy, where they stood waiting for further instructions.

"The kidnappers don't want anyone here when they bring Shakira," she said. "If they see any of us, they will detonate the bomb on her."

Dele groaned. "This is so unfair. These criminals."

"They promise they will not harm her if we obey. The money will be dropped under the window thirty minutes before she arrives, by which time the school and church should be deserted. We can come for Shakira thirty minutes after she gives them the money."

Dele's heart pounded. "We have to do as they say. Please."

"We don't have much of a choice," Runo muttered. "Everyone needs to stay calm." She started to walk away, but Dele called her. She arched an eyebrow. "Yes?"

"Joshua. He did it?"

Runo stole a glance at Eddy. "We don't compromise an operation. And no one is a sacred cow where I work." She moved to where Pastor Goodwill stood with his ministers.

Dele watched her go and wondered where he stood with her. From the first time she served as Shakira's housekeeper, there had been a silent animosity between her and Joshua.

Eddy blew his breath through his mouth. "One has to be careful around this lady."

Veronica approached the men, her fingers entwined. "I thought I should invite you to the prayers. We've been told we all have to leave by ten in the night." She shrugged. "We can pray till then."

Dele sucked in his breath. Ten! Another twelve hours or thereabout? He had never joined any prayers for more than thirty minutes.

"Huh, I may join later, but I believe I should stick around till the plans are finalized."

"Okay, sir." She pointed toward the end of the hall. "We are in the conference room."

"Okay."

She left as the two uniformed policemen welcomed two of their colleagues who had CCTV gadgets. The four entered Pastor Goodwill's office behind the altar area.

"They want to fix cameras, though I don't see the use. Those people are not coming anywhere close to this place. They will strap a bomb to her and remote-control it."

Dele sighed. "I wonder what she must feel, knowing she could be blown to pieces at a madman's whim."

Eddy shrugged. "We see it every day. Some survive."

"What do you mean some survive?"

"It's our job, bro. Just pray someone doesn't panic."

Dele shuddered. He may not be important to anyone, but at least his life was safe back in Lagos. His home, or where he squatted with his sisters and referred to as home, was safe and secure. He didn't eat as well as now, but he got a meal a day most days. Maybe he had wanted too much, but now he appreciated the little he'd had.

"Panic?"

"Yeah." Eddy blinked. "The person with the remote. May see the money and get all excited. Boom! And Shakira is gone." He sighed. "She too may detonate herself if she panics."

Dele couldn't hear anymore. "I think I'll join the prayer team. Let me know when you need me."

Eddy mumbled, "Sure."

Dele hurried off. Now he had prayer points for the team. Eddy was right. As fidgety as he was now, he could press a wrong button and blow the building up. He wiped the sweat from his palms onto his new chinos pants.

This party would soon be over, and he would go back home. He decided on two things: if Shakira came out alive and well, he would turn his life around, serve God from the bottom of his heart, and get a proper job, any honest job. This experience had gone on longer than he envisaged.

He met ten people in the prayer team. To Dele's consternation, the leader handed over the coordination to him as soon as he stepped in. If Veronica had been right, this would go on for another twelve or so hours. He didn't know what to do.

When the room got quiet, and the members waited on him, he said with a hoarse voice, "Let's pray no one will panic."

The people stared, unable to understand the request.

"You see, these kidnappers do not have the Spirit of God, and they may panic, do something wrong. They may get excited and shoot, or like I said, out of confusion fire or detonate the bomb. Anything you can think of may happen and everything goes wrong." He trembled. "We may all be dead by tomorrow morning if these evil people go on a rampage. Most important is the life of my dear wife." He fought tears. "Pray nothing will happen to her."

He wept while fervent prayers commenced.

A heaviness overwhelmed him, and he knew he couldn't deceive anyone but himself anymore. Light entered his heart, and he fell on his knees, crying and seeking for God's mercy and forgiveness.

"I am nothing. I am a liar and a thief, and I have not done anything to deserve Your mercy! Help me. Forgive me. I am sorry!"

The intercessors surrounded him and laid their hands on him. He couldn't lead any longer beyond what he had. The supplication got more intense. The men and women mentioned his name and Shakira's intermittently. They called on the Almighty to intervene and save with His mighty hand.

Dele knew something more had happened to him. His time to come clean was here. It didn't matter if Shakira returned or not. His salvation wasn't based on her rescue, it was now. He trusted God for her smooth release and the capture of the evil people behind it, but he wasn't going back to Lagos to his old ways.

He stood amidst the raised voices and shouted, "Praise Him! He has done great things. He has set me free. He has set us free. I see freedom!"

Everyone in the room screamed with delight. They clapped and thanked their Maker, lifting holy hands up in the air. Tears streamed down many of their faces. Dele doubted they understood his cry of joy. He hadn't seen any visions of deliverance as they might assume. His soul had been set free, and they never would guess.

Chapter Forty-Six

It was too risky to defy the orders of the evil workers, so Runo and everyone else congregated at the house to wait out the release.

Dele, flanked by Pastor Goodwill and Veronica, who seemed glued to his side right from the time the prayers ended two hours earlier, sat on the couch and murmured silent prayers. The police officers who installed the camera in the pastor's office sat in their vehicle stationed a mile from the church premises and monitored Shakira. They communicated the progress to Runo through their radio. She would join them once they confirmed she had delivered the ransom money and was back inside the church alone.

The wait was the worst part of the night. His heart thudding at an alarming rate, Dele counted the cost of a loss. What would happen to him if Shakira wasn't returned or came back dead? Eddy had hinted at the possibility. Her country's embassy may wage war on this town and the country. Her family may blame him for assisting her at all, but deep down he knew it would affect him in the least way, and this he dreaded. He had nothing to lose. He may even be seen as a hero, and he hated the idea. The foundation of his heroism was faulty, and would he be bold enough to denounce it?

He spoke to Pastor Goodwill. "Can we worship?"

Goodwill nodded. "Yes."

Runo curled her lips. "Softly, please. I need to hear what the guys on the other end of the radio are saying."

Pastor Goodwill raised a solemn song and soon it filled the room. Some people went on their knees, others lifted their hands in the air.

Dele didn't know how long it continued until Runo screamed, "She's out!"

It was music in the ears of a dying man, water to a thirsty soul. The church members jumped on one another, shouting, "Hallelujah!"

Everyone hurried to the different vehicles which had conveyed them to the house and drove to the church. The police car with the two monitoring officers was parked outside the gate. One of the policemen directed the cars to the side of the road several feet away from the entrance.

Dele, Eddy, and Runo hurried to the men.

One of them spoke. "She's alone inside the church now. The bomb belt tied on her has been removed."

"I will go and get her," Runo said. She opened the door of the police vehicle and removed the bulletproof vest and helmet she wore. "I'll be back." She tucked in her service pistol and walked into the premises, her hands raised.

Dele paced, praying. It seemed like forever, but when he checked his watch it took only five minutes before Runo resurfaced with a limp Shakira. She was fainting on the officer's arm. He scooped her up and rushed to the car Eddy drove.

"Disperse!" Runo shouted. "Go home. Everyone. She's fine."

Pastor Goodwill and the leaders rode behind to the house. A nurse from the police clinic waited with a drip line for Shakira. It seemed she had not eaten since her kidnap.

Veronica, who had joined the team from the church, helped to get Shakira in bed. After her condition was ascertained as stable, Runo asked everyone to leave.

"We will check again in the morning," Pastor Goodwill said.

Runo shook her head. "Much later in the evening will make more sense."

"Okay, madam." Goodwill gave a simple bow and left with his members.

The three remaining in Joshua's team sat in the parlor with the police nurse.

Runo squeezed her eyes shut. "Ah, aren't we grateful it all went well?"

Dele could feel all the emotion he'd kept at bay burst. He laughed until he cried. "Yes. Thank You, Lord. What would I have done?"

Runo cackled. "Your cover almost broke there, you know. Mine sure did."

"They think you are a housekeeper from the police, just like I'm a police nurse," the rotund woman with twinkling eyes said.

"It makes sense that Shakira's housekeeper would be a policewoman." Runo stretched and stood. "I tasted the soup the lady from the church brought in the morning. Anyone interested?"

She got a chorus answer from her colleagues, but Dele still didn't have an appetite. "I think I'll sit with Shakira a while." He stood.

Runo waved him off. "Sit down and get some food in your stomach. She's asleep."

The nurse nodded. "And will be for the next few days."

Dele frowned. "Sleep for days?"

"The trauma was too much, so we'll keep her lightly sedated and bring her out little by little."

Runo left and returned with a tray full of fruits and food Veronica brought in the morning of the previous day, when the tension in the house was too much for anyone to eat.

"We can feast now. She got out!" She threw a punch in the air. "This is my first operation as an OIC, and I nailed it. Wow."

Eddy threw a salute in her direction. "Great job, officer in charge."

They dished out the meal of boiled white rice and goatmeat pepper soup into plates and served it round.

Dele didn't know he was hungry until the food touched his tongue. He gobbled it in record time and took more.

The officers may have noticed and found his gesture funny, but none showed interest. Their topic of discussion captivated their interest much more than Dele's hunger pangs.

"I saw it in my email," Runo was saying. "Of course, I had Shakira to rescue so I didn't pay attention. But I got the gist of it quite alright. I don't know what would make such a promising person turn evil."

"Greed," the nurse said. "We get so exposed to these criminals, and they have a lot to offer. Imagine if you could earn an extra five to ten thousand dollars every month."

"But you will get caught sooner or later. I have never seen one single officer get away with it." Runo groaned. "Dollars that will ruin a lifetime career."

Dele paused and listened. Eddy ate on without saying anything, but his gestures showed he was following the conversation between the ladies.

"Hmm, this one got away, my dear. He just took the wrong taxi, and he's in the neighboring country." Runo started to interrupt, but the nurse continued. "Which we all know by now he is a citizen of. From there he moves on. He'll disappear much the same way the criminals he aids do. The guy works with an international organization and has citizenship in at least three countries."

Runo rolled her eyes. "I never could have imagined. His arrogance just put me off. I mean, he acted like he owned the world. And everyone in it."

Dele cleared his throat. "Who are you talking about?"

"Joshua." Runo jerked her head back. "I was right. He compromised us."

Chapter Forty-Seven

Shakira came out of the daze three days later. She felt weak and sick to her stomach. Given a choice, she would have preferred to live through the next few days after her release, but no one had sought her opinion.

The nurse was kind and did her job, but it didn't make the decision to tranquilize her without her consent right. She wanted to explain that she needed medical attention beyond sedation.

Runo walked into her room on the evening of the third day, a weak smile about her lips. "I'm glad you're awake now."

Shakira pulled herself up. "I think I have a headache."

Runo sat on the edge of the bed. "The nurse says you'll be fine from now on. We wanted you to rest and gain your strength back."

"At least can I have some solid food? I'm starved."

Runo chuckled. "I prepared chicken onion soup. And we have fresh bread."

"Sounds good," Shakira said. "Why did I need to be sedated? I was fine."

"Your kidnapper put some drug in your veins. We wanted it out of your system."

Shakira gasped. "Why would they do so? What was it?"

"We don't know. But you're fine now."

"I want to go home, please. I can't stay here any longer." She covered her face and sobbed into her hands. "I can't."

Runo patted her back. "I understand. You'll soon go back home. I will ensure the process is expedited."

"Thank you." Shakira sniffled. "I never should have come here."

"You know being here sped up our investigation. We were stuck at a point. Only to discover we had a snitch in the team."

"Oh. I'm sorry."

"None other than Joshua."

Shakira's head shot up. "The same Joshua, your boss?"

Runo grimaced. "He wasn't my boss. He liked to think he could order everyone around, but we realized he did so to cover his betrayal."

"How horrible."

"You remember the first time he came was when Florence entered your class. The second time you were taken."

Shakira inhaled sharply. "He works with Florence?"

"We're not sure yet, but he does get paid for snitching."

"Where is he now?"

"He crossed over to the neighboring country. We suspect he will leave West Africa or go into hiding."

"How mean of him. To see me go through what I've been through and still snitch?"

"There are a few things I wanted to discuss with you. When our colleagues searched Joshua's office, we found several documents meant for you. Including your passport."

"Oh, thank goodness."

"The marriage certificate, well, and some letters from your family." Runo stood. "Let me get the soup warmed."

Shakira leaned forward. "Can I have the letters?"

"They're not here yet but I've requested for all to be sent." Runo stopped at the door. "I think you should take a shower. Come out to the parlor. Dele is anxious to see you too."

Shakira nodded and Runo left. She remembered being bed-bathed by the nurse, and it made her realize how much she needed a good shower. She put her feet on the mat by her bed and tested her strength to stand. It was good. She stretched, yawned, and went to get cleaned up.

Contrary to the bathroom in the previous places she stayed in Nigeria, this had a nice shower and a tub. She chose to soak in the tub. The warm water helped to sooth her. She shuddered at the thought of what her life had become in the past month, and in the last four days in particular.

She believed her abductors must have drugged her because she could only remember being tied to a chair all day and all night. They didn't gag her, but she never had the urge to scream. She wasn't blindfolded either, and she couldn't remember a single face. And there were several men and women who came in and out of the room she was placed in.

When she thought she could face the others, she stepped out of the bath and wore her robe over her nightdress. Steaming chicken soup with two small rolls of fresh bread had been served on a tray and placed on the center table.

Dele jumped to his feet when she entered the room. "I'm so glad you're back on your feet."

Shakira grunted. "Thanks to the decision to turn me into a weakling."

He showed amusement. "You could barely walk when they returned you to the church."

She sat on one of the single chairs and picked up the bowl of soup. "This smell good."

"Runo has been great. Since the nurse left yesterday."

She took a sip. "Tastes good. Not too spicy."

"God has been so faithful, and I give Him all the glory, Shakira. A lot has happened in the past three days. Almost as though we just got here."

She continued her meal, unwilling to get into any chat with him. What preoccupied her now was the plan to go back home. She was done with

Nigeria, the investigation, and the people. The conversation she wanted to have now must be directed toward her return home. She wanted a timeline, and she wanted it fast.

"I know we have many unspoken issues between us, and we should try to resolve them—"

She raised her hand to stop him. "I don't have issues with you. Not anymore anyway. You brought me here and tried to take advantage of me." She swallowed. "All is forgiven. My life is changed now, and I am grateful to God for the encounter I had. But those are in the past. I'm leaving. Going back to my family." She took a chunk of chicken and popped it in her mouth. "Real good."

Dele cleared his throat. "Runo didn't tell you."

She arched an eyebrow. "Tell me what?"

"What her colleagues found in Joshua's desk."

She dropped her spoon. "A marriage certificate for a marriage that never happened?"

"And divorce papers from your husband." He swatted at the air. "Joshua seemed to have wanted you around. He communicated with your family. Told them you had remarried and settled down—"

Shakira flew to her feet. "What are you saying?"

"No one knows his motives, but he was working for both sides, the law and the criminals." He moved to her. "Shakira, think about this. What do you stand to lose? We can make a living here, and after a few years return to the States together." He put his hand on hers. "Look, I got saved too. While praying for your return, God touched—"

Shakira screeched, "Don't you dare touch me!"

Chapter Forty-Eight

Runo came into the parlor, her arms folded across her chest. "You told her."

Dele scratched his neck. "Someone had to."

"None of you care!" Shakira battled tears but couldn't help it. "You are all trying to use me to get what you want for yourselves."

"Sit down, Shakira, and let me explain this to you." Runo took a deep breath. "And I want to tell you the whole truth."

She didn't want to hear it, but she was at their mercy, so instead of taking her seat she leaned against the wall. "Say whatever you want."

Runo shrugged. "Much of what is happening now is no one's fault. The search for Florence Odu, the real one, had gone cold, and when her identity resurfaced in your case, the investigators thought they would get a break." She leaned away. "We didn't want any part of it. As it was, no one seemed to know where FO was. She disappeared into thin air. When you came here, we had to decide whether to acknowledge you or not. For the first week, we had you trailed and realized you had come here to find the criminal who killed your daughters."

Shakira stuck a fist in her mouth. How could they be so callous? "You arranged for my money to be stolen at the airport and my passport taken here too?"

Runo smirked. "Of course not. You came here without direction. If you had not met the good Detective Dauda at the airport, you don't even want to know what could have happened to you."

Shakira yelled, "But you had someone watching me all the time."

"To know your mission. As soon as we were sure you came to look for the woman, we decided to step in." Runo arched an eyebrow. "Joshua was just a sad case. Everywhere in the world there are bad men in uniform, and many times we don't know when someone has tipped over the edge and is conniving with wanted persons because of greed. And don't ask me how they connect because I don't know."

Shakira burst into tears and covered her face with her hands. Dele moved over to her and pulled her into his arms, but she shrugged him off.

"Shakira, please. It breaks my heart to see you hurt. We will work everything out, and you'll be fine."

Runo snorted. "He's right, Shakira. We will work things out. You only need to be patient and to trust us."

Shakira straightened. "I want to leave. Joshua gave me the option and said your office would facilitate it."

"Joshua lied a lot to you, but yes we planned to facilitate your return when the investigation is over, or at least we can be sure we don't need you anymore."

"What? I'm not gonna wait till this investigation you have no clue is going anywhere is coming to an end!" Shakira gasped. "You know what? I want my passport back. Do you have it, Runo?"

"I don't. It's in our office at the headquarters. But even if you have it, how do you propose you will leave here? You don't have any money, and your accent easily gives you away." She threw a dirty glance at Dele. "You will fall into the hands of some hungry hustler, and your life will end up on another rollercoaster."

For a moment Shakira marveled that Dele did not have a comeback. The problem before her was bigger than his reaction to Runo's sarcasm, though, and she swallowed hard. "Can you help me, please. I don't want to be a part of this anymore. I want to go home."

"I wish I could, Shakira." Runo sighed. "My advice is for you to sit tight and allow us to do our jobs. You have a nice house here, a job to keep you occupied, and protection. The mole is gone."

"She's right, dear," Dele said. "Try and live a normal life, and we will continue to pray the investigation wraps up quick."

Her eyes lit up for a second. "All the clothes and shoes in the wardrobe, can I sell them off? I could use the money for my ticket back."

Runo snickered. "First, no one cares if you've never worn any of those clothes. The moment you put them out for sale, they'll term them as 'used.' And money from it won't even buy your flight ticket to Lagos."

Shakira's lips quivered. There was no way out. She had not been on social media since she left home, hoping to cut off anyone who tried to get in touch with her. And with her last experience, nobody knew what happened to her phone. She was cut off. No money, no means of communication, and people she couldn't trust had her trapped in a house in a town bordered by another African country and the ocean.

"I want to retire. Maybe I will know what to do in the morning."

Her companions gestured her release. It felt much like a prison, where she was at the mercy of her guards. She hobbled to her room and closed the door. It didn't help that she couldn't remember anything after she was snatched up in a sack in the church and taken to an unknown place for over thirty hours, and then remanded to her bed for another seventy-two. She would go crazy if she didn't do something about her situation.

There had to be a way to contact her embassy.

Chapter Forty-Nine

Shakira at first thought she was dreaming, but she soon realized the cold hand on her forehead was real. She moaned, and when she saw the male face close to hers, stifled a scream and fumbled for the alarm button under her pillow.

"What do you want, Dele?" she exclaimed. "Get out of my room!"

He murmured, "Shh, calm down. I just want to talk."

Her eyes were wide open now, and she saw his face well because she never switched off the lights to sleep. He still wore the outfit of the day before, a blue cotton tail shirt over blue jeans. It must still be night. She'd cried herself to sleep despite her effort to brainstorm the options open to her.

She snapped, "I don't want to talk. Please leave."

He stepped back as though stung. "I only want to help you. I have a conscience, you know. You asked me for help, and besides, this is my country. I ought to help you."

He didn't say it, but she heard loud and clear the insinuation of him getting help from her if he found himself in her country as well. But she couldn't snub any offer of assistance.

She removed her hand from the button and sat up. "What do you want?"

"To help."

"How?"

"Listen, I'm not sure Runo wants you to leave now, but she won't force you to stay." He ran his hand over his head "I don't think you should go back. Your husband has started divorce proceedings and—"

She stifled the urge to use bad language. "Get out of my room if you have nothing to say."

"Your phone is gone, the woman you came to catch is still wanted, and you don't trust anyone around you. I understand how you feel. I have been there most of my life. And I have a plan."

"Get to the point, Dele," she said between gritted teeth.

"We raise an offering for your ticket back home."

She flinched as though stung. "No."

"How else will you leave? Runo will play delay games till you end up being here for another year or month. You want to leave as soon as tomorrow, right?" He paced. He had her attention, and much as she hated it, she listened.

"Yes," she whispered.

"You can use my phone to go on social media and send messages to your family and friends."

He made sense, but could she trust him? From the beginning, he had done only the things he would benefit from. What had changed?

"What's in this for you?"

Dele paced. "I will be doing something good for you, and it makes me feel so blessed to be there for you."

She shut her eyes, thinking. Was there anything she would lose if she agreed to his plan? "But how will they send money to me? I mean, if I ask my family?"

"There are fast-cash services through the banks." He shrugged. "You have to trust me to collect the money and give you—"

"No. No way."

"I can discuss with Pastor Goodwill to—"

"No. We're not taking money from the church again." She rubbed her temples. "I can't do it again."

He threw his hands up in the air. "These are the only ways. Don't you want to leave? You know my sisters; they don't have money, or I could have asked them."

She snickered. "Even if they had money they wouldn't give it to you."

"I have my ways, Shakira."

She narrowed her eyes. "Just like now?"

"Come on, I'm trying to be a brother. A friend."

She shook her head. "Please leave. I need to think about it. Besides, my passport is not here. Runo has to get it—"

"Your passport is with Runo. She got it with the divorce papers and our marriage certificate."

She choked. "We don't have a marriage certificate. And—she lied too?"

He shrugged. "If you ask her for it, she will give it to you."

"How do you know?" she said. "Everyone lies. Who can I trust?"

He returned to her side. "You can trust me, Shakira. I know I haven't earned it but give me a chance."

She covered her face with one hand and waved him off. "Just go."

"I know you may think I'm a con or something, but if there's anything you'd do to repay me for helping you, it's a photoshoot."

Her hands dropped from her face. "A what?"

"Wedding photoshoot."

She threw her pillow at him. "Get out!"

Chapter Fifty

The following morning, Shakira asked what the plan would be going forward, and Runo shrugged.

"We wait for further instructions from HQ."

Shakira wanted to scream out her frustration but knew it would be of no use. She wished she could discuss the previous evening when Dele entered her room uninvited, but he'd thrown in accusations about Runo keeping the truth from her. She couldn't trust the policewoman any more than Dele and the others. She had believed in Joshua and the system with all her heart, and he'd let her down.

After two days of no news from Runo's HQ, Shakira decided to take a risk on Dele. She hadn't gone to school because it was too traumatic, and though Runo believed Joshua had been a part of the whole wicked operation and now was gone, she couldn't be sure there wasn't another double agent in the team. So she opted for Shakira to stay off the school premises in the meanwhile.

With nothing to do most of the time, Dele had developed a habit of working on the landscape and keeping it neat.

Shakira found him trimming the climbing blue dawn flower off the fence with a kitchen knife. She'd never allow anyone to use her knife for such a job, but she remembered this was not her house. The early morning breeze hit her face, and she hugged her robe closer. It wasn't seven yet, and she thought it was a bit early for gardening, but she'd noticed Dele's routine.

"Runo doesn't have any plans for me as it is."

Dele directed his focus away from the plant. "I didn't notice you come. Good morning."

"Good morning. Runo has no plans for me."

He lowered his hands. "From the start. She's only doing her job."

She cringed. "Her job doesn't include telling me the truth?"

"This is Nigeria, Shakira. A police officer does not owe you the truth. She has not done anything wrong as a matter of fact."

"I'm so confused. Without the school job, am I just gonna sit like this till some unknown person at headquarters decides I've suffered enough?"

Dele shrugged. "You have a choice."

"Between a hard place and the deep blue sea."

"All I have asked is a few pictures. We will rent a gown and a suit—"

She covered her ears. "I don't want to hear it. I am not married to you, and I won't pretend about it."

"Okay." He sighed. "No pictures, but I still want to help you."

Her shoulders relaxed and she lowered her hands. "I hoped you'd feel so." She shuddered. "I have made many mistakes, but I have also realized this."

"You will tell Runo you have decided to return home. You give up on the search for the woman."

"It's the truth."

"She may want to protest, but you have to insist."

"I will."

"Good. I will stand by you. I know she'll talk about money."

Shakira drew in a shuddering breath. "I know what to say to her."

"Good." He returned to his landscaping duty. "We'll talk more about it when I'm done here."

Shakira hugged her arms. "I want to talk about it now, please."

"I—okay. Once she agrees, we'll go to your social media platforms and send messages to your friends for—"

"No way. You said you'd have to get the money."

"Yes. The other way is to talk to Pastor Goodwill."

"Oh no!"

"You have to decide, Shakira. I don't have any money to loan you or I would have."

She chewed on the insides of her cheek. "What about Detective Dauda? Can he help?"

Dele shook his head. "I doubt it. He is just a policeman."

She rocked back and forth on her heels. This was tough. She would never know if he was ripping her off as he'd done at first unless she agreed.

"Okay. We'll ask my friends for money. How much do you think?"

He shrugged. "We can check online for tickets."

"My return ticket was stolen in my luggage, but couldn't I call the airline?"

"We'll call, and they can advise on what to do. Maybe you'll have to pay a token or something."

"I have defaulted, though. I didn't show up on my return date."

He wiped sweat off his face. "Should we see Runo now?"

"Yes." She dragged in a long breath. "Thank you."

Chapter Fifty-One

Runo listened to their explanations and asked the same questions in different ways. Shakira presented her reasons and when she was done, Runo reluctantly brought out the documents and her passport. She offered no apology, which Dele found wrong, but since Shakira demanded none, he made no fuss.

Shakira laughed and squealed at every success point in the plan. Dele had never seen her so excited. She sent messages to her sister and friends, and to Deon. Everyone agreed to send some money. With her lost ticket and no-show penalty, she had to pay some amount, but she was issued another ticket. Within a week, she got enough money to fly to Lagos. Her flight to Houston would be the following day, but she had booked the hotel Dauda took her to for the night. The police detective was to meet her at the airport and drive her there.

Dele did not want to ask for anything, and she offered nothing. Altogether, he received a little more than two thousand dollars on her behalf, which was far more than she required, and he handed all to her. On the morning of her departure, he and the police officers offered to take her to the nearest airport in Calabar about thirty miles away, partially to escort her for safety reasons, and also to prevent her having to use public transportation.

There was general talk about the trip and the investigation. Shakira's voice was louder than the others' and Dele's lower, which showed his state of mind, but she didn't seem to notice. At the airport, Shakira hugged each of them after checking in.

"We'll hang around till the flight takes off," Dele said.

Shakira beamed. "Oh, wow. So kind of you." She pointed toward the departure lounge. "Seems I'm the only one who can cross over here, though." She giggled and waved.

Runo waved back and Eddy saluted, but Dele couldn't find it in him to return any of the gestures. His stomach churned as he leaned back against the wall.

Runo arched an eyebrow. "Are you okay?"

He nodded. "Just sad to see her go." The policewoman snickered.

He watched Shakira smile at the airport officials, who made small talk with her and commented on her passport. She collected the passport from an official and tucked it in her bag, collected her hand luggage from the security conveyor belt, and strolled off. She didn't even spare a backward glance.

Everyone noticed, but Runo stifled a giggle. "Girl can't wait to get out of here. I thought she'll wave one last time or something."

Eddy smirked. "She'll do more than wave if the flight is canceled and she needs a place to sleep tonight."

"Ah, no more drama, please. I'm exhausted," Runo cried. "Glad to see her go. This was what I suggested all along."

Eddy shot a quick look in the direction of Shakira's retreating figure. "She just clogged the investigation. Not like we've made any progress."

There were no seats in the check-in area, so they trooped to the parking lot to sit in the car and wait for the plane to be airborne before they returned.

"You're so quiet, Dele." Eddy threw a punch in his direction. "Missing her so much? I'd thought you'd leave with her."

Dele grunted. "It's better she went alone."

Runo opened the car door when they got to it. "What's your plan?"

Dele waited till they were all seated inside before he responded. "I'll leave by road tomorrow morning."

"By road!" Eddy chuckled. "Why?"

Dele shrugged. "I don't have enough money for a flight."

He didn't have any money. Since he promised to help Shakira, he had silently prayed she would think of him and ask about his plans. Or better still, offer to buy him a ticket to Lagos. She had done neither.

Runo gasped. "Huh, Shakira did not think of buying you a ticket?"

Dele couldn't help but jump to her defense. "She has a lot to spend on."

Runo snickered. "She took our wardrobe full of lovely things."

Dele snapped. "Her clothes and money were stolen when she arrived."

"I'm glad she's on her way. We can focus energy on finding the rogues behind her tragedy." Eddy grunted. "At least we've confirmed they are in the area."

"We knew they were a long time ago—"

"Wait, sorry, an announcement was made."

"They've called boarding," Eddy said.

"We might as well set out," Runo said.

Eddy scratched his chin. "There's a place down this road where they sell the best palm wine in the world. Can we just stop by?"

Runo threw her hands up. "Sure."

Dele would have preferred to see the plane up in the sky before they left the airport, but he didn't protest. They found the place Eddy spoke about and bought a keg of palm wine and some dry-roasted wild meat.

About an hour and a half later, as they settled down to enjoy the delicacies bought near the airport, Shakira sent a message to Dele from the new cell phone she bought out of the funds she received. She had arrived on time, and Dauda had taken her to the hotel.

Dele sighed with relief. "She's in Lagos."

"Oh, hallelujah!" Runo took a swift gulp of the local palm drink. "Hmm, the best of the best."

Eddy laughed. "Too much of it will get you so drunk, you won't remember where you are."

"I'd like to retire into my room," Dele said softly. "I have a long journey ahead of me tomorrow."

Runo lowered her glass cup. "Are you going to see her before she leaves?"

Dele smirked. "No. I don't plan to even if I get into town on time."

She shrugged. "Okay."

It was too early to go to bed. He had his bag packed, so he just sat and stared into space. He didn't even have enough money to get to the bus station. He toyed with the idea of calling Pastor Goodwill, but what would he say? He'd vouched not to lie about his identity to anyone any more. Where would he get about five thousand naira from? He thought of Dauda. His friend could get the money, but at such short notice?

He pulled off his shoes and lay on his back. For the past month, all his basal needs had been met. Couldn't he trust God just one more time?

Runo knocked on his door. "You have a visitor. The sister from the church."

He sat up. "Veronica?"

"I guess."

What does she want? He didn't want to see anyone from the church or answer any questions. He had hoped to keep Shakira's return quiet. But she thought she owed Pastor Goodwill an explanation. Though she didn't blow the cover, there were many unanswered questions.

Chapter Fifty-Two

Veronica sat on the edge of the couch, her hands clasped in her lap. She stood when he walked in, an uncertain grin on her face.

Dele grunted. "Good evening, Sister Veronica."

"Good evening, Pastor Dele."

"Please, have a seat."

An awkward silence ensued after both sat on opposite sides of the room. Dele imagined Runo was in her room, and Eddy had gone wherever it was he went for the night. The trip had not been long, but the roads were bad and the whole day emotionally draining. The last thing he wanted was an inquisitive woman, but perhaps she needed counseling. Whatever was the case, he wasn't ready for it.

He cleared his throat. "Did you want to see me for something?"

"Yes, and no." She held his gaze. "Pastor Goodwill told me your wi— Ms. Shakira was leaving today."

He didn't expect to talk about Shakira.

"She left already."

She sat forward. "I knew she wasn't your real wife from the start."

He arched an eyebrow. "What do you mean? She is my wife, and she's had to go back to attend to family matters. I am leaving in the morning myself." He bit his tongue, wishing he hadn't told a lie again.

"Why didn't you leave together?"

"Huh?" He got defensive. "Because we decided to do it this way."

She smirked. "Hmm. There have been rumors going around."

He didn't want to get impatient with her. *What does she want?* "I don't listen to rumors. I don't care about them."

"I don't either, but because they involved you, I was interested."

"People always say what they wish."

"I didn't believe any of the rumors, of course."

She was baiting him, but he refused to bite. He wasn't surprised there would be whispers around. Not many people could keep secrets, and with all the action involving the local police force, there would be a lot of talk.

"So how may I help you?"

She twisted her fingers on her lap, drawing his attention to how nervous she seemed.

"I wanted to talk with you privately."

He allowed his eyes to roam around the room. "We are alone."

"Yes, I know." She paused. "I know."

He didn't know what to say or do. This was the most awkward moment of his whole encounter since he met Shakira. A woman from the church he professed to be a missionary of was sitting across from him, twisting her fingers, unable to say what she had to say? Very strange. Maybe she had a confession to make? A sin, or a disease, or even a crime?

"I'm in love with you, Dele. I have been since the first day you arrived."

If she hadn't spoken so fast, he would have jumped to his feet quicker. "Of course not!"

Nothing could have prepared him for such a silly claim. To imagine he had been paraded as a missionary, married to a beautiful American woman who had a passion for souls in a backyard-town in Nigeria? And this girl had thought of nothing but "love" for him. It was the most ludicrous thing he'd heard. Would this drama never end? Could he ever return to his normalcy?

He assessed her. Her face wasn't striking, but she had a beautiful figure, he'd noticed from the start, and she had great sense in fashion and make-up. She knew what best suited her. Even now she wore a beautiful red blouse over a red and gray color block skirt with gray sandals. He remembered a white figure-fitting dress she wore once, and on another occasion, a tunic over skinny jeans. Her clothes popped. Her hair too. She always had something new, either braided or styled.

Dele paced. This was weird. In the past, he'd been in and out of a few relationships, but nothing serious. The ladies he'd dated wanted more than he was willing to give, and the relationships broke off after several months. Never had a woman made a move on him. How would he tell her he wasn't interested in the least?

She sat with her head bent, and he noticed how light her scalp was with her beautiful Ghana-braid hairstyle. Her skin was as light as Shakira's. He shook his head. It was improper to acknowledge anything about her features.

He cleared his throat. "I'm sorry, but I am not interested in a relationship with you. Disregard any rumor you heard, I am not even available."

She murmured. "I'm not saying this because of rumors. I've not heard anything about your marital status."

He couldn't hold back anymore. "Then what did you hear?"

She raised her head and caught his gaze. "Shakira knows the people who kidnapped her. She followed them from America. She didn't come here for ministry." She paused. "Did you know?"

The police on the investigation were not good with keeping secrets after all. He couldn't lie about this, so he nodded.

"It confirms you are not married to her, then."

"It confirms nothing." He sighed. "Look, Veronica, you're a beautiful lady, and I see you love God. You will find a man who wants you and loves you. I am not the one." When she said nothing, he continued. "I am going back to Lagos tomorrow. We may never cross paths again."

Her eyes seemed to tear up, and he took his eyes away from hers.

"I don't mind moving to Lagos."

"For what?" he yelled. "How else do you want me to say this, young woman? I am not your man and never will be!"

He veered away from her. He wanted to walk into his room and let her find her way out, but it seemed gross to act in such a way with a lady.

"You're wrong," she whispered. "I'm convinced. I have my signs."

Her words annoyed him. He swung around, his fists clenched. "You know what, it takes two to tango. I am not the one. Whatever signs you got, deal with it." He breathed in. "Now, if you don't mind, you have to leave. I have a long trip tomorrow."

She didn't give up. "You are not married to her. You'll never see her again."

"Say whatever you wish." He walked to the door and opened it. "Thanks for stopping by."

For a moment, she seemed to struggle. She must have believed her visit would be a long one, and they'd be all cuddly at the end of it. She stood and bit her lower lip. On a second look, Dele thought she was pretty in a way. Her lips were full, and her eyes were small and almond-shaped. She had high cheek bones too. Her figure he already knew was attractive, at an average height of about five feet four inches.

No. I'm not thinking about this.

She walked to the door and stood right in front of him. "If you change your mind, or you need me for anything, I'll be here. Anytime." She stepped across the threshold.

It wasn't something an honorable man would say or do, but it came to Dele and he decided to score his point with it.

"I need some money for my trip tomorrow."

Chapter Fifty-Three

enya Brawn drove around the arrival area of George Bush Intercontinental Airport, Houston, waited several seconds, and would have driven on had Shakira not seen her blonde-dyed hair in time. When she sent messages online to her family and friends the week before, she'd noticed Kenya's new hair.

She waved with all her strength, dragging her luggage with her. "Kenya!" She doubted her sister would hear, but she saw her.

Kenya found a parking space just as a shuttle bus pulled out. She left the engine running, as she could only be there for a few minutes.

The two sisters ran into each other, crying and laughing. Kenya smacked her butt. "How could you Shakira Graham Smith? You nearly killed all of us."

Shakira sobbed. "I'm sorry. So sorry."

"Come on. Here. Give me your bags."

Kenya put her suitcase and hand luggage into the trunk of her Ford C-Max. The sisters hugged once more inside the car before Kenya drove off.

Shakira beamed. "I see you got yourself a new car too!"

"New hair, new car." Kenya waved her left hand and a glittering diamond engagement ring. "New man!"

Shakira screeched. "Oh! You go gurl!"

"Yeah. I can't believe it all worked out."

"Who is he? Someone I know?"

Kenya giggled. "No. Well, I met him in church."

"Tell me something. In church. You now go to church, Kenya?"

"You drove us all to church, Shakira. Mom was devastated. Deon near killed *hisself*! We all ran to God A'mighty for help."

Shakira chuckled. "And you came out with new hair, a new car, and a new man?"

"Yeah, right, babygirl! And new faith too. I accepted Him right into my heart."

Kenya's words broke Shakira down. Her sister must have been the toughest to crack in the family. She'd been married thrice and divorced just as many times. Never believed in anything but herself and what she could get out of life. If Shakira had thought she was selfish, Kenya was egotistically so. The only times Kenya did anything for anyone was if she feared for her life, gained from it, or Shakira was involved. Otherwise, Kenya Brawn lived only for Kenya Brawn.

"I'm so happy for you, Kenya," Shakira sobbed. "I know I was mean and stupid to leave, but I found God too."

Kenya grabbed her hand and squeezed it. "Oh, it's alright. I mean, you were gone for a year, but now you're back. Like the prodigal child."

"A year! I didn't stay away for all of six weeks."

"Like forever. Come on, Shakira. We thought you'd died."

"Thank God I'm alive, and I'm back home."

"We give Him praise. Hallelujah."

Shakira sniffed. "Tell me about everyone. How's Deon?"

"Great. He moved out of the house into a condo downtown." Kenya shrugged. "Thought it was useless to stay alone in the house with such memories."

"I'd do the same, I guess." Shakira inhaled. "Does he call you?"

"I make it my duty to call him once a week. Check him out." Kenya shrugged again. "He seems okay."

"Aww, thank you so much, Kenya. You're the best sister in the world."

"Your only sister. I've watched over you since the day ya crawled outta Mom's body, all eight pounds of cuteness."

"Thank you." She pressed her lips together. "Deon doesn't want me no more, right? He sent divorce documents."

Kenya groaned. "He told me about it. I was confused, though. He said he got to speak with a man you were with. Dele? And he spoke to you once?"

"Yes." She sighed. "I don't know what to think. Does he want to see me? He sent five hundred dollars when I asked him for money to return."

"A man's money is where his heart is. But until you see him, I don't know what's on his mind, dear. He has said many things."

"Many things like what?"

"He wanted you back so bad at a time, then he told me he was done. Then he sends you money. I don't get it too."

Shakira covered her face. "I will do anything to get him back. I was foolish, but I've learned my lesson." She wiped tears off her face. "I don't want to cry so much."

Kenya smirked. "Oh, you will cry a lot in the next few days. Get ready for it."

Both ladies laughed, and Shakira threw Kenya a playful punch. "Yeah, right." She sniffed. "At least I'm home."

"This Dele guy—who is he?"

Shakira explained the whole ordeal. She was done playing games and didn't hide her foolishness in going along with people she knew nothing about. Her life at the time was on a verge. She wanted to die or die trying.

Kenya exclaimed at her audacity. "Are you sure he didn't abuse you in any way?"

"Yes." Shakira exhaled. "He was a gentleman. In the end he treated me with kindness."

"So no one has been caught. Not the robbers at the airport, not the other ones, not the kidnappers? And not Florence Odu?"

"No one."

"Do they catch criminals in this country at all?"

"The police force seemed busy. Not sure what they're doing, though." Shakira shook her head. "I don't want to talk about it anymore."

"You should write a book. *Sojourn of a Mermaid to Nigeria, the Land of Nowhere!*" The two sisters laughed. Kenya drove up to her apartment block. "I thought it'd be better if you stayed with me till you can sort out what next."

"Thank you, Kenya."

She parked in her space, and they took out Shakira's bags. "Mom will be here later in the evening. I haven't told Deon you're back today."

"I sent him a message but didn't get any reply."

"He'll come through, I pray."

Chapter Fifty-Four

*S*hakira didn't see Deon for another three months, and it wasn't a private meeting as she'd hoped the first time would be. Kenya thought it was inevitable, but Shakira feared the outcome of such a meeting because she discovered after a fainting spell, and a visit to her doctor, that she was pregnant.

It hadn't shown yet, but it was there and soon would. Her doctor dated the pregnancy back to her visit to Nigeria.

She told Kenya of the doctor's findings when the latter came back from work.

"When I was abducted, I was drugged." She wept. "I couldn't remember anything all of the thirty or so hours. The police nurse checked me when I was rescued, but never mentioned any such thing."

Kenya paced. "Why would this happen? Your life is supposed to be back on track."

Shakira wailed. "Deon would never take me back!"

"You could abort it." Kenya sighed. "I mean, it's the right thing to do. You don't know how it got in there."

"Do you think Deon would ever believe?"

"Shakira!" Kenya shook her. "Think about yourself. You can't have this baby!"

"I can't kill it, can I? It is a sin against God. I will never do anything to harm the life of a helpless child."

"A helpless child fathered by some African criminal! No one wants such a child."

"I don't know what to do, Kenya." She wept into her hands.

"I'm fixing an appointment for you with Dr. Brickam, 'cause I dunno what to do either." Kenya picked up her cellphone. "I'm not gonna sit here and watch you ruin what's left of ya life, though."

Dr. Brickam saw Shakira the following day and, after one session, scheduled another time. Her therapist had a lot to work with her on, and the baby in her womb was one of them. She needed to get her confidence back. Dealing with grief remained an area of longstanding research, and human beings always surprised. Shakira had taken her grief to another level. The doctor wanted her to find some form of closure for her grief, and to figure out how she'd handled it.

What remained most important to Shakira was her marriage, or whatever was left of it. She had questions to ask, and some to answer. Deon had reached out only once, and she'd given an excuse not to see him. Since then, he had not called or requested another meeting.

Kenya stayed out of the situation, especially because she believed Shakira had no business being pregnant for someone she didn't know anything about.

A couple of months with the psychologist, however, seemed to have prepared Shakira to see her husband for the first time since her return home. Nervous and giddy at the same time, she waited in Dr. Brickam's office for him to arrive.

"I'll excuse you two when he gets here," the doctor said. "Speak your heart. Tell him the truth."

Shakira nodded, and moments later, Deon walked in.

To her relief, he stretched out his arms and she ran into them. He had changed a lot. He'd lost some weight, and his face had stress lines where they'd never been before. She had promised herself not to cry, but she did. Her sobs wracked her body, and to her delight, Deon cried with her. Seeing him, touching him felt right. It was right.

When they both could talk, he touched her hair. "I like the style. You look African."

She touched it too. She had walked into one of the African salons and had it made. "Thank you."

"I knew you needed time to recover from the trip. It's why I didn't want to bother you."

Deon, so dear and so considerate, she thought. "Thank you, darling." She stroked his face. "I missed you so much."

"You had to get your groove back, I understood."

"Deon, darling." She took his hands in hers. "A lot has changed with me."

"I can imagine. We've both changed."

"I found Jesus, Deon." She searched his face. "He brought me back from the brink of destruction. He saved me. Showed me the way back home."

He cupped her cheeks. "I found Him too, darling. Thank God for our salvation."

She laughed. "Thank God." She pulled him to the couch she'd been treated on several times, and they sat closely, their hands locked. "I have so much to tell you, I don't know where to start." He simply stared, so she spoke on. "I want to come back home to you. I want to build our family with you."

"Me too." His voice cracked. "It's what I always wanted. A life with you."

"I'm so sorry I left. I couldn't forgive myself for what happened to the girls, and I took it out on you."

"You took it out on yourself too, which was just as unfair because it wasn't your fault." He tickled the parting on her braided hair. "I don't care about any of this anymore. What matters now is that you're back, here with me."

He drew her close and took possession of her mouth. For several seconds, the kiss continued. She didn't want it to end. It had been so long.

His touch was like a lifesaver. She didn't know she'd missed it so much as she clutched his face and allowed him to slant his mouth over hers.

But it had to end. She didn't know what he would say when he heard the whole story, and Dr. Brickam had encouraged her to tell all.

She withdrew, but he continued to kiss her face. "I love you, Shakira. I thought you'd never come back to me. I had dreadful dreams. I saw you die in the jungle."

She stood because it was the only way to get away from him. "Deon. I love you too." She sucked in her breath. "But there is something I need to tell you."

He walked to her and pulled her back in his arms. "I'm ready to take anything as long as you come back home to me." He cupped her cheeks. "I got a condo downtown, right above a bar." He chuckled. "I wanted a lot of noise because the quiet was killing me." He kissed her forehead. "But I started searching for another place, back in Katy where you're used to. I want you to see a couple—"

"Deon. Deon, I'm pregnant."

Chapter Fifty-Five

eon went still like he was frozen. Within a few seconds his palms grew cold and wet, yet still on her cheeks.

"I don't know who it was. I was kidnapped and held for about thirty hours. They drugged me." Tears streamed down her face. "I only learned about it when I returned and had fainting spells."

His mouth hung open as he stared into her eyes. She swallowed but couldn't look away. At least she was still in his arms, and he had her face in his palms.

She blinked. "Kenya thinks I should take it out. But I wanted to hear from you."

Not quite true, because she had no plans to abort the baby. Deon's gaze dropped to the floor, but he held onto her face until she freed herself of him and placed her head on his chest. He wrapped his arms around her, and not until then did she hear his silent sobs.

"I'm sorry," she cried. "I'm sorry."

"It's not your fault, Shakira. I should have come after you."

She stepped back. "No, darling. I was wrong to go in the first place. It was crazy to plunge into such a journey."

He sniffed. "I was going mad, Shakira."

For another several minutes, they held each other and cried over the mistakes of the past. Deon was the first to recover.

"You cannot have an abortion, Shakira." He wiped her tears. "If you don't want to keep the child, we can give him up for adoption."

Shakira jolted and would have laughed, but a sob escaped instead. "I thought of adoption."

He lifted her. "It's not showing yet."

"It's a little above three months."

He pressed a kiss onto her stomach. "We will overcome all of this, Shakira. I know."

She slid back until her feet touched the floor, and they exchanged another hungry kiss.

"When are you coming home?" He nuzzled her neck. "Today?"

She nodded vigorously. "Yes. Yes."

He chuckled. "To the condo above the bar?"

"Anywhere you are, darling." She giggled. "I'll follow you to the moon."

"This baby." He led her back to the couch, and they sat together. "I'm thinking now, we need to get its DNA. It may help track the criminals who did this to you."

She gasped. "Deon! You're right. I mean, it never occurred to me." She hesitated. "But I doubt the country would have any records of such a thing. I saw the police force. They are not well-equipped."

"Oh, wow. It won't make any sense then."

"But we can still do it. No harm in sending the information." Shakira shrugged. "I'll call Detective Dauda and tell him about it."

The detective was happy to receive any information which could aid their investigation, but they had to wait. Shakira and Deon wanted to get back together and settle down before they did any more about the case.

Deon took her to his condo, and she liked it.

"Reminds me of your bachelor days when I'd come in to help with cleaning." They stood in the middle of the room and kissed. "Good old days."

"Are here again," Deon moaned. "Wait, do I have to marry you again? I mean, I'm ashamed about it, but I sent you those divorce documents."

"I tore them up, Deon. We are still married."

He carried her to his bed. "Thank you, Mrs. Shakira Smith."

Chapter Fifty-Six

Shakira reclined on a rocking chair she got from a thrift shop a few weeks earlier. It had become her favorite seat in the room. She munched on a corn snack she was sure would give her heartburn but couldn't resist and reread an update from the police officer in Nigeria.

Detective Dauda was glad to receive the baby's DNA two months later. Not only did it match one in their records, it opened the case a lot wider. Shakira's baby was fathered by the notorious identity thief known by many names, including Bayo Odun, Bayuz Dunzland, Green Cobra, Chancer Epp, and Who Dollar Epp.

Chancer Epp, the name on file, had been on Interpol's wanted list for three years across two continents. No one knew he had entered Africa after he was chased to the ground in Asia and escaped. With the result, though, the career criminal was back home.

Deon walked in from work and gave her a peck on the lips. "How was your day, sweets?"

She shrugged and watched him go to the refrigerator to pour a glass of orange juice for himself. "I want to go public with my story, Deon."

He turned to face her. "You do?"

Since she moved back with him, she hadn't worked because Deon wanted her to recover from the past few months, and with a baby on the way, they both agreed it would be better to wait until it was born and she could start over.

She crunched on her corn chips. "With the result of the DNA test, I mean, I think it's important to speak out."

Deon put the juice back and went with his filled glass to sit on the chair he placed across from her recliner so he could massage her feet.

"This will open the wound, darling. Are you ready for it? And with your condition, do you want the world to know?"

She hadn't thought about all this. "I just want to help. The police explained Florence used a stolen ID. The real owner of the identity has been missing for almost five years!"

"They must have killed her."

"Maybe. And this guy is the leader of the ring. He appears and disappears across countries."

Deon sipped his drink. "That's the reason why we should stay out of their faces. Let the police handle it."

"The police in Nigeria are not equipped. They want to do the job, but there's so much restraint." She sighed. "They end up taking deals from these criminals and snitch on their own investigations."

"It's pure greed, Shakira. They are on government payroll."

"But they are paid peanuts. Can you imagine a sergeant earns as little as two hundred dollars a month?"

Deon gasped. "Two hundred? Wow."

"Exactly. They're not motivated. Only a few have a good conscience. I was there. I saw it."

He rubbed the back of his neck. "What about the baby? You want the whole world to know you were drugged and raped by this criminal?"

"Maybe we should speak with Detective Dauda and hear what he has to say."

Deon finished his drink and set the glass on the coffee table. "I feel more comfortable with Fraser. He's been interested till now."

"Fraser. He has called just once since I came back."

"You know what?" He lifted her left foot and kneaded it. "Talk to the detective in Nigeria, and I'll call Fraser. We can compare and decide afterward."

Both Fraser and Dauda acknowledged the problems faced by the Nigerian police force, and how difficult it was to penetrate many of the hiding places the criminals had. The borders were porous, and the interiors were not properly developed with a good road network or communications facilities. Most important was the simple truth about the level of poverty in most areas outside the city limits. Hunger drove many to sell their souls. These criminals had access to a lot of money, and they would pay any price.

After comparing the facts, Deon agreed the least he could do was leave his comfort zone and help with the investigation.

Shakira granted an interview Fraser set up and gave as much information as she could. She described in detail Florence's new physical features. As much as she tried to recall details about her kidnapping, she couldn't, but it was obvious now that the most wanted man in the fraudster ring had been in Efayaw for the period she was there, or at least part of it.

"I don't know if I was right." She watched part of the interview in the local evening news. "I mean mentioning all the names."

Deon cuddled her on the couch. "What names?"

"All the names. From Sean who sent me to Mo, to Glory. I was like a name drain." She giggled. "Was it right?"

"I'd do the same, Shakira." He noticed the news anchor had moved on to other updates. "Too many shady people."

The following day, Deon arrived home waving a sheet of paper. "Honey, they got a break. A bust of the ring." He gave her a quick kiss on the mouth. "Fraser faxed this to me."

Shakira took the paper and stared at the picture of the woman who confronted her in the church school classroom.

"O-moh-tay O-me-tee-kow?"

"Her real name." He sat opposite her and took her left foot in his lap. "The man Sean did a lot of business for the ring. He's bitter. They owe him.

Fraser said he was the name drain." He laughed. "Mentioned four other gang members and where to find them."

Shakira stared at the picture of the Nigerian woman Florence Odu aka Omote Ometeko. This was the closest to any closure she imagined she would ever get.

Chapter Fifty-Seven

After snubbing his teaching job for more than a month, Dele Thomson didn't think he had a chance to return to it. His dream of manipulating Shakira to get an American visa was terminated by his desire to do right. She had not been in touch since the text message she sent to inform him Dauda had picked her up at the Lagos airport and taken her to the hotel for the night. At least he proved he could be noble. He promised to get her back home, and he did. Not a word of thanks had come off it.

For the umpteenth time, he stared at the marriage certificate in her name and his. Dauda had joked he could present it at a visa interview, but when he spoke to an immigration agent, he learned Shakira had to send a letter of invitation ahead.

"These would just be supporting documents."

Any remaining hope that Shakira could help had been crushed. Still, he didn't destroy the marriage certificate. Maybe her husband would divorce her, and, one day just for old times' sake, she would invite him to her country.

Since his return to his sisters' place, things had gotten worse. The five thousand naira Veronica gave him had covered his transportation back and left little change. Bessie and Tami intermittently threw tantrums, which included threats to throw him out if he didn't contribute. Daily he went out in search of a job, any job, but there was none to be had.

He took his new faith in God seriously, but his prayers continued to bounce off the walls. Five months after the drama, he still had nothing. He volunteered in a nearby church twice a week, but this wasn't his ideal. He couldn't afford to pay for transportation anywhere farther away. The church was small and couldn't put him on their payroll. It was just a frustrating cycle.

His phone beeped, so he picked it up. No one called, by and large, except Dauda or a couple of old school friends on rare occasions. But he was subscribed to a news organization that sent daily news updates.

Bored, he opened the text and read through the headlines. One caught his attention. *DNA results of Shakira Smith's unborn baby reveal notorious criminal is back home.* The text messages didn't detail the news, and he didn't have any data to operate his phone, so he put on his shoes and half-ran to a business center a block away. The owner was his friend.

"Please, I need to use the Internet. It's urgent."

The friend snickered. "Get a job, Dele!" But he let him use a computer for free.

Dele searched out the newsfeed and read the story. The face of the woman Shakira had described was on display.

Dele gasped. "I know this woman."

He took her picture with his phone and sent a "call-me-back" request to Dauda.

The detective called about five minutes later. "Dele, hello."

"Hello, Dauda. Are you free?"

"What's up? Free in what way?"

"Can you come around to my place today? There's something I need to show you."

There was a pause on the other end. "It's been a busy morning, but I'm getting off at five today. What happened?"

"The woman Shakira came after—her picture has been released. We know her."

Dauda grunted. "We know her?"

"Yes. You remember the prostitute Queen? She was all over the place for a while, and then she disappeared."

"I can't recall."

"If you see her picture, you'll know her. They say her real name is Omote Ometeko."

"We have a security report on the woman." Dauda hesitated. "But I can't discuss it with you."

"I know. But I remember her well. Boys in those days talked about saving up to patronize her."

Dauda chuckled. "You probably hid it from me, so I won't arrest all of you. If it's the woman you mentioned, I can't remember the face."

"She does look a little different, though."

"Listen, Dele, I have to run. But thanks for bringing it to my attention."

"Sure." Dele coughed. "Huh, can I get a little loan from you, Dauda? Maybe two grand."

"I'll credit your account shortly."

"You're a blesser. Thank you, Dauda."

After Dele hung up, he continued to read the story. Shakira was pregnant! And she had come out to tell her story. He thought she was bold and appreciated her strength and resilience. He got a credit alert for the loan almost right away and returned home. He couldn't appreciate his old friend enough. There had been many unpaid loans, and he prayed one day he'd have the ability to repay them.

He took a bus to the bank and got the money. From there, he decided to take a little expedition. If Shakira could stand in front of a camera with a bulging stomach and relay her horrid experiences, the little he could do was check out his suspicion. It gave him great pleasure for the first time to take out a loan not because he needed the money for himself, but to pursue a worthy cause for another person's sake.

Shakira would probably never contact him again. She might never thank him for this, but he'd always feel good about his effort to help solve the case. He had seen Omote before. Some ten years back, he had worked at the harbor and followed a few sailors about town. Dauda might not remember her because he was an officer of the law, but he couldn't not recollect.

The One Sister brothel had changed in years. Back then it was a single-story nondescript building. Now it had signage one would think represented a B&B, and another story had been added to it.

Inside, there was a reception area with potted plants around a classy ceramic-tile island. The air conditioner was not too chilly, and the room smelled like lavender. A corridor led away from the area with rooms labeled in fancy gold numbers. In those days, things were not so organized.

"Huh, good afternoon." Dele winked at the pretty young receptionist. "I need a room."

The girl smiled. "Do you have a particular room in mind?"

"Queen's. Is she still here?"

"Queen? Yes." She nodded. "Room twenty-three."

Dele frowned. "Just to be sure. I know she left some years back. Was hoping she's back."

"We have a Queen in room twenty-three. But I can call to confirm she's free."

"Can I see her picture?"

The girl laughed. "Ah, sir, you don't know Queen. Who gave you her name?"

He chuckled. "Believe me, I knew a Queen. I was young then and didn't have the money to pay her, so I always thought of when I could come back."

She corked her neck. "How many years?"

"Ten."

Her eyes widened. "I was in primary school ten years ago."

He leaned forward. "So what are you doing here now?"

"A job." She giggled. "Customers always ask me the same question, but no one has ever given me a job at the bank."

"What's your name?"

"Honey."

"Nice name." His eyes twinkled. "It's quiet. Or is it the time of day?"

"Yes, sir. Timing. Most of the ladies are asleep. But if you're sure about Queen, I'll call her up for you."

He narrowed his eyes. "You're not scared I'm a policeman or something? You just speak freely."

She arched her eyebrow. "Are you?"

"No."

She shrugged. "Even if you are. My madam knows how to take care of the authorities."

Against his better judgment, he was impressed. "Okay, so you were not here ten years ago when Queen reigned. How can you know if she's still here?"

She beamed. "I can show you a catalog."

She opened a photo album and flipped through it to a page. "This is Queen."

He leaned over and stared at several pictures of a dark-skinned model in bikinis and minis. "She's quite pretty, but not the one."

Honey closed the album. "So do you want another room? Queen is one of the best here. There are other great ones."

"Give me top three."

"Glory, Princess, and Lolly."

"In any particular order?"

She giggled. "In no particular order."

"Queen is not in the top three?"

"Top five, maybe."

"Can I see the pictures?"

She opened the album again. "Room thirty is Lolly."

Dele stared at a young woman who might not have been more than twenty, pretty and curvy. "Next?"

"Room eleven is Glory."

Glory resembled the Queen he knew, and for a minute Dele was taken aback. He wanted to take a shot of her and send it to Dauda. Back in the day, he couldn't remember if Queen had a relative. But Shakira had come to meet someone here. Could be this one. If it was, then they had to take her in for questioning. Someone here knew where to find Florence Odu aka Omote aka Queen.

"You like her?"

"She looks great." He winked characteristically. "Let me see number three."

"She's just a few rooms away. Room five is Princess."

If anyone knew Queen, it would be Princess. Despite the make-up, she couldn't be younger than fifty.

"Quite—aged."

Honey giggled. "She hates being told so, but she's good. Been here longer than anyone too. She may know your Queen."

Dele licked his lips. "My Queen, I like the way you say it. Wow, I was after my dream, but alas." He pulled out a two-hundred-naira note. "Thanks for your time. And if I see another job for you, I'll be in touch."

Honey took the money and batted her false eyelashes. "Thanks. I appreciate."

Dele breathed freely again outside the One Sister house. He called Dauda.

Chapter Fifty-Eight

Dele came back for Lolly. Dauda went for Glory, and a young vibrant police detective called Ofem paid for Princess. Honey beamed as she received the regular five thousand naira for each of the women.

Five minutes afterward, Glory and Princess were led out of their rooms by the policemen, wanted for questioning. Honey gasped as the ladies were taken away.

"Tell Madam what happened. They are police," Glory shouted to her.

Honey frowned. "What happened?"

Dele came up behind them. "You said your madam knows what to do. Don't worry about it."

Honey clasped her hand over her chest. "Ah, you're police. You lied."

"No, but sorry."

The ladies were helped into the unmarked police jeep outside the One Sister house before the three men got inside. Ofem took the wheel and switched on the police siren. Through light traffic, they arrived at the Criminal Investigation Department (CID) in Alagbon and went as a group into a conference room.

"Please sit," Dauda said, closing the door.

The two women sat beside each other, but the men remained on their feet.

"This is an informal inquiry, but I am going to have it recorded." Dauda set a small recorder on the table. "It is just a routine investigation. You ladies have not done anything wrong. We only want information."

Dele didn't know much about police procedures, but he was glad Dauda allowed him to be a part of this. He liked his friend for one thing: his ability to take action at a moment's notice. Dauda was one of those people Nigerians liked to refer to as an "action man." After the call to him, he'd told Dele to give him a few hours to organize a simple raid. He'd gotten verbal authorization, which could boomerang depending on the "madam's" level of influence, and had taken the One Sister women to CID instead of his office. Nothing was scripted at the moment until it became official.

Dauda held his hands loosely behind his back and faced the women. "I want you to cooperate. I'm not going to use force on you. I will take you back to your hotel once we're done here. And depending on you, this will take only a few minutes."

He did not give them any opportunity to respond. Princess had her eyebrows drawn upward in a sharp tilt, and all Dele could see were Glory's eyes. She had eyes like Queen's.

Dauda brought out three pictures of Queen. One was taken in her hey-days, when she was the queen among the ladies of the night. Another was of her in America, and the last, the most current photograph gotten from the file footage at the airport as she fled after the incident in Shakira's house.

Princess's face lit up at the photographs just a second before she regained her composure.

Dauda arched an eyebrow. "Do you recognize her?"

Glory averted her gaze and pressed her lips together.

"We worked together in a bar. At One Sister. Long ago." Princess's eyes darted. "Her name is Queen."

"Thank you, Princess." Dauda narrowed his eyes at Glory. "What about you?"

"I don't know her."

Dauda pushed the pictures closer to her. "Look at her. Are you sure?"

Glory folded her arms across her chest. "Yes. I don't know her."

Dauda returned his attention to Princess. "You said you worked together. When?"

Princess rolled her eyes. "Ah. Long time. Ten or twelve years."

"And when last did you hear from her?"

Princess bit her lower lip. "It's long. She left Nigeria . . . since. I think she went to Libya, then Italy. I don't know again after that."

"What can you remember about her? What kind of girl was she?"

"Hmm. Queen wanted to see the world, make a lot of money. She can't live in this Nigeria," she faltered. "Can I know what happened to her?"

"We're doing an investigation on her. She may be in serious trouble, and we don't want her to get hurt."

Glory mumbled. "It's a lie. They are looking for her."

Dauda arched an eyebrow. "Do you want to tell us something we don't know?"

"I don't know her. I'm just saying my own."

"Okay." He gestured to Ofem. "Please take Princess back to where we got her from. I'd like to continue with Glory and don't want to waste Princess's time."

Princess giggled. "Thank you."

Glory started. "What do you want to ask? I said I don't know the woman." She stood. "Please, let me go too."

Ofem led Princess out, and Dauda closed the door.

"Glory, for your own good, you need to tell the truth. You can't escape anymore." He pointed at Queen's pictures. "How is this woman related to you?"

"Related?" Glory scoffed. "Someone I don't know?"

Dauda removed two more pictures from his bag. One was of Glory at a much younger age. The other had two people in it—Glory and Queen.

Glory's eyes widened. "Ah!"

"You need to talk to me. Is she not your sister?"

The woman trembled and flitted a glance at Dele. Both men waited on her with blank faces. Dele wished he could help her, but the only way was for her to cooperate with the police.

"She is." Glory twisted her fingers. "She said she will send for me when she has money, but she did not."

"When last did you speak with her?"

Glory kept quiet for a long time. Dele watched her lips work up a word then fail. Her jaw twitched, and the twisting of her fingers increased.

"Glory?" Dauda leaned forward. "When last did you speak with your sister, Queen?"

Glory raised her head and caught his gaze. Her voice was like a child's when she spoke. "Yesterday."

Chapter Fifty-Nine

Glory spoke for a long time. She was a master witness and articulated her report well. Dauda allowed her to give a detailed account of her relationship with Omote and her husband, Chancer, whom she knew as Bayo.

"When did you meet Bayo?"

"Five years ago. He was supposed to come here and take me back to America with him."

"Why didn't he?" Dauda asked.

"He cheated me. He was married to Omote, and yet he still got intimate with me. And I get to the airport and he is not there."

"Didn't you have your passport and ticket?"

"No. It was with him. He went back. Omote call me and said sorry. Next time she will send someone else to come and take me."

Dauda squinted. "So you've waited ten years for your sister to come for you?"

"Yes. She said she has come for me herself."

"When did she tell you this?"

"Yesterday."

Dauda nodded. "Before yesterday, when did you speak with her last?"

"Two years ago."

"She's lying," Dele interrupted. "She told Shakira where to find this woman."

Dauda raised his hand to stop Dele. "Listen, Glory, you can make this simple or hard. You have not done anything wrong until you give false information, then you will be held as an accomplice." He leaned forward. "And your sister's sins are far and wide. You don't want to get tangled."

He moved back and leaned against the wall. "How did you get to know Shakira Smith? The American lady you accommodated for a few days."

"Mo sent her to me. I don't know what she wanted, but I was to take her to meet Omote in my mother's village."

"Why didn't you?"

"We had many customers. I told her to wait, and she said she will find her way."

Dele gasped. "She's lying, Dauda."

"I'll send you out if you keep interrupting," Dauda snapped.

After a couple of hours, Dauda wrapped up the questioning and put Glory in a cell.

"It's unlawful, Dauda," Dele protested on their way out. "You know you can ruin the whole investigation by doing the wrong thing."

"Oh, my fault." Dauda chuckled. "You seem to forget this is not my investigation. It is not my jurisdiction either."

"Her madam will call some big shot, and they will ban you from ever talking to her again."

"Haha!"

Dauda's car was parked in the lot, and he got into it with Dele.

"I know there's a lot of under-G work in the force, but—"

"But this is a jungle, bro. Police work in this country is wound up. Let me do it the way I know. You want to go by the book, you'll never get anything done. Never! Unless you're the Inspector General, maybe."

"Who's going to free her?"

Dauda shrugged. "I don't know. Maybe when Ofem returns. It's his office."

Despite the gravity of the matter, Dele laughed. "You lock a woman up under another person's custody? Dauda!"

Dauda entered the evening traffic. "What do you say we go out for a drink? It's on me."

Dele snickered. "Who else would it be on? Anyway, I stopped drinking. I told you."

"Oh, yes, the religion thing. You mean you've not gone back?"

Dele rolled his eyes. "You're impossible."

"I'll drop you off then go find big boys who still know how to drink."

"Go home to your wife," Dele bit out. "Huh, should we contact Shakira to let her know what's going on here?"

Dauda shrugged. "Her number's on my phone. Find it."

"Okay."

Dele got the phone and found the number. He was tempted to commit it to memory and call her when he could, but that might not work. He'd played with the idea of connecting with her on social media too, but hadn't gotten around to it.

The conversation was brief. When he hung up, he returned Dauda's cellphone to its place on the dashboard.

Dauda snorted. "So fast. Hard feelings?"

"We went straight into business. She first thought it was you."

"I heard your recap. What did she say?"

Dele groaned. "She said police went to find Mo after her interview."

"Oh, good. Did she cooperate? Glory made it clear Mo knew more than she did."

"Mo is dead. She was found decaying in her apartment."

Chapter Sixty

Dauda and Dele chatted for several minutes after they got to his sisters' house.

"You see why we need a strong grip on this Glory girl. If I let her go now, she'll take a bus to Efayaw and disappear into the creek. End of story."

Dele slapped his back. "You are a good policeman. So smart of you."

"The girl? She's as dangerous as her sister. She just hasn't gotten the opportunity."

Dele sighed. "Poor Mo. They must have sent their gang members to finish her because of what she knows."

"A deadly gang, those ones. I'm keeping Glory locked up. I have no other choice." He took his phone. "Let me tell Ofem not to let her go."

"I guess I should let you go home. Thanks for today."

"You're welcome."

Dele got out of the car and waved his friend off. He had never felt so fulfilled in his life. Maybe he should pursue a career in the force as well. There was nothing more fulfilling like catching bad guys in the society. It was like picking stones out of the local brown beans.

He opened the door and found Bessie and Tami seated in front of the TV, but it was switched off. Their angled posture told him something had just happened, a discussion gone bad, or a tragedy. Either way, he'd learned a while ago never to prod.

"Good evening, ladies."

They didn't answer. He strolled to the kitchen, hoping there would be some food for him. Many times, he'd gone to bed hungry. He'd also learned not to ask if there was nothing to eat. He walked to the bathroom, and when he came back he found them in the same position.

He took his cellphone and opened one of his favorite games. Because it never ended well to put the sound on for his games, he had switched them off for good.

"The electricity bill came today," Bessie muttered. "You're paying it tomorrow morning so the power will not be disconnected."

He knew she addressed him, but because she hadn't mentioned his name, he didn't respond.

"It's eight grand. I think you should give me, I'll pay it," Tami sneered. "Before we will be hearing a long story in the dark."

The sarcasm grated. Dele raised his head from his game. "Are you talking to me?"

Bessie snickered. "Who else gives nothing in this house and expects to be housed, fed, and clothed?"

"I don't have eight grand."

He returned to his phone. His head pounded as he got ready for it. Both sisters were physically violent. Bessie hadn't been able to keep a man because she would at some point do something crazy, like throw hot water or rocks. Tami's last boyfriend ran from her when she threatened him with a kitchen knife. A throw pillow landed on his head, and because he expected something from them, he flung it right back.

It landed square on Tami's face. She flew to her feet and screamed, "Was I the one who threw the pillow at you? Are you mad, Dele? Are you crazy? How dare you!"

Bessie got on her feet too. "In fact, I am sick of this. I will not take any more of this nonsense." She marched into the bedroom.

Tami continued to scream. "What kind of useless big brother are you? Your life has no direction, and you think you can get away with it just because we accommodate and feed you!"

She moved closer, less than a foot away. So close, Dele imagined she would hit him. He sucked in his breath in anticipation.

"Are you not the one I am talking to?" Tami screeched. "All your mates are married and living respectable lives, and you have no shame. You can't even contribute to your daily living. You have to depend on your two little sisters. Shameless man!"

"Two little sisters who earn a living selling their bodies!"

His words triggered her more. She swung around and beat her chest. "At least I pay my bills and don't beg like you. And who are you to point fingers? Your cup is full. No, no. You won't get away with this."

She searched the room, wild with rage, and, unable to find something strong enough to cause him harm with, stomped into the kitchen.

"She's gone for a knife," Dele muttered.

He tucked his phone in his pocket and headed for the door. Better to leave before she stabbed him to death. He opened the door and stepped out a moment before a bag hit his shoulder. He swung around to know his attacker.

Bessie picked up another bag and flung it at him. "Good, you know you're out of this house. Worthless creature."

He saw his clothes sticking out of both traveling bags and picked them up. "Bessie, listen."

Tami came barging out with a kitchen knife. "Where is he? Where is this mad idiot?"

Bessie grabbed her by the waist. "He's going. Leave him."

Dele ran to the road but slowed down to watch his sisters shout at the top of their lungs. A few neighbors shouted back, and some switched on their security lights to peer out. Well, his sisters had done their bit, he guessed. There had to be a time when this would happen, and he had to get going. He'd hoped for too long. Sometimes he argued fate had not been kind to him, but for years these two girls had accommodated and fed him.

He'd put up with their insults because he thought he had no choice. But he did.

He called Dauda. "I'm so sorry to disturb you. Are you home yet?"

"Actually, no. Ofem wanted me to see my prisoner. I'm on the way there. Why?"

"Oh, well. Can you stop by and pick me up? It's a long story."

To Dele's surprise, Dauda laughed. "They threw you out? Finally! I'll be with you on my way back."

Dauda picked him up close to midnight, three hours later. He was hungry, tired, and almost sure he would spend the night by the roadside.

"You should have picked me up on the way to Ofem!" he admonished his friend when he arrived.

"No." Dauda opened the trunk and threw his torn bags inside. "I wanted you to learn one more lesson about life."

Chapter Sixty-One

"**N**onsense. What lesson have I not learned?"

"How many times have I told you to move out of your sisters' place and find something to do?"

"Did I not look for something to do several times?" Dele yelled. "How many rejections have I gotten from everywhere! If I don't know someone, I must give a bribe."

"Calm down, bro. Shouting doesn't change your life." Dauda drove into the night. "My wife will have a fit when we get home, but I'll calm her. You have to make a plan, though. Maybe a couple of days more, then you have to find somewhere else."

Dauda's wife was a petite woman some ten years younger than him. They had a one-year-old son and lived in a studio apartment provided by the police force in the barracks.

"Let me go in first and tell her we have a guest."

He came back about half an hour later with a thin film of sweat on his forehead. "Women! Hmm, come on." He opened the trunk.

Dele joined him at the back of the car. "I can sleep in the car tonight."

"Just what she suggested. Come in."

They carried a bag each and entered the house. Dauda at one time had built a partition to separate his bed from the sitting area. The room was crowded but clean. Too much furniture crammed into too little space gave little chance for moving around. The air conditioner was on and made it chilly. Dauda dropped the bag with him on the couch and Dele followed suit.

"Don't make noise, the baby is not yet asleep," Dauda whispered.

"Close to one in the morning?"

Dauda stifled a chuckle. "Shh, or I'll throw you out too."

The men sat on the two single couches.

Dele yawned. "Thanks for having me tonight."

"Lower your voice. Madam is awake too."

"Oh, sorry." Dele glanced toward the partition.

Whoever fixed it did a good job. It was neat and featured framed pictures on the walls, but it had no door, although it was designed in such a way that one couldn't see anything more than the wall beyond it.

"I thought officers of your caliber got better living accommodation."

Dauda sighed. "We've been at it for almost two years. Some big shot in the force expects me to bribe him before I get a two-bedroom apartment, which I am entitled to."

"How can?"

"I applied for it, it passed every level, and got approved. You know, these approvals come with a condition of availability." Dauda shrugged. "The man said none is available, but I pass by empty apartments every day."

Dele stretched, and his stomach grumbled. "Country of sinners."

Dauda lowered his voice. "Are you hungry?"

"Haven't eaten today."

"Really?"

His friend walked out and returned with a plate of ground rice and melon soup. Dele gobbled the food like his life depended on it while Dauda watched.

"When last did you have a good meal?"

Dele sighed heavily. "Maybe three days. The girls leave crumbs for me. Two slices of bread, a wrap of food here, one spoon of soup there."

"Ah, but guy, you were so enterprising in school. What happened to you?"

Dele licked his fingers. "After the folks died, you know the story. Uncles took everything from us. We had to scrape and scratch to survive."

"But you were smart. I mean, I don't understand." Dauda packed the plates and took them to the kitchen. "You can wash your hands over there." He pointed to a washing basin at the corner. When he came back, Dele was dozing.

"Dele." He tapped him. "You need to have a plan. You know you can't stay here for long."

"I know." Dele shrugged. "I'm thinking I'll go to our church tomorrow, but the place is small, and I don't know if the pastor will allow me to sleep in the hall at night."

Dauda teased, "You can tell him you're doing night vigil every day." They both laughed. "But on a serious note, Dele. You must make a plan. Find a woman, for goodness' sake. You're a shadow of what you were."

"A woman, huh!" Dele sneered. "A woman is the last thing on my mind. I don't have a job or accommodation, but I should start talking to a woman?"

"Yes. You will be surprised. If you get a good one, she will help you order your life."

"Where do such women exist on this earth?" Dele scratched his head. "I haven't found one. The moment you don't have a car, a house, and a good job, you're toast."

"I don't think so. When I met my wife, I was just a policeman without purpose or direction. Since we got married, believe me, I have grown."

"But you had a good job as a policeman. What are you talking about?"

"What about the scripture 'he who finds a wife finds a good thing.' Eh?" Dele dropped his head to his chest. "I don't know, Dauda."

"Anyway—" Dauda stood. "I'm going to bed. I'll see you in the morning, but it will be better if you think about this well. All the 'Lagos boy smart guy' attitude you had has taken you nowhere. If you can't get a job, get a woman. Goodnight."

Dele watched him walk around the partition. He heard mumblings then everything went quiet. Did he think Dauda had a good woman? Her food tasted really good, and at least she allowed him to sleep on her couch, if only for one night. If he'd be able to sleep.

He thought of Shakira, but she had moved on. She was never for him. He admired her bravery. He would want a woman like her, but would such a strong woman want him? Dauda had been right. As a young man he was proactive, motivated, and excited, but with every disappointment of his dreams, the Dele Thomson willing to take on the world had disappeared and this pathetic beggar took over.

Dauda was the only one who remained at his side. Had he overstayed his welcome? He needed to go somewhere. At this point his university honors degree in environmental science had done him no favors. His pride and discriminating behavior had to be thrown away. He would work as a cleaner if it was the next available job. The only things he would never do were to beg on the streets or take to arms and become a criminal.

He covered his face and sobbed into his hands.

Chapter Sixty-Two

hakira stared at her cell phone for several seconds after she hung up. It had been five months since she heard from Dele last, and she was glad. But as Deon had predicted, her interview opened many cans of worms. Sean, Mo, and the other Nigerian women she spoke with had all been visited again by law enforcement teams.

Poor Mo had been found with her throat slit and left to rot on the floor of her stinking apartment. The investigators ruled it an inside job. She had let the person in. Had not struggled. She probably didn't see the knife before it cut her.

Shakira sighed. Who else would she hear from soon? Several victims' groups had called her. Charity organizations wanted her to grace their campaigns. One pro-life group would not allow her a moment's rest until she agreed to grant an interview. Hers was a compelling story. Coming forward with it had changed her life again.

She rubbed her stomach and stared at the huge box she'd been working on when her phone rang. It was the first so far of three or four cartons she wanted to pack. An organization involved in sending welfare items to

Africa had agreed to cargo hers along with theirs. She had specific places she wanted the boxes delivered to. Two must go to Efayaw, to Goodwill's church. One was labeled "Kem's family." Kem had a three-year-old sister, Latoya's age now. All of Leila's clothes were going to her.

Deon had done a good job of storing all the girls' belongings at a storage facility when he moved from Katy. The day he took her there, she'd cried for joy and appreciation. It spoke volumes of how much he cherished the memory of the girls. So when she announced the day before that she wanted everything sent to Nigeria, he'd gone to fetch them for her.

She placed the rest of the clothes and many of Leila's toys into the carton. In his magnanimous and thoughtful way, Deon had given his old clothes in addition to hers, which were fast becoming too tight for her. Kem's family would have something for everyone when they got their package. She sealed the box and labeled it, then started with the next one. She filled four boxes altogether, as she had expected, and called the organization.

Deon came back home to find her asleep on her recliner. His gentle massage of her feet brought her to consciousness.

He leaned over and kissed her mouth. "I see you've done all the boxes, Babe. Good job."

"Yeah," she moaned. "It took me all day. Have you been home long?"

"No, darling. Just got on your second foot. You were talking in your sleep, I didn't want to disturb you."

"Talking? What was I saying?"

He mimicked her voice. "Come home, Deon, darling. I love you. I miss you."

She giggled and threw him a punch. "You wish."

When he finished, he curled up with her on the recliner. "I thought I'd meet up and join you with packing. Missed it."

"It was quite satisfying, and full of memories."

He traced his fingers over her face. "You cried?"

She whimpered into his chest. "At first. Then I remembered Kem and how she died. How strong her mother was. How brave her father was too."

"I wish I could have met them."

She giggled. "Maybe, Deon. One day if you want to be a missionary to Nigeria."

They laughed together. He caressed her arm. "Real missionaries this time, darling. When we have an actual call."

"Yeah. And we are quoting the Bible correctly."

She heaved a shuddering sigh. The ability to crack jokes about her sojourn was one of the things Deon had worked on achieving, and he had. They had inside jokes about the airport thieves and Dele Thomson she never imagined she could laugh about.

"Are you alright? You sound drained."

"A little. All the emotions." She stared at his handsome face. "And guess who called in all of it. Dele."

"Hmm. What did he want?"

"I told him the little I know about Mo. Seems the work is on them over there. We can't do more."

Deon cupped her face. "We have done much more than anyone expects. He thinks you should return, doesn't he?"

"Not at all. He can't ask it of me. He said he read the interview and felt he hadn't done enough to help."

"Oh, I get it. He wants to come here?"

"Deon!" Shakira chuckled. "No. He can't ask that of me either. I left him without a dime, so he's likely hanging onto the police officers to get whatever he can off them."

"I don't trust a man like him."

Shakira kissed his mouth. "He's far from us, darling. And he means nothing to us."

He kissed her back hungrily, the way he had kissed her since she came back. "None of them mean anything to us." He rubbed her stomach. "Not even this child."

She clasped his hand on her belly. "Not even this child," she repeated then took it higher up where she wanted it.

It was part of her therapy since she opted to give the baby up for adoption. She denounced everything attached to her awful experience. She loved her strength and ability to give up the baby at all. Dr. Brickam had taught her to love the sinner and hate the sin, and so she detached herself from the life growing within her. Not because she hated it, but because it was her responsibility to provide life, and nothing else for the child. She and Deon had signed the documents for adoption. They would not even be told the sex of the child, nor would they see it before it was taken to its new family.

For the moment, though, she couldn't be bothered. The only person in her life right now was Deon. He was her hero, and as he fumbled with her clothing, all she could think of was how to please him.

Chapter Sixty-Three

Dauda found Dele fully dressed and leaning against the wall when he woke up about four hours later.

"Bro! You didn't sleep at all?"

"Can a man carry fire in his chest and sleep?"

"Hmm." Dauda walked toward the bathroom. "Let me finish and we can talk."

"Okay. Thanks."

The policeman was done within ten minutes and dressed to go out. Lagos did this to people. If he wasn't out before six in the morning, he could as well bid the morning farewell, because the traffic was insane from any part of the city.

Dele picked up his two bags, and Dauda raised an eyebrow. "You're leaving for the church?"

"No. We can talk on the way. Please thank your wife for me."

"Okay. She's still asleep."

Both men contemplated the partitioned room as Dauda's wife hummed a soft tone, and Dele winked despite himself.

"You need a lot of wisdom with women." Dauda opened the car and they got in. "She wasn't happy you came, so I promised she won't even see you."

"I wonder what you'd have done with me this morning if I was still snoring on your couch when you woke up."

Dauda bared his teeth. "Kick your behind." He laughed. "So where are you headed?"

"Efayaw."

"What?" Dauda pushed at Dele's shoulder. "Why? What did you forget there?"

Dele gave a brief recount of his association with Veronica. "I think I should move there. See what can happen between us."

"Are you sure? You don't know this woman."

"You said if I can't get a job, I should get a woman! Where will I find one?"

"Not this one!"

Dele frowned. "You confuse me. Why not her?"

"Someone you deceived into believing you're married, told off, and then skinned five thousand out of?"

"Yeah, I wanted to ask . . ." Dele scratched his head. "If you could give me a loan? Maybe twenty thousand?"

Dauda laughed. "You must think I harvest naira in my backyard. Where do you think I will get this twenty thousand from?"

"I promise, Dauda, I will never ask you for money again. Please. I want to give Veronica her money back, and then talk to her about a future."

"I don't have twenty thousand. I don't have two."

Dele worked up the courage to ask for a lower amount, but he saw the way Dauda's jaw twitched. Maybe he had finally overstayed his welcome.

"Can you drop me at the bus station?"

"It's what I planned to do."

He could never find any fault with Dauda. He owed his friend for past favors, and he could imagine how difficult it was to have a wife who didn't support his charitable ventures. He would take his chance on Veronica. Efayaw was way far from home and everything he knew. They spoke a different language, ate different foods, and lived a different lifestyle. But he could adjust. He would.

Alone in a strange land, he was throwing himself at the mercy of God. His "Lagos boy" sense had not worked for him in Lagos. Double-dealing and swindling people for peanuts would no longer be his lifestyle. If Veronica would not have him, then he would find a job, any job, and make something of the rest of his life.

The stony silence in the car made it clear to him he was done with his birth city. If Dauda removed his support, then he was better off anywhere else.

The bus station already bustled with people eager to leave town in the early hours. Dele collected his bags from the trunk and walked around to Dauda.

His friend peeked through the window. "If you get stuck, call me."

It was the kindest thing he'd heard in a long while. Despite his refusal to lend him money, Dauda still offered help.

"Thanks, bro. Thank you for everything."

He stepped back and watched Dauda drive off. "My Father in heaven, to Your mighty hands I commit my life."

The cheapest available fare to Efayaw was more than thrice the amount he had, the leftover from the loan he got from Dauda the previous day.

"Can I see the driver?"

The cashier gave him a wry look. "In the shed over there. Ask for Zuki."

He walked over, muttering silent words of prayers. "Favor, Lord. I pray for favor from Zuki. He will answer me and help me."

Thoughts of the prodigal son after he'd squandered his inheritance in the strange land came to his mind. It couldn't have been harder to ask a stranger for help.

Zuki was a short, slim, clean-shaven man who, despite being older, looked strong and healthy. Dele couldn't determine his age. He sat with two other men, and they drank gin from the bottle and chatted in the local Efayaw language.

"Zuki?"

"Yes?" The smallish man rose. "Who wants him?"

"I'm Dele. I'm going with you to Efayaw."

"Okay. Pay over there."

"I know. Huh, I want to see you, please."

Zuki said something in his language, and the others laughed. He stepped out of the shed, and Dele realized he couldn't be more than five feet and a few inches, but he commanded a presence with his strong jaw and keen eyes.

"You told your friends I want to beg for money."

Zuki snickered. "Good, you speak the language."

"I don't."

"Then how did you hear what I said?"

For a moment Dele wondered too. All the while he stayed in Efayaw, he'd found their language too fast and complicated. All he could speak was the simple greeting.

"I don't know." *How did I understand?* "But I need your help. I have to get to Efayaw and I don't have any money."

"Go to your family and borrow."

"I don't have anybody. Please, it's a long story." He paused. "I will work for you. Anything."

Zuki sniggered. "Work for me. How?"

"I can load the vehicle."

"For how much?" Zuki waved him off. "I cannot help you." He spoke a string of words Dele didn't understand and went back into the shed.

Dele walked to the bus scheduled for the trip and waited. He would work, whether Zuki agreed to pay or not. He prayed someone would take pity on him. There had been times people spoke of angelic visits. He sought for one now.

The bus filled up faster than expected, and Zuki came around to inspect it. Dele stood to one side with his two bags.

"Ah, this man. Have you paid?"

Dele swallowed. "I couldn't."

"If not that my wife said I should be kind before we will see angel and pass him and not help him." He assessed Dele. "This one you understand my language, and you don't know how." He peeped into the bus. "I have one more passenger." One or two people already seated told him there was no more space. "We will find." He assessed the bags. "Oga, you will take only one bag."

Dele didn't care about any of the bags. They were his clothes, and he could do well without. Like a man being pursued, he sorted through the bags and picked his best. The other bag he gave to one of the "boys" working in the station.

Ten minutes later, squeezed in between two consenting passengers, his journey to the unknown began.

Chapter Sixty-Four

Efayaw nights had always been calm, and Dele, though cramped from the journey, took a deep breath and knew he had done the right thing to leave Lagos. His heart thudded as he found his way to Pastor Goodwill's church. It was too late to meet any gatherings, but the security man, if he were still the same, should remember him.

The man did. *One more lie, I'm sorry, Lord*, Dele thought, struggling not to lie. "I just came in from Lagos, but I want to spend a night of prayers."

The security man opened the gate and church. Overwhelmed by his new direction and the sudden fear Veronica would turn him away, his lie to have a night of prayers became a necessity. He didn't want Veronica for want of nothing else to do, he realized he wouldn't have come this far if he didn't find himself attracted to her.

Over the previous night he'd thought of her, their last time together. How her eyes widened for a moment when he demanded money, and how her lips trembled when she apologized, saying she didn't have much but just five thousand. Five thousand was what he needed to get back! As he later put the money in his wallet, he had felt a twinge of guilt.

He'd wanted to call and thank her but didn't have her number, and still didn't.

"If you'll have mercy on me, Lord, let her pity me."

He didn't have a place to stay, but he planned to speak with Pastor Goodwill about this. He was coming clean. In the morning, he would visit the pastor and tell his story in full. No more of this "hide and seek" lifestyle. Then he planned to go in search of the woman after his heart. He was a prodigal, and he wanted to make things right.

Schools had vacated weeks earlier, so when morning came the premises were still deserted. Dele woke up early, though he'd hardly slept. The thudding of his heart each time he thought about Veronica had not abated and he greatly desired to see her.

It was too early for the pastor to visit with anyone, but the house servants let him into the guest parlor. Because he wasn't a stranger to this home, he requested a bath and a bed, so by the time Goodwill attended to him, he had groomed himself to an extent.

Taking the prodigal son's approach was his intent. The man of God hugged and welcomed him, and he broke down and wept.

"I'm not who I said I was."

When his emotions were under control, Goodwill allowed him to tell his story in full.

"I have nowhere to go. Please help me."

"I can't believe all the drama here was staged." Goodwill groaned. "Up till now, we pray for you. We thought you had gone back to America."

Dele couldn't hide his shame. To have sold such a lie so convincingly made him feel cheap.

"I'm so sorry, pastor." He breathed hard. "I'm ready to work for you, if only you can give me a place to live until I find my path."

"But you are not a pastor."

"I will do whatever you want me to do. I will carry your bag and Bible, run errands, drive you around, do anything."

Goodwill smirked. "Wonder what members will have to say when they see you again. After all the lies we fed them." He rubbed his eyes. "Dear Lord, what do I do?"

"I can stand before them and ask for forgiveness."

"No. You cannot." A flash of rage crossed the pastor's face. "We took their money, Dele. Do you know what people will think about such a thing?" He sighed. "Many of the people here live below poverty level, yet they give of the little they make. I have never deceived my members to take money from them. You made me do it."

"But it's not your fault. You didn't know."

Goodwill shook his head. "The only way I can let you stay here is if you continue to pretend. And when you have made some more money, go elsewhere. Move to another town."

"Sir, no. Please."

The pastor walked out. Dele dropped his head to his chest. He would not do this. He couldn't. He had traveled over four hundred miles of bad roads and dangerous terrains to change his life. Maybe he had hoped for the pastor to throw him out, but not to offer him what he'd vowed never to do again.

He found one of the servants of the house and got Veronica's number. If she rejected him, it would be final, but in this country people fought hard. He had burned all bridges to be here, and there was no going back.

"Hello, Veronica. This is Dele."

Her voice was low. "I know. I have your number."

"Where can we meet?"

She paused. "You are in town?"

"Yes. And, please, I want to apologize for the way I treated you last time. I am sorry. I know you may not want to see me, but I beg you to." He swallowed. "I don't have words."

"Are you at your old house?"

"No." *Where should I say I am?* "I just came in last night." He took a deep breath. "I don't have anywhere to stay."

When a man was down, there was no other place to go but up. Dele didn't care what Veronica thought of his shameless admittance. She met him at a fast food restaurant and bought the food. He didn't eat much, not because he wasn't hungry, but because seeing her made him lose his appetite. It became clear he didn't want to live without her love. The feeling had grown like a seed from the day she made the move on him, and he had suppressed it. Now seated across from her, he imagined he might have to go on his knees and beg her. Dauda's reference to "finding a good woman" had never made more sense.

Veronica was aloof. After breakfast, she took him to her brother's house then excused herself to go in to work at a federal government office.

"I'll see you in the evening. Huh, does pastor know you're back?"

"Yes. But, I—it's a long story. I'll tell you later."

"Okay."

Her brother worked in the military and only used his one-room apartment whenever he wasn't on the waterways patrol. Dele was glad to have the nice small place to himself. Veronica had not rejected him outright. She hadn't fully accepted him, but this was as good a start as he had hoped for.

"Veronica!"

Her name was a sweet song in his ears. He spent the rest of the day loving the thought of loving her. If she still wanted him, he would work hard to make her proud. Nothing else would matter.

Chapter Sixty-Five

Veronica was not only a true Christian, she was lovelier than he had given her credit for. When she returned in the evening, they went for a walk and he professed his love for her in a tremulous voice. He had never been so afraid of rejection in his life. The beautiful woman who brought him to this humbling realization also made him feel like a king when she accepted his proposal.

"Veronica, I want to marry you. I'm done with being stupid."

She laughed. "I knew you would come back one day."

They spent the evening discussing each other. He told her the pastor's stand, and she agreed he couldn't follow such a path.

"You'll keep running." She shook her head. "I know he won't want to see you around him either. So you need to find another church and lay low. With time, the story will come out, and you can make amends."

Her opinion about his next direction was just as simple and helpful.

"We have some contract jobs in my office. I can make enquiries."

Dele grabbed her hand. "I will appreciate this. Thank you. I don't mind any job. I will work as your messenger or cleaner."

She giggled. "They are junior and middle management contract jobs, sir."

Within a day and a half, Dele's life took a new turn. He kept telling himself he would never have known he could make something of his mess if he hadn't taken a leap of faith. Being with Veronica became the highlight of his life, and by the end of a month he could pay for his own accommodation, a small room much like Veronica's brother had.

His life took shape in the twinkle of an eye, and he had his dignity back. With hindsight, Pastor Goodwill allowed him to tell his testimony in his church and to apologize, though it didn't go so well. Many people felt offended and manipulated.

"People will forgive and forget with time, don't worry," Veronica assured him in her customary way. "And Shakira's boxes arrived today. It's just the right time. The way God works."

"Yes, I guess." He cleared his throat. "Maybe I can be allowed to make the presentation of the cartons. Save face."

Veronica nudged him. "Pastor will make the announcement. Loosen up. People forgive. Anyone could have fallen into the temptation."

"I hope so."

She greeted a few of her friends even as some unforgiving members strolled by with canny remarks. "By the time the boxes are opened and the gifts are shared on Sunday, people will be thanking you for bringing her."

He smirked. "Amen."

She didn't have a car, but they had plans to buy one soon. As they got to the main road to catch a taxi, she tapped him. "Do you mind going on to your place? I'll catch up later. I need to get something from the evening market."

It was after the mid-week evening service, and they would have gone to her house or his for dinner.

"What do you need to buy at this late hour?"

"Dried fish. I made the soup without it." She cringed. "I'm sorry. Go on. I'll catch up with you."

He winked. "Let me come with you. It's not like I'll have dinner before you return."

"Aww, thanks, dear."

The evening market was sometimes open until almost midnight, but it filled up pretty quickly, and one could find as many things as in the day market. Dele hung around as Veronica haggled with the fish seller—until he caught a glimpse of a most unlikely person.

Glory.

He grabbed Veronica's hand. "Are you done? I see someone I know." He kept his gaze on Omote's sister, afraid she would disappear.

"I'm done. Yes." Veronica collected her bagged fish and said, "Shall we?"

"The lady over there. In the next stall with the man. I know her."

"Should we go over and—"

"No. We follow them. They mustn't—she must not see me." He whispered in her ears, and her eyes bulged. "Yes."

"Come behind me then."

Chapter Sixty-Six

ele held Veronica's hand and ventured on the craziest thing he'd ever done. They followed Glory and the man with her. The couple hid from the criminals, and, though almost caught several times, they managed to follow them out of the evening market down a dark street until the two drove off on a motorcycle.

When they got back to Dele's room, they were exhausted.

"I'm calling Dauda right away." Dele breathed hard. "He knew she would leave Lagos if she were released."

Despite the time of the day, Dauda picked up on the second ring. "Hello, Dauda. Good evening."

"Hello, Dele. How far?"

"I'm great, thanks. All is well." He'd brought Dauda up to date on his life from time to time, so he knew his friend was expecting another update. "I saw Glory. Here in Efayaw."

"The same Glory we know?"

"Yes."

"I knew it. I told Ofem not to let her go."

"Why did he?"

Dauda hissed. "You know where she works. Ofem couldn't even keep her more than a night. Her boss does have influence in some high places."

"So she may have been here for a month?"

"It's possible. I tried to keep tabs on her, but I do have a job at the airport."

"We followed her, but she got on a motorcycle and disappeared. I can't believe she's here. Probably her sister is too."

"You know what, Dele, send me your address. I'm coming in. Don't tell anybody."

"Dauda, you're sure you should?"

"I'm more involved in this case than you think. And I don't want anyone in my office to know." There was some noise in the background. "Listen, send the address. Expect me tomorrow." He hung up.

Dele stared at his phone. "He's coming tomorrow. Why, though?"

"He must be in this more than you know."

"Exactly what he said."

"We just have to keep our fingers crossed. Those criminals are in hiding, and the moment they know someone is close on their trail, they may get violent." Veronica shrugged. "They must think everything is clear now and the authorities think they've left Efayaw."

Dele grunted. "I'll send Dauda my address. If he wants to do this without official backing, it's his decision."

Dauda arrived the following night. Dele and Veronica met him at the bus station and took him to dinner at a restaurant in town, after which they went to Dele's apartment, and Veronica went home.

The guys relaxed and chatted late into the night.

"Don't you have to be at work?" Dele asked.

"I took a casual leave. I am bored stiff at my job. It's depressing."

"Well, I wish you luck. I don't know how you plan to track down these people. You have this place for as long as you wish."

Dauda checked out the small though well-furnished place. It was the perfect place for a single upwardly mobile man. He had a queen-size bed, a couch, carpet, and a table. Another small table accommodated an electric stove, and beside it a table-top refrigerator. His flat screen TV was bracketed against the wall facing the bed. On the other side of the wall was a room unit air conditioner.

"You have a great place." Dauda punched his shoulder. "In just a month, you've done so well. You see?"

Dele bumped shoulders with his friend. "I have you to thank."

"I'm happy for you. The lady of yours is nice too. I'm glad I was right."

"You were so right. Finding a woman is a good thing." Dele chuckled. "And this woman in particular drives me crazy. I'm saving to marry her in a couple of months. I can't wait."

"You'll see the difference. The moment you marry her, your life will improve even more."

"Amen. Now, what's your plan with these criminals?"

Dauda stretched out on the bed and groaned. "Road transportation in this country is a demon."

Dele laughed. "For a day after, your legs will be asking you if they belonged to your body."

Dauda did not respond, and when Dele looked at him he was fast asleep.

"I work, bro. And I leave early."

The policeman didn't hear, but it didn't matter.

———

Dauda woke up on time the following morning and got Veronica to take him back through the path they'd trailed Glory on before she reported at work. In daylight, the street didn't seem as long, but it was downtown and could lead anywhere.

Veronica pointed at an unremarkable house on a narrow street. "They got on the motorcycle here. They must have parked it earlier."

"What kind of street is this? What is it known for?"

Veronica shrugged. "Nothing. Just a low-income area. Some people come here to take accommodation because it's cheap."

Dele checked his watch. "We have to get to the office."

"Right." Dauda took another look around. "I'll wait till you get back from work, and we can walk around a bit, if you don't mind?"

"Okay." Veronica nodded. "Dele?"

"Sure," he agreed somewhat reluctantly. He wanted to spend the evening with his woman, but Dauda had been a true friend indeed.

Chapter Sixty-Seven

The three walked the length and breadth of the street later in the evening and found nothing but a night club. It was a shifty unmarked building one could mistake for anything but what it was. They'd walked past, but on their way back they saw two people walk in.

Dauda stopped. "I wonder what this place is."

Veronica shrugged. "Doesn't look like anything."

"Did you see the two people who went inside now?"

Dele frowned. "Maybe it's a bar. Or a local point-and-kill joint."

"People could live inside, you know," Veronica observed. "Those people who walked in may live here."

"The way they were dressed—I don't think so." Dauda arched his eyebrows. "Can we check it out?"

Dele shrugged. "Why not?"

"I don't know." Veronica hesitated. "This is not a fantastic street to be loitering on."

Dauda shoved his hands in his pockets. "I have a loaded gun. Anyway, we could take you back. I'll return with Dele. Or alone."

"No. Let's check it out together. You don't speak the language, and the people here won't readily respond to you."

"Thank you, I appreciate it." Dauda walked to the door and knocked.

A burly man stepped out of the shadows and spoke the local dialect. Veronica giggled and responded. They exchanged words for a bit, then Veronica pulled Dele forward and spoke a string of words he didn't understand. The big man led them to a side door and opened it. He said something and Veronica took Dele's wallet from his back pocket and pulled out a couple of five-hundred-naira notes. She squeezed it into the bouncer's hand, and the three were allowed in.

The inside was dark except for colored lights which illuminated a dance floor. Two poles featured two naked girls dancing for an audience that drank, smoke, and paid little attention to them. It was impossible to determine how large the room was, or how crowded. Loud rock music filled the atmosphere, but none of the patrons danced.

Dauda found an empty table close to the door and produced a pack of cards. Dele gasped. "You are ready for this, aren't you?"

Dauda guffawed. "You know my profession, after all."

A waitress dressed in a baby doll negligee walked over, chewing gum. "Drinks?"

Veronica spoke first. "Ginger beer with plenty of lemon and ice."

The waitress snickered. "We only serve alcohol."

"A bottle of dry gin," Dauda ordered. "Three glasses. Plenty of ice."

"Fifteen thousand." She chewed. "Anything else?"

"No, thanks," Dele said. When she left, he spat out, "Fifteen grand, for what?"

"We should leave. There can't be any good come from here." Veronica reached out and held Dele's hand. "I'm scared."

"Don't worry." Dauda cleared his throat. "Is there anything I should know about the way we got in?"

Dele shook his head. "Not here. We're shouting."

"I told him you were sailors. I wanted to rip you off and didn't want to go where people know."

"Well, not a bad reason to let us in." Dele tapped the table. "When do we leave here, I'm tired."

"I want to walk around." Dauda stood. "I'd say you wait for me outside before the girl brings the drinks. I don't have her money."

Dele nodded. "Okay."

Dauda walked toward the dance floor, and Dele saw him flirt with one of the girls, waving a note at her. No one paid attention to him.

Dele stood and pulled Veronica up.

"I need to use the restroom. I've been trying to control it," Veronica said then hurried off in the same direction as Dauda.

The waitress returned with the bottle of gin and a bill.

Dele waved toward the dance floor. "The guy buying is dancing." But Dauda was no longer there. "I think you should come back later."

The waitress hissed and left with the order on her tray. Dele had been in a night club on several occasions, but this didn't fit any he knew. The naked girls on the poles, and the complete darkness except for the colored lights were unfamiliar. This was the first time he'd seen one where the drabness outside resembled nothing of the action inside.

Veronica returned after almost ten minutes. "We can leave."

"What took you so long?"

She shuddered. "Let's go, please." She gazed around like someone was in pursuit.

He took her hand and led the way. They got to the door they entered through and found it locked with an arrow pointing along a dark narrow corridor to the exit. They trudged down several meters and found a door which opened to another street. They slipped out and gulped in fresh air.

"Should we wait for Dauda?"

"Do you know where we are?"

The chorused question showed their anxiety. Veronica answered Dele's first.

"I know where we are. But will Dauda come out of there and meet us here?"

"I don't know, Nica," Dele addressed her with his shortened pet name for her. "Maybe we wait a little."

"This is not a good street to hang around either."

"You know what? Let's go. Dauda is a big boy, and he has a gun."

The street was dark, dirty, and the road was bad. The couple stepped into puddles several times until they got to a main street and took a taxi to Dele's place.

Veronica trembled nonstop. She complained that her skin crawled, and she needed a bath. Dele sat outside while she had one. She called to him when she was done, and he entered the room to find her in his pajamas and curled up on his bed.

"I was going to take you home."

"No, please," she whimpered. "I'm afraid to be alone. Please."

He stared at her, clueless as to what to do. He was tempted to take her into his arms and do more, yet he couldn't take advantage of her in such a way. As it was so close to midnight and with Dauda still away, he decided on the most honorable thing to do.

"Okay. I'll sit outside my door and wait for Dauda to return. He'll sleep on the couch, and me on the carpet."

She didn't protest his plan. "Thanks, darling." She drew up his duvet to her chin and closed her eyes.

Dele kept his word and took his single chair to sit and wait for Dauda outside his door. His friend did not return until two hours later. Dele had dozed off on the chair and startled when Dauda tapped him.

"Why are you outside?"

"Veronica refused to go to her house. She's terrified of being alone."

Dauda led the way inside. The lady on the bed was fast asleep and snored softly. "Did she tell you what she saw?"

Dele shook his head. "No. She didn't say anything. She was just so scared."

"I need a bath. Then I'll tell you."

Chapter Sixty-Eight

Dele couldn't remember the last time he was so exhausted, but he fought sleep while Dauda took a shower.

His friend tapped him awake for the second time, and they both sat on the couch. "I've found them. All of them. Chancer, Glory, Omote. They were all there."

"What? What are you going to do?"

"We need to go back. Tomorrow, we—"

"Please, just let's keep Veronica out of it. She was so terrified. I've never seen her so shaken like this."

Dauda tipped his head to one side. "It's because she saw them. She went in search of the restroom and opened a door where they all were smoking and drugging themselves. She excused herself, ran out, and bumped into me. I calmed her down and told her to leave."

"She didn't tell me a thing."

"She peed on herself, Dele. Poor girl."

Dele's mouth dropped open. "Oh no."

"She was shaking so much and peeing as she told me what she saw. Said one of the men managed to pull her onto his lap and feel her up." Dauda swallowed. "I bought the gin. Poured it on the front of my shirt and entered the room. Feigned I was dead drunk. They threw me out."

"I thought you reeked of alcohol when you arrived." Dele scratched his head. "I don't think I want Veronica involved anymore, please. I will go anywhere you want, but not with her."

"Well, I thought she'd not want to go back either. I need undercover policewomen who can dress like whores and fire good shots."

"I know one." Dele gave him Runo's phone number.

———

The operation was supposed to be simple. Runo could speak the local dialect, act any part given to her, and shoot like a sniper. She asked Dauda to give her one day to get another capable woman and a man, and to alert a back-up team.

Veronica couldn't go to work the following day, afraid someone at the club would recognize her, but she gave good directions to the building.

Dauda spent the day in the main market where he got clothes and disguises for himself and the other undercover force members. Veronica called in sick, but Dele went to work and later returned to find Dauda ready for a showdown.

"I didn't think it would be this easy to find them," Dele told him over a meal of boiled white rice and fish stew Veronica had prepared. "I thought they were in a creek or something."

Dauda took a gulp of water. "Believe me, where we saw them yesterday was the least likely place. Besides, I think they have become careless. After avoiding law enforcement for so long, they begin to relax. Seen it happen too many times."

"But their case is still unsolved."

Dauda snickered. "These criminals are used to hiding. But they hate it. They want to go in and out as they please. Hurt people as much as they want and make all the money in the world. They are not smart. It's the reason they are common criminals and not professors of science."

Veronica sat with them on the couch with her food. "I hope this will wrap it up. Someone might have gotten wind of our visit yesterday and snitched."

Dauda stood and stretched after his meal. "There are two possible problems: the bouncer at the entrance, and the chance they'll be there tomorrow night."

"The bouncer is a big fool. Men like him take instructions, and anything outside of this confuses him." Veronica rolled her eyes. "Even I thought what I said was too stupid to convince anyone."

"Runo will handle him. She's an amazing policewoman." Dele finished his meal and blew Veronica a kiss. "Thanks, darling. It was delicious."

Dauda paced. "If they aren't in the club tomorrow night—"

"They will be," Veronica said. "One of them referred to soldier ants, saying they'd all disappeared, and that a man can now enjoy his life in peace."

Dauda sneered. "I told you they get careless."

Chapter Sixty-Nine

Leon threw the front door open and waved a letter in Shakira's face. "It's a yes, darling!"

She didn't have enough time to turn before he picked her up and planted a kiss on the back of her neck.

"No! This deserves a real kiss." And she gave him one.

"My first six-figure paycheck job. After taxes. Can you believe it?"

"You deserve it. All of it. Every cent." She kissed his face. "When do you start?"

"I asked for a month."

She gasped. "A month. Honey—"

He separated two cruise tickets from the letter. "Barbados calling. We are overdue for it. You know it. No arguments." He kissed her on the mouth. "No complaints."

She pulled out of his embrace. "Well, I have something to show you as well. Two things." She pulled him to the couch they replaced the recliner with after the baby was adopted and opened her laptop. "I got the venue for the creche! The agent sent me the contract."

"Wow! Great news!" He browsed the documents. "And it's the amount we want to pay. The condition is perfect. This is awesome, Shakira."

"Yes, it is. Since we're going to Barbados, I'll decorate when we return." She snuggled closer. "And on to other breaking news." She navigated to a separate tab. "Fraser sent me the link."

Deon's eyes widened. "What on earth? They brought her in?"

"Yes," she whispered as her eyes teared up. "They did."

Deon hugged her neck and cried with her. When they both calmed down, Deon read the article.

Omote Ometeko extradited: Woman returned to face prosecution in the death of two Texas children.

Omote Ometeko, accused in the deaths of two children in Katy, Texas, arrived in the United States today, along with wanted notorious identity thief, Chancer Epp, also known in his native country of Nigeria as Bayo Odun. Ometeko, 38, is charged with two counts of felony murder and will be tried in the deaths of three-year-old Leila Smith, and eighteen-month-old Latoya Smith. She faces up to life in prison for each count, if convicted.

"I can't believe it, honey. She's finally here." He stared at the picture of the woman he last saw almost three years earlier.

"I called Dauda. He told me they were found in a night club. A gang of six. Only this one and the man were wanted here." She giggled. "Dauda thanked me. He believed I was somehow responsible for it. The system back there would have played around with the case for years." She sniffed. "I'm glad our girls can have the justice they deserve at last."

Deon pressed her head to his chest. "They will. And now we deserve Barbados. She'll be locked up where she can harm no one, while we soak in the sun and make a new baby." He kissed the crown of her head.

Shakira's phone rang, interrupting a juicy comeback she wanted to give Deon. It was Kenya with a shrill voice.

"I just got off work and saw the breaking news on *Crime International.* She's here. Florence Odu has been caught and extradited. Are you in front of your TV?"

Shakira laughed with tears in her eyes. "I heard. I don't want to watch it on TV, but we know. Thanks Kenya. For everything."

"Thank God. It's all I can say."

"Yeah."

"I read she confessed she was on social media and didn't know when the girls ran water in the bath." Kenya's voice cracked. "I'm so sorry, darling."

"Thank you."

"Do you want me to come over or something? I could make lasagna. Is Deon back from work?"

"Thanks, Kenya, but it's not necessary." Shakira nodded before she answered. "Yes. Deon's here."

"Bless your souls, Shakira, dearest. Justice is served."

"Yes." She hung up because Kenya could just keep going on. "Kenya," she told Deon.

"I know."

Getting married wasn't as simple as Dele had thought. He was heady more than half of the time, and despite Veronica's protests and offer to give him part of the money he needed for the wedding, he stood by his plan. She deserved a great day, and honeymoon, and lifestyle. He wanted to pay for it. It was one of his vices, stubbornness.

After the daring bust at the night club, where Chancer Epp got shot in the leg, and Omote almost got away again, Dele had decided the woman of his dreams was worthy of a greater life than he'd planned.

Veronica had set herself in the way, hidden in an abandoned building on the street, in case any of the criminals escaped. As it turned out, Glory and Omote slipped out of the club just in time, but Veronica, from her hidden place outside, alerted the back-up team to them.

The news went around for weeks, and other raids were carried out as a cartel of drug dealers and international thugs were caught and indicted. The extradition process began for the felonious woman and her husband, and Dauda went back to his job at the airport. Dele's focus went back to making enough to give Veronica a fitting wedding and married life.

His dream did not materialize until over a year later. He had a new three-bedroom apartment in a middle class area of town and a small car.

His three-month contract job had only been renewed once before his boss recommended him for a permanent position, and he got the job. He had benefits with the new appointment, and his paycheck allowed him to save more.

Most important to him was that Veronica got her dream wedding, and they could pay for a one-week honeymoon trip to the beautiful Obudu Ranch Resort.

One week after they got back from the honeymoon, still basking in the euphoria of being married, Dele got a visitor at his office.

It was Detective Dauda of police force airport area command, Lagos.

"Dauda!" he shouted. "What are you doing here?"

Dauda laughed. "I came to visit you. What do you think?"

"You were here for my wedding two weeks ago. You didn't say you'd be back so soon." Dele wagged his finger at him. "Or did you get another lead of a den of thieves? We're doing our best to keep Efayaw rodent-free."

Dauda beamed. "Nothing so excessive. I have news, though. I didn't want to say it on the phone."

"Oh. But you fly all the way from Lagos to tell me?" Dele leaned forward. "My heart is beating fast. What is it? Good news? Great news?"

"An American visa for you."

Dele laughed, toying with his diamond wedding band. "Much as I dream to visit the great country someday, I am no longer desperate. And anyone giving me a visa must give my wife one too."

"I am so impressed by you, Dele." Dauda sighed. "You are back to the Dele Thomson I knew. So incredible."

"And I thank you, Veronica, Shakira, and God for straying into my life, and everyone who threw me away when I needed help. My sisters—"

Dauda frowned. "Didn't attend your wedding."

"They sent well wishes at least. No hard feelings there." Dele clapped. "Now, you must tell me what brought you here."

Dauda opened his bag and took out an envelope. "I got this letter yesterday from force headquarters in Abuja."

"A promotion for you?"

"No." Dauda chuckled. "Appreciation for my part in the operation which brought Bayo Odun to book. I knew there was an incentive within the force for anyone who facilitated his arrest."

Dele threw him a punch. "And you never told me."

"Oh, you know how our system works. I didn't believe they'd give anything."

"Did they?"

"They did." Dauda took out a check from the envelope in his hand. "This letter landed on my desk a minute before I got an alert in my salary account."

"Congratulations! Oh, so now you decide to fly down here to spend and be spent? Where's your wife?"

Dauda laughed. "Please, Dele, let me finish. Take a look." He handed the check to Dele.

Dele's head shot up. "Dauda!"

"Yes. You deserve it. We did this job together. Half of what I was paid is in there."

"Half a million naira, Dauda!" Tears gathered in his eyes. "My friend." He grabbed him by the neck in a tight hug. "You didn't have to do this."

"I had to. Heaven would not forgive me if I didn't."

Are You Saved?

All that is written in this book may not be of much use to you if you haven't yet given your life to Christ. We cannot make difficult decisions unless we have the Righteous and Wise One to help and choose for us. The Bible says "greater is he that is in you, than he that is in the world" (1 John 4:4 KJV), and "we wrestle not against flesh and blood, but against principalities, against powers, against the rulers of the darkness of this world, against spiritual wickedness in high places" (Ephesians 6:12).

This is why I want to encourage you to make this important decision if you haven't yet given your life to Christ. I made this decision over twenty-five years ago, and I haven't regretted it even for one day. Please pray this prayer of faith if you are willing to surrender your life to God:

Lord Jesus, I honor You. I praise You, and I acknowledge that You are Lord. I know I am a sinner, and I ask that You forgive me all my sins. I want You to be my Lord and personal Savior. Wash me clean and give me grace to serve You wholly from now on. Come into my heart to reign supreme. In Jesus' name, I pray. Amen.

Praise God, you are born again.

Now that you have prayed this prayer of faith, I encourage you to:

Get a Bible and read it every day. (Start with the first four books of the New Testament to familiarize yourself more with your new commander in chief, Jesus Christ.)

Pray every day.

Attend a living church.

Introduce yourself to the pastor and seek further teaching. (You can join a foundation class and activity group in church. You will thereby make yourself available to work for God.)

Tell others about your salvation.

May God help you in Jesus' name! Amen.

Acknowledgments

I want to thank God for this book, which I wrote during one of the toughest years of my life. Perhaps it also helped me to identify with the heroine's journey of being "banged up" in a foreign country.

Special thanks to my husband, Afolarin, and my kids, especially Orey, who placed a fine for every day I delayed in finishing up the first draft. I paid five dollars altogether. To Ife, who put her education at risk to ensure I got this book going.

To my loving mother, Tinuola, also a writer, who keeps me challenged. "Keep writing," she says all the time and does anything to make sure I do, including financial gifts that I find quite embarrassing but sometimes need.

I also appreciate my siblings, who are very special and supportive in every way.

I met Tamar Sloan on my YA novel team, and she blew my mind away. She's done it again with her content edits of this book.

Last but not least, a big thanks to the publishing crew at Morgan James who made this dream come true. Terry Whalin consistently ensured I was in the right place. Thanks so much for your guidance, patience, and professionalism. Also, thanks to Aubrey, Margo, Angie, Jim, David, and the entire team. I celebrate your creativity and kindness.

God bless you all.

About the Author

Sinmisola "Sinmi" Ogúnyinka is a writer and producer who enjoys creating stories across different cultures.

In a 2013 collaborative effort, she wrote and co-produced the Nigerian movie *Red Hot*—with award-winning Nigerian director Teco Benson—which went on to win an international award. Since then, Sinmi has freelanced for several online blogs in addition to writing her own short stories.

Sinmi has a bachelor's degree in economics from her home country, is a Craftsman (Mentorship Program) of the former Jerry B. Jenkins Christian Writers Guild and is currently pursuing a master's degree in creative writing.

When she's not at work in her day job or crafting stories in her unique style, she enjoys singing and dancing karaoke with her four kids and husband where they currently reside in Philadelphia.

Sinmi has written and self-published more than forty books, including an award-winner titled *The Days After That Night*.

You can connect with Sinmi on Facebook, Twitter, Instagram, and LinkedIn, and follow her blog at www.sinmisolao.wordpress.com.